Currency Girl

C J Bessell

Other Books by C J Bessell

This Series
Jacob's Mob

The Copper Road Series
Pioneers of Burra
For the Love of Family

Margaret Chambers Duo
Margaret
Burnt Bridge

ISBN: 978-0-6451051-6-2

Currency lads and lasses were the first generations of native-born white Australians.

It was a derogatory term, which meant they were subordinate, or worth less than their British-born counterparts.

Chapter One

16th March 1833, Launceston

Jessie watched as her sister, Charlotte repeated her wedding vows. She glanced at her father who was sitting in the row ahead of her. He appeared to be calm and relaxed as he sat there holding her stepmother's hand. She grimaced. How could he allow Charlotte to marry? She was only fourteen, and wouldn't turn fifteen for another month.

She knew – she knew it wasn't her father's doing. Her stepmother, Sophia couldn't wait to get rid of them all. Her father had married her four years ago and Jessie wondered why. Well, she knew her father had needed help to raise his five children - but why did Sophia marry him? She hated all of them. And what was she going to do without Charlotte for protection? Jessie swallowed as tears threatened to overwhelm her. Life was going to be just awful. Not only that, but Sophia had somehow convinced her father to move to New South Wales. They were going in two weeks.

"Move," said William prodding her.

Jessie glared at her youngest brother. "You move," she said poking him in the ribs. It was only then that she realised the wedding ceremony was over, and Charlotte and her new husband were leaving. She got to her feet and followed the procession from the church. Well, that was that - Charlotte had escaped.

By the time she exited the Church, Charlotte and Tom were climbing into the waiting spring cart. Panic gripped her as she hurried to speak to her sister before she departed. "Charlotte. Charlotte, wait."

Charlotte smiled and reached a hand out to her. Jessie grasped hold of her. "Can I come with you?"

Charlotte laughed and tossed her head. "You know you cannot. But we're not going anywhere just yet. I'll see you back at the house for our wedding supper."

Jessie let her go as Tom clicked his tongue and the cart started down the street. In her panic, she'd forgotten there would be a wedding party back at the house. She sighed.

"What's this," said Sophia from behind her.

Startled, she turned around and gaped at her stepmother.

Sophia put her hand to Jessie's face and ran her thumb across her cheekbone. "You look piqued my dear. Are you feeling unwell?"

Jessie swallowed and resisted the urge to swipe her hand away. "No, I'm fine thank you."

"Aren't you well Jess?" said her father as he came to stand beside his wife. He put his arm around Sophia's waist and peered at Jessie.

"I'm fine."

"It's all been too much for her, George," said Sophia in her silky smooth voice. "I think it best you rest in your room when we return home. No festivities for you."

"Hrmph," said George turning his attention back to his wife. "Come, my dear, I'll drive you home. The children can walk."

Sophia dropped her hand and smiled smugly before walking off on George's arm. Jessie wanted to burst into tears. She swallowed the ache that stretched across her throat and sucked in several deep breaths.

She was still blinking back her tears when her eldest brother, George arrived by her side.

"Come on, we have to go."

Jessie nodded and followed him to the front of the Church, where William and her sister, Mary were waiting. Mary looped her arm in hers and gave her a reassuring smile. Jessie sighed, as the four of them started walking home. They didn't have far to go and it was a lovely sunny day. In no time the two boys had run ahead and left Mary and Jessie to walk alone.

"Didn't Charlotte look beautiful," said Mary picking a daisy flower that was poking out between two fence pickets.

"Yes she did," said Jessie kicking a large stone aside. "I wish she was coming with us though."

Mary sighed. "We'll be fine without her." She started plucking the petals from the daisy, muttering under her breath as she did so. "He loves me, he loves me not."

Jessie glanced sideways at her. She didn't think Mary had a sweetheart and anyway she wasn't even fourteen yet. Papa wouldn't let her get married. "Well, at least I get to escape Sophia for a while. What are you going to do stuck here with her?"

Mary tossed the plucked flower aside and shrugged. "She's really not that bad. Anyway, I expect I'll be busy. We have to sell whatever we're not taking with us, and get the house ready for Charlotte and Tom to move into." She looped her arm in Jessie's again and smiled. "If I was you, I'd be more worried. What are you going to do while Papa gets his wheelwright shop up and running? You won't even have a house to live in."

Jessie wasn't remotely concerned about that. She'd be away from her stepmother and anyway Mary didn't need to worry. Sophia didn't hate Mary the way she hated her. She'd often wondered why she picked her out from her brothers and sisters. She thought it was because she looked like her mother - at least that's what Charlotte said. Although why that should bother Sophia was beyond her.

She shrugged. "I overheard Papa saying that we'd be going to his mother's place."

“Grandma’s?” said Mary coming to a halt. She stared at Jessie for a moment before they started walking again. “Well, now I’m jealous. I remember her visiting us once after Mamma died. She was just the most wonderful Grandma you could wish for.”

“Really? I don’t remember that.”

“You were only little. Trust me, you’ll love her.”

They turned the corner into their street. “Come on I’ll race you,” said Jessie.

Without waiting for her sister’s response, she hoicked her skirt up around her knees and started running as fast as she could. It was only a short sprint to their house, which was a single-fronted timber house. It wasn’t any different from the other houses in the street, except for the huge camellia bush out the front. It was Sophia’s pride and joy. Jessie was nearly there when Mary easily outstripped her. Mary was laughing when she came to halt by the gate.

“You can never beat me.” She was panting as she opened the gate and waited.

Jessie was gasping for air as she reached her sister. One day she’d beat her, but not today. She was a good four inches shorter than Mary, and although they were both of a similar build, Mary was already budding into a young woman. Jessie hastily tucked a few wayward strands of honey-blond hair back under her bonnet. It wouldn't do to give Sophia any further reason to rebuke her.

Mary looped her arm in hers as the two of them walked up the path and then down the side-way. Voices wafted to them through the open back door. It sounded like quite a few friends had come back to the house to celebrate. That was nice for Charlotte and Tom. Jessie didn't expect any other family would be there. Her father's family were all in New South Wales and hadn't made the trip down for the wedding. Most of her mother's family were dead. She thought she had two Uncles who lived in Launceston, but she hadn't seen them in years.

She followed Mary into the house and they were immediately accosted by Sophia. "There you two are. You took your good time getting here," she said glaring at them. "I need your help in the kitchen.

We've got guests to feed and I can't be expected to do everything on my own."

"I'm sorry mother Sophia," said Mary lowering her eyes.

"Several platters are in the kitchen ready to take into the dining room. Jessie, you can get the plates and cutlery from the dresser," she said before turning and heading for the parlour. She stopped in the doorway and stared at Jessie. "You still look unwell child. Once you've done that you can go to your room."

Jessie was feeling perfectly well but knew it was easier to agree with her. "Yes, mother Sophia."

After giving them one final glaring look, Sophia disappeared through the door into the hallway. Jessie rolled her eyes at Mary before heading into the kitchen. She presumed Sophia would want to use the best china. She opened the dresser and got a stack of plates out. They were lovely rose-patterned plates that had belonged to her mother – she didn't care if they weren't the ones Sophia wanted. She headed for the dining room and placed them on the sideboard and then went to fetch more.

After dropping off the last of the plates she retrieved the cutlery from the dresser and placed them beside the plates. She sighed as she made her way to her room. There was no point complaining about being sent to her room. Her father knew she was being punished, for God only knew what, and he'd said nothing. She carefully removed her Sunday best dress and hung it down her end of the wardrobe. She would only be sharing a room with Mary from now on, and even then only for the next couple of weeks. How strange it was to think she wouldn't see Charlotte every day from now on.

Jessie slipped into her everyday dress and flung herself on her bed. She lay there for a few minutes listening to the voices coming from the parlour. It sounded like everyone was enjoying themselves, including Charlotte she hoped. She reached under her pillow and retrieved her copy of Swandown's Adventures. She smiled as she opened it and began to read about the tabby cat's life – perhaps she could escape as Swandown did.

Jessie wasn't sure how long she'd been engrossed in her book, but was nonetheless surprised when her bedroom door opened and Charlotte came hurrying in. She closed the door behind her and smiled.

"I thought I'd find you in here. What have you done this time?"

Jessie snapped her book shut and grinned. "Nothing, except look sickly."

Charlotte giggled as she sat down on the bed beside her. "Here, I brought you this." She produced a napkin wrapped around a piece of cake. "It's my wedding cake."

"Thank you," said Jessie taking the cake and sniffing it "Mm, it smells good." She took a bite and licked her lips. It was sweet and the fruit tasted like it had been soaked in brandy. Not that she knew what that tasted like. But she remembered having a Christmas cake last year that had brandy in it. It sort of tasted similar. "Yum," she said cramming another mouthful into her mouth.

"I'm going to miss you, Jess," said Charlotte tucking a wayward strand behind Jessie's ear. "But I promise I'll arrange for you to visit."

Jessie put the last of the cake down and licked her lips. "Can't I stay here with you? I won't be a pest."

Charlotte shook her head. “I’m sorry, but no.” She stood up and walked over to the wardrobe. “It wouldn’t be fair to Tom to have my little sister come and live with us.” She removed her new blue travelling costume from the wardrobe and held it against herself. She smiled as she twirled around to face her young sister. “What do you think?”

“It’s lovely,” said Jessie getting off the bed and joining her sister. She ran the fine wool fabric between her fingers. “You can’t desert me, Charlotte. Who knows what that woman will do to me without you here to stop her.”

“You’re being dramatic. She’s not that bad,” said Charlotte. “Here, help me out of my wedding gown.”

“To you maybe, but she hates me.” Jessie began unlacing the gown, all the while trying to think of a way to convince Charlotte to let her stay. “I can cook – well maybe not that good, but I’m getting better at it.”

Charlotte stepped out of her gown and carefully hung it in the wardrobe. “Papa will never agree.”

“What if he did?”

"He won't. Please don't badger me on my wedding day."

Jessie sighed as she helped Charlotte into her travelling costume. It fitted her slim waist and clung seductively to her hips. Jessie couldn't help but admire her. "You look beautiful."

"Thank you," said Charlotte with a smile. "I hope Tom agrees."

A knock on the door surprised them both. "Come in," said Charlotte spinning around.

The door opened and their father poked his head around the door. He grinned before entering the room proper and closing the door. "I thought I might find you both in here."

"Jessie's been helping me get changed."

George raised his brows and then immediately concealed his thoughts. "You looked beautiful today, Charlotte," he said placing an affectionate kiss on her cheek. "I wanted to give you this, but I was waiting for the right moment." He pulled a small velvet box from his pocket and handed it to her. "It was a gift I gave your mother on our wedding day, and I know she'd want you to have it."

"Oh, thank you, Papa," said Charlotte taking the small box. She ran her fingers over the soft velvet before she lifted the lid. "Oh, Papa it's beautiful." She pulled a glittering brooch from the box and held it out for Jessie to see.

"Was that Mamma's?" said Jessie.

"Aye it was," said George taking the brooch. "Here let me pin it on you." He pinned the small sapphire brooch to her dress and smiled. "I bought her this brooch because it matched the colour of her eyes. I loved your mother so very much."

"Then why did you marry Sophia?" said Jessie with her voice dripping in disdain.

George spun around to face his youngest daughter. He sighed. "After your mother died, I never wanted another wife. I was beyond distraught, but I had no choice. You all needed a mother, and so I married her."

"Do you love her?" asked Jessie, still not content.

"I have never loved anyone the way I loved Mary," he said in a serious tone. "You remind me so much of her, with your honey-blond hair and blue eyes."

"Do I?" said Jessie as her eyebrows raised to her hairline. Charlotte had said so, but her father had never before said such a thing.

"Aye, very much so. You, more than any of my children look so like your mother."

Jessie felt her cheeks warm. For some odd reason knowing that she looked like her mother pleased her. She had no memory of what she looked like. There was just this vague feeling she had whenever she thought of her – but she couldn't remember what she looked like.

"It's why you must try not to annoy Sophia," he said as he headed for the door. "When you're ready, Charlotte, your new husband is waiting for you. Oh, and Jessie, go and get yourself some supper. You must be starving." He disappeared through the door shutting it behind him.

A frown creased Jessie's forehead as she stared at the door. What did he mean that's why she shouldn't annoy Sophia? What a very odd thing for him to say. She shrugged as she followed Charlotte from the room. One thing he was right about, she was starving.

***

Chapter Two

Bound for Pitt Town

Two weeks later Jessie found herself boarding a schooner bound for Sydney. Despite her best efforts, she hadn't been able to convince Charlotte to let her stay. She glanced at her two brothers and her father who were standing at the rail with her. If only Mary had been able to come as well. Jessie sighed. Her life had taken a most unexpected turn, and there was nothing she could do about it.

She wound her fingers in the fabric of her skirt as the wind filled the sails and the ship sliced through the waves. Would she ever see Launceston or Charlotte again? She didn't think so, and she blinked back her tears of despair. Life was so unfair.

The journey to Port Jackson on board the Elizabeth was short and uneventful. But nothing had prepared her for the busy port of Sydney. There were several tall-masted ships and at least a dozen smaller vessels moored at the docks. Men were loading cargo onto one ship, and everywhere she looked was a bustle of activity. Jessie clung close to her father as they made their way along the docks. It was only a short walk before they were on the streets of Sydney.

Jessie remembered going to Hobart Town once, but it wasn't a lot busier than Launceston. In contrast, the streets of Sydney were crammed with horses and carts and people. She gripped her bag firmly in one hand and hurried to keep pace with her father. He was striding purposefully down the street, and the three of them had to hurry to keep up.

"Come along," he said as he crossed the street and headed down a narrow alleyway.

Jessie was surprised that he seemed to know his way. He'd been away several times in the last year, and she now suspected he'd come to Sydney. Perhaps, to make arrangements for them to move here permanently? She didn't know. The alleyway joined another street and her father turned right towards the harbour. Half way down the street he came to halt outside an imposing three-story building. Jessie noticed the sign on the door as her father opened it and gestured to them to enter – The Commercial Hotel.

The hustle and bustle of the streets were immediately silenced as they entered the hotel. Jessie followed her father and brothers down the wide-panelled hallway. She'd never been in a hotel in her life, and the smells of ale and stale tobacco smoke assaulted her. She grimaced and screwed up her nose. A woman wearing a grey dress with a crisp white apron came down the stairs and greeted her father.

"A room for the night if you please," said George. "The name's George Smith – I've stayed here before."

"Indeed," she said looking us all over with an appraising eye. "I do seem ter recall yer, Mr Smith."

She went over to the counter situated opposite the stairs and took a key down from the shelf. "Second floor - third on the right." She handed the key to George and smiled warmly. "Supper'll be served at six in the dining room if yer interested."

"Thank you," said George turning the key over in his palm. "Aye, we'll be down for supper."

"Very good, Mr Smith."

George gave the woman one last look before heading up the stairs. "Come along," he said over his shoulder.

Jessie gave the woman a friendly smile before following her father up the stairs. She'd seemed like a nice lady, and Jessie wondered if she perhaps owned the hotel. She'd heard of women running businesses – of course, nothing like a hotel. She knew Mrs Johnson who ran her own seamstress business. But now that she thought about it, most of the businesses in Launceston were run by men.

Her father unlocked the door to one of the rooms and waited for, William, young George and herself to file inside. It was a small dark room, with one large bed and a small trundle under the window. A fireplace and a washstand completed the room. It smelled musty and damp. Jessie looked at the threadbare rug and patched quilts with distaste. Obviously, this was not the best accommodation available.

"George, see if you can get a fire going in that grate," said George dropping his bag and glancing around the room.

"Yes, Papa."

"I have some business to attend to," said George opening the door. "Do not open the door for anyone, and stay in the room. Do you understand?"

Jessie nodded before plopping herself down on the trundle bed. She was glad she'd packed her book – she would at least have something to do until supper time. She sat and watched George as he set and lit the fire.

"Do you know where we're going?" said William sitting down on his bag.

George put another log on the fire before turning around. "Pitt Town."

Jessie's eyebrows raised and she shook her head. "No, we're going to Grandma's."

"I don't know where you heard that," said George straightening. "Papa's setting up his business in Pitt Town, so that's where we're going."

Jessie stretched out on the trundle bed and gave her brother a knowing look. "I heard him say he was taking us to Grandma's."

William looked from his brother to his sister with an exasperated look on his young face. "Where're we going to live?"

"Pitt Town," said George.

"Have it your way," said Jessie rolling onto her side. "But I know we'll be staying with Grandma until mother Sophia gets here."

A frown creased William's forehead. "Who's Grandma?"

"Don't listen to her, she doesn't know," said George in a voice dripping with the superiority of an elder brother.

Jessie eyed her brother and then shrugged. "Suit yourself." It annoyed her that George always thought he was right and acted so superior. At twelve years old, he was only three years older than her, but he always acted like he knew everything. She knew she was right, and he'd soon find out. She couldn't help the smug smile that crept across her face.

It was nearly six o'clock before their father came back. He hustled them downstairs to the dining room for supper. It was a rushed affair, and no sooner had they finished than he hurried them back upstairs.

"You all need an early night," he said removing his jacket. "We'll be leaving very early in the morning."

"Where're we going?" asked William.

Jessie suppressed a giggle. Poor William – he'd been left so confused by their conversation this afternoon. She climbed into the small bed, keeping one ear open to hear her father's reply.

"Pitt Town."

There was no mistaking the 'I told you so' look that young George cast in her direction. It took all her self control not to poke her tongue out at him.

"And then," said George settling himself in the big bed beside William and young George, "I'll be taking you up to the MacDonald River. You'll be staying there with your Grandma and Grandpa Joe until I've got a house sorted."

It was now her turn to give young George a smug look of 'what did I tell you.'

***

True to his word, George had them out of bed and packed ready to leave before six o'clock the following morning. After a quick breakfast of porridge, and coffee for their father, they stepped out into the cool autumn morning. The grey gloom of the dawn still clung to the buildings and Jessie shivered. She had a thin cloak wrapped around herself, but it was Charlotte's old one, and no longer gave much warmth or protection from the wind.

A dray was waiting for them loaded with their sea trunk. Jessie wondered where that had come from. That must've been the business her father was attending to yesterday afternoon.

"Jessie and William, you two get in the back with the luggage," said George as he climbed up onto the driver's seat. "There're two blankets in the corner, Jessie. Wrap them around yourselves if you're cold."

Young George climbed up beside his father and gave his sister a withering stare. Jessie ignored him. She was still trying to throw her leg over the back of the dray and her stupid brother was the last thing on her mind. She finally got herself in the back and grabbed one of the blankets. She bundled herself in it and then sat down in the corner beside the trunk. She hoped it would give her a bit of protection from the cool breeze that would swirl around the dray as soon as they started moving.

"All settled?" said George swivelling around to check on his two youngest children. "Good."

With a click of his tongue, the dray started down the road. Jessie sighed as she huddled out of the wind. Six months ago she could never have imagined the direction her life would take. She felt like everything she loved and was familiar with had been snatched away from her. Would she ever see Charlotte again? This question had plagued her over the past two weeks, and every time it surfaced she pushed it away. She sucked in several large breaths as a hard knot formed in the pit of her stomach.

Her father skillfully manoeuvred through the morning Sydney traffic and onto the road to Parramatta. The crowded streets of houses soon changed to a landscape of farms and orchards. Jessie wondered how long it would take to get to Pitt Town. She had no idea except she thought it might be on the river. An hour or so down the road the sun peeked its head out from between the clouds and Jessie started to feel a bit warmer.

They arrived in the town of Parramatta around mid-morning. Jessie came out of her huddle to get a better look at the township. It was situated on the river among undulating hills with tree-lined streets of houses. Her father pulled the dray over on the side of the road under a large gum tree.

"Get down and stretch your legs if you like," he said as he leapt down from the driver's seat.

Jessie tossed her blanket aside and waited for William to climb out. She followed him and stretched. Her legs felt stiff and cramped and she stamped them up and down as she tried to get them working again.

"Why don't you come and sit up front with me, Jess," said George checking the horse's harness. "You boys can ride in the back for a while."

"I'd like that," said Jessie smirking at young George.

She waited beside the dray while her father finished checking the horse. He grabbed her by the waist and easily lifted her onto the seat.

"You need to eat more child, you're as light as a feather."

Jessie didn't think so. She was wearing one of Mary's hand-me-down dresses, and it already fitted her perfectly. If anything, she thought she was a bit on the chubby side. She shrugged and pulled her thin cloak more firmly around herself. She was sure she'd grow taller – she was already nearly as tall as Mary who was four years older, but she didn't want to get any fatter.

"Are you all ready?" said George climbing onto the driver's seat.

"Yes Papa," said Jessie with a grin.

With a click of his tongue and a shake of the reins, they were off again. They left the town of Parramatta behind and the countryside turned to gum trees and bush. Jessie was surprised at how many carts and wagons were on the road. It was a busy thoroughfare, and her thoughts turned to her new home in Pitt Town.

"Is Pitt Town on the river?" she asked.

"Aye," said George glancing at her. "It's on the Hawkesbury. I think you'll like it."

She'd heard of the Hawkesbury River but had no idea what it was like. "Is it like the Tamar?"

"No, not really. At Pitt Town, it's lined with river gums and grass grows right down to the edge. It's not as wide as the Tamar there, but it does get very wide further north."

Jessie nodded as she tried to imagine what her new home was like. "Have we got a house there?"

George laughed. "No, not yet. That's why we'll only be staying the night and then I'm taking you to your Grandma's. But don't worry," he said grinning at her. "I'll arrange one as soon as I can. Then mother Sophia and Mary will join us."

Jessie wasn't looking forward to that. Well, it would be nice to have Mary by her side again, but she wasn't missing mother Sophia. Maybe it would take a while to find a house and for her father to get everything arranged. In the meantime, she'd be spending her time with her Grandmother, and according to Mary, she was going to just love her. She glanced briefly behind her at her two brothers. She screwed up her face – of course, George would also be joining her at their Grandma's, and he could be a pain.

***

Chapter Three

MacDonald River at Grandma's

The overnight stop in Pitt Town was uneventful. It was a much smaller town than Jessie had imagined. There was a church, a school and several streets of houses, and a few shops situated along the riverfront. It was nowhere near as large as Launceston. Still, it seemed nice enough. Her father showed them where his new wheelwright shop was. Young George and William carried on like it was something marvellous, but Jessie couldn't see what the fuss was about.

By mid-morning, they'd finished their tour of Pitt Town and they all piled back into the dray. According to her father, they'd be at Grandma's mid-afternoon. They followed the main road north towards Wiseman's Ferry and crossed at the confluence of the Hawkesbury and MacDonald Rivers. A short hundred yards or so on George turned the dray down a narrow track that wound its way towards the river.

Jessie hung over the side of the dray – she wanted to be the first to glimpse the house. The track was thickly treed and bushy, and as much as she strained to see through the undergrowth, she had to give up.

"Is it much farther?" she asked in a tone laced with disappointment.

"No, we're nearly there," said her father over his shoulder. "You should see the house around the next corner."

With renewed enthusiasm, she leaned over the side of the dray and peered through the trees. She was soon rewarded as they turned the next corner. "I see it." She grinned at the tin roof glinting in the afternoon sun, before sitting back down in the dray. She couldn't help the shadow that crossed her face a mere moment later. This was going to be home for the foreseeable future – without her father or her sisters. She hoped Mary had been right about their grandmother.

A few minutes later the house came into full view, and Jessie was left with her mouth agape. It was a large rambling homestead with twin stone gables and a wide shady veranda. It was nothing like she'd imagined. Not that she knew exactly what she'd expected – but this wasn't it. George pulled the dray to a halt at the front door and looked around at his children.

"Well, this is it," he said jumping down and stretching his legs. "Come on. Grab your bags and come and meet your grandmother. Do you remember her?"

Jessie and William both shook their heads.

"I think so," said young George climbing down from the dray. "Did she come and visit after Mamma died?"

"Aye she did," said George ruffling his son's unruly dark hair. "Come."

The front door opened and a balding man with wisps of grey hair at the sides stepped out onto the veranda. He smiled before calling back over his shoulder. "Tis them, Maggie."

A moment later a small wizened woman wearing an apron and mob cap came hurrying out the door. "George, oh George it is ye. An' the children." She rushed down the steps and threw her arms around George.

"Ma," said George hugging her close. "It's good to see you again. Do you remember the children?"

"Aye, of course, I do," she said letting him go and turning her smile on her grandchildren. "My how they've all grown. Look at ye young George." She grabbed his face in her gnarly hands and kissed his cheeks. "Oh ye'll be a man afore we know it." She let him go and turned her attention to Jessie.

Jessie swallowed and smiled. "Hello, Grandma."

"Ye must be Jessie," she said wrapping her in her arms. "Of course, ye couldn't be anyone else." She let her go and held her at arm's length. "Ye look just like yer dear mother." She had tears in her eyes when she released her and turned her attention to William. "An' William. Ye were just a wee lad last time I saw ye." She engulfed him in a hug and kissed his cheek. "I can't believe you're all here. Come, come inside."

"Nice to see ye again, George," said Joseph stepping from the veranda and shaking hands with his stepson. "I trust everything's in order?"

"Aye."

Jessie left her father and Grandpa Joe to their conversation and followed her grandmother into the house. If she'd been amazed at the exterior, she was equally surprised by the interior. The sitting room was crammed full of furniture. You couldn't fit another sideboard or cabinet in if you tried.

"Come," said her grandmother. "We'll get ye all settled first, an' then we can sit an' get better acquainted."

The sitting room opened onto a cluttered dining room, with another parlour off to one side. A short hallway led to the rear of the house, past a study with a desk piled high with papers and such.

"I think this room will suit ye boys," said Maggie opening a door and stepping into one of the many bedrooms.

Young George and William followed her inside. Jessie peeked through the door and nodded. It was a large bedroom and well furnished with two beds, wardrobes, a washstand and two comfy chairs. A rug was spread out on the floor in front of a small fireplace. Jessie wondered if her grandmother had an obsession with furniture. Every room she'd seen so far was crammed full.

"Well, what do ye think?" asked their grandmother.

"It'll do us great thank you, Grandma," said young George dumping his bag unceremoniously onto one of the beds.

She smiled and heaved a sigh. "Good, well ye can unpack ye things an' put them away. Come, Jessie an' we'll see ye to yer room."

Jessie followed her down the hall to the next bedroom, which was down the end on the right-hand side.

"I didn't think ye'd want a room next to yer brothers," she said opening the door and gesturing Jessie to follow. "This is one of my favourites."

Jessie followed her into the most wonderful bedroom. The sun was shining in through the window onto a pink floral counterpane. The wardrobe and tallboy had been whitewashed and a small desk with a pair of chintz-covered chairs sat in the corner. A plush rug covered most of the floor, and a painting of the river hung over the small fireplace.

"It's beautiful," said Jessie trying to take it all in. "Is this truly to be my room?"

Maggie smiled widely. "Aye. I'm so glad ye like it. Now, why don't ye unpack ye things an' then come an' join us in the parlour."

"Yes, Grandma," said Jessie as she opened her bag and prepared to unpack her meagre belongings. Most of her clothes were in the sea trunk, which she presumed her father would bring in later. She heard the door close softly as her grandmother left the room.

She sighed and sat down on the bed. This was all far more wonderful than she'd imagined, and she wished she could enjoy her stay – but she had this horrid feeling in the pit of her stomach. This wasn't real. She'd only be here for a short time and then she'd have to join mother Sophia and the rest of her family in Pitt Town. She pressed her lips together and swallowed. Her life would never be the same again and it was just so unfair.

She sat there wallowing in her self-pity for some time before finally turning her attention to unpacking. She only had a few clothes with her, which she put away in the tallboy. Her only other skirt she hung in the wardrobe and hoped the wrinkles would fall out overnight. She slid her bag under the bed and looked around the room. If only Mary was here to share it with her. She sighed as she opened the door and retraced her footsteps back to the parlour, following the sound of voices.

"Ah here she is now," said Maggie as soon as Jessie entered. "Come an' sit beside me here. Are ye all settled then?"

"Yes," she said with a nod before perching herself on the sofa beside her grandmother. Her father and brothers were already seated and had small plates with cake. She glanced around and noticed a table with a tray of cake and a glass of milk.

"Help yerself," said Maggie smiling at her.

"Thank you." She slid a piece of cake onto a small plate and took a sip of the milk. It was cool and delicious, and all of sudden she became aware of how thirsty she was. She gulped down several large mouthfuls before placing it back on the table.

"Now, the boys have already been introduced, but ye haven't," said Maggie putting her cup down with a clatter. "This is Grandpa Joe."

"Hello," said Jessie smiling shyly at him.

"Nice to meet ye young Jessie," said Grandpa Joe with a warm smile.

"Now ye'll stay the night won't ye George?" said Maggie. "Ye don't need to get back to Pitt Town tonight."

"Of course, he will," said Joe putting his plate down. "I'd like ye to take a look at my spring cart. There's a problem with one of the rear wheels."

"I'll gladly take a look, Joe. But I'd rather get back tonight."

A young woman came into the room wearing a grey skirt and a crisp white apron. She glanced about and looked intently at Maggie.

"Not yet Eliza," said Maggie appearing to read her mind.

She gave a bob and left. Jessie looked after her and wondered who she was. She didn't think any of her Aunts or Uncles were living here. They were all married, well except for Uncle Joseph, but then he was nearly as old as her father. She settled herself back in the sofa and half-listened to the adult's conversation. She'd never met any of them, or her cousins or anything, but her father had told her about them. His brother William lived in Pitt Town and Jessie expected they'd visit him. She wondered if there were any cousins around her age. Life in Pitt Town was going to be different that was for sure.

***

After they'd finished their tea and coffee, her father and Grandpa Joe brought the trunk inside. Young George and William's clothes and things were put in their room, and Maggie joined Jessie in her room. She didn't have that many more clothes to put away, but it was nice to have her grandmother's help.

"Ye can finish yerself I think," said Maggie easing herself into a chair.

"Yes," said Jessie hanging her Sunday best dress in the wardrobe.

"Ye don't seem very happy about staying here with us," said Maggie eyeing her granddaughter.

Jessie swung around and looked at her. She was about to deny her feelings about moving to Pitt Town and leaving her sister behind, but one look at her grandmother's face and she changed her mind. She seemed to genuinely care about her. Maybe she'd understand.

"It's not you Grandma."

"Well I didn't think it was," she said with a scoff. "Come sit down an' tell me what it is."

She sighed as she sat in the other chair beside her Grandma. "I'm never going to see my sister, Charlotte again. And I hate that my whole life has been turned upside down."

Maggie smiled. It was a smile like she was remembering something, and her eyes had a far-away look in them. It only lasted a moment, and then she settled herself back in the chair. "Ye know life's like that. But ye never know what good things will happen because of it."

A crease furrowed Jessie's brow as she tried to understand how anything good could come of it. "I don't think so."

"Ye know, something happened to me that changed my life forever. An' I never saw any of my family ever again," she said leaning forward. "An' I never will again."

"Doesn't that make you sad?"

"Well of course it did at the time. But, if it hadn't happened I wouldn't be here. An' I love it here with Grandpa Joe."

"What happened?"

"I had a very good friend named Hannah," she said looking off into the distance. "She'd been pestering me to go to Bowerbank's drapers with her."

"Please Maggie, come with me."

"Alright, but only to look at calico for yer new bedgown. Nothing else," I said crossing my arms and frowning at her. "I know ye. An' I'm only coming with ye because I need some ribbon." I'd been caught by Hannah before. She'd say she only wanted to do one thing, but she always had another agenda. I had no intention of getting dragged all over town with her today.

"Oh thank ye, Maggie," said Hannah smiling with delight.

And so the two of us headed down Newgate Street together, arm in arm. We were both wearing typical dresses of the day with aprons and caps. There was nothing unusual about us whatsoever. When we went into the shop, Mr Bowerbank served us himself. He showed Hannah several prints.

"I'm going to look at the ribbons," I said, having every intention of doing so on my own. But, Mr Bowerbank accompanied me to the ribbons and helped me with my selection.

"There's nothing here I like," called Hannah from the other side of the shop. "Ye get what ye want and I'll meet ye outside."

Without waiting for a reply Hannah raced out of the shop. I was annoyed, and angry with myself for once again getting caught up in one of her hair-brain schemes. She obviously hadn't wanted to buy any calico at all, because there was a lovely selection.

Mr Bowerbank frowned. "Excuse me," he said, and he went over to the calico prints.

A moment later he started yelling. "Thief, thief."

He raced out of the shop, leaving me standing there with my mouth agape. Surely Hannah wouldn't have done such a thing? Seconds later, his brother appeared from the back room and accosted me. I was still trying to wrestle free of his rather firm grip of me when his brother returned dragging Hannah by the arm.

"You're mistaken, Mr Bowerbank," said Hannah. She looked like she was on the verge of tears, and yet I didn't miss the look in her keen eyes. She was looking frantically around the shop. "Oh, look Mr Bowerbank, is that not the length of calico ye think I stole?"

Sure enough, sitting on top of a pile of towels was one of the prints she'd been looking at. Mr Bowerbank inspected the cloth without releasing his grip on her.

"I think not," said his brother dragging me with him to look at the calico. "I saw her drop it. She had it under her apron. I'll hold them both while you go for the constable."

"I was in shock I think because I just stood there while he ran for the bobby," said Maggie shaking her head.

"What did they do to you?" said Jessie staring open-mouthed at her grandmother. She couldn't imagine any of her friends doing anything so awful.

"They carted us off to prison, an' then to court," she said with a shrug. "We were found guilty an' sentenced to seven years transportation. An' so here I am." She smiled ruefully. "I was distraught at the time. I was furious because I hadn't stolen anything an' yet I was as guilty as Hannah in the eyes of the law." She paused. "But, Jessie, don't ye see? If that awful day hadn't happened I wouldn't be here. I wouldn't have had the many happy years I've had married to Joe."

Jessie nodded. Although she couldn't imagine being separated from all that she loved like had happened to her grandmother. What did she really have to complain about? "I think I understand. But I still don't like it." There was a petulant note to her voice.

"You'll see," said Maggie rising to her feet. "Come now, our supper will be waiting for us."

***

Chapter Four

MacDonald River

Jessie awoke the following morning in her new room with a new life ahead of her. She lay there looking at the ceiling before finally climbing out of bed and facing the day. Her father had left the previous day, and now it was just her - well, her two brothers, Grandma and Grandpa Joe as well. She dressed in a warm pinafore and pulled her apron over her head.

There was a small mirror on the tallboy, which didn't allow her to see her whole self. She peered at her reflection. She still looked like her. She pulled her long straight hair back into a braid and tied it with a length of ribbon. Her blue eyes looked critically back at her before she shrugged and headed off to find the kitchen.

She soon discovered that the kitchen was situated off the veranda near the dining room. French doors opened onto the wide veranda, and the out-kitchen, and what she presumed to be the washhouse were within easy reach. She went down the short path and opened the door. The warmth from the hearth and the smell of freshly made toast assaulted her.

"Ah, ye must be Jessie," said the young woman she'd seen yesterday in the parlour. She was kneading dough on a wide bench and smiled warmly at her. "Sit down and I'll get ye some breakfast. I'm Eliza."

Jessie was momentarily surprised. She looked around the cluttered kitchen, with its large table in the middle of the room. "Hello," said Jessie trying not to let her confusion show. "Umm, where's everyone?"

Eliza wiped her hands on her apron and put the dough aside. "Oh, well Mr Smith's already down the paddock I 'spect with your brothers. Mrs Smith's just finished her breakfast. You'll probably find her in the sitting room." She pulled a loaf of bread from the crock and prepared to slice it. "Sit down. Will bread and jam do?"

"Yes, thank you," said Jessie slipping onto one of the chairs. She was curious about Eliza but didn't want to appear to be rude. She watched her as she sliced the bread and decided to just ask her. "So, do you work for my Grandmother?"

She turned and gave Jessie a rueful smile. "Ye could say that." She slipped the bread onto a plate and put it on the table. "I don't suppose it's a secret…I'm a convict."

Jessie didn't know what to say. A convict? While there were lots of them in Launceston, she'd never actually had anything to do with one. Of course, she knew her Grandma had been one, but still, she didn't know what to think. "Oh."

Eliza placed a pat of butter and a pot of jam in front of her. "It's alright. I mean your grandparents are the kindest most generous people."

"Thank you," said Jessie reaching for the butter. "Have you been here long then?"

"A while. I'll be free in another year." She wiped her hands on her apron and went back to kneading her dough. "Once you've finished that, go and see your grandmother. She'll want to show ye around I'm sure."

Jessie nodded as she munched her breakfast. She was mesmerised by Eliza's kneading and would've loved to have a go herself. She eyed her as she worked. "Are you making bread?"

"Aye."

"Would you show me how?"

Eliza looked at her for a moment – and then shook her head. "You'd best ask your grandmother."

"Alright." She finished eating her breakfast; all the while her eyes were firmly on Eliza and the breadmaking. She didn't understand why she should ask her grandmother's permission. She shrugged as she popped the last of her bread into her mouth. "Thank you."

Eliza smiled as she left the table and headed for the door. Jessie made her way back into the house and through to the sitting room. The door was open and she spied her grandmother sitting at a small desk writing. She didn't look up or react as though she'd heard her. She pressed her lips together and knocked on the door.

"Oh Jessie," said Maggie swinging around in her chair. "There ye are. I was wondering when ye'd surface."

Jessie felt her cheeks warm. She hadn't meant to be late getting up this morning and fully intended that it wouldn't happen again. She made her way over to where her Grandma was sitting and peered at the parchment in front of her. "What are you doing?

"Ah, I'm writing to yer Aunt Mary," she said glancing at a straight-backed chair sitting beside a small cabinet. "Pull that chair over an' join me."

Jessie nodded and dragged the chair closer to the desk before sitting down.

Maggie smiled at her. "I'll just finish this off. Would ye like to write to yer sister?"

Jessie screwed up her face. It wasn't that she wouldn't mind writing to Charlotte – she had lots to tell her…but.

"What is it?"

"Well," said Jessie slumping in her chair. "My writing isn't very good."

"All the more reason to write to her then," said Maggie reaching for a sheet of parchment and a quill. She slid them across the desk, "go on then."

Jessie spent the next hour composing a letter to her sister. All the while Grandma chatted away about all manner of things. "Tis such a shame that ye don't know any of yer cousins. But, I've invited yer Aunt Mary for a visit. I do hope she can come."

Jessie paused before dipping her quill into the ink pot again. "How many Aunts and Uncles do I have?"

Maggie sealed her letter and a crease furrowed her brow. "Well, it's rather complicated," she said. "Yer Aunt Charlotte's gone, God rest her soul. She was yer father's true sister. Then there's yer three Uncles, as well as Uncle Richard – Charlotte's husband."

"What do you mean by his true sister? Does he have others who aren't?" She knew about her Uncles – her father spoke about them often, but he rarely mentioned her Aunts.

Maggie sighed and peered at her granddaughter. "Aye. There's Sarah an' Mary, who I've just written. They're Joe's children. Then there's yer Uncle James – but ye'll not likely ever meet him. He's off whaling."

Whaling – that sounded so exciting. "You mean he actually hunts those big beasts?"

"Aye he does," said Maggie eyeing Jessie's letter. "Have ye finished?"

"Almost."

Maggie got to her feet and stretched. Jessie watched her as she went to the door and called for Eliza.

"I asked her if she'd show me how to make bread," said Jessie. She eyed her letter critically. It wasn't her best writing, but at least she'd managed to tell Charlotte everything that was going on.

"Did ye? Why ever for?"

"I really like cooking," said Jessie swivelling around so she could see her grandmother. "I'm not that good at it though. And the bread-making looked like fun."

She smiled at Jessie before sticking her head out of the door. "Eliza, Eliza," she bellowed. "An' what did she say?"

A distant 'I'm coming Mrs Smith' reached their ears. Maggie smiled again before sitting at the desk with Jessie.

"She said I'd have to ask you," said Jessie folding her letter and carefully slipping it into an envelope. "Can I?"

"Well, I suppose we need to find something for ye to do," said Maggie with a shrug. "Alright, but just don't go picking up any of her bad habits. She swears like a teamster an' I won't have ye speaking in such a way."

Jessie had no idea what swearing like a teamster would sound like, and she hadn't heard Eliza say anything bad. She was curious but tried not to look too excited at the prospect. "Thank you, Grandma. And I promise not to pick up any bad habits."

"Good," she said with a stern expression on her face.

"Sorry Mrs Smith," said a breathless Eliza coming to a halt beside the desk.

"Quite alright Eliza," said Maggie with a wave of her hand. "Has Mr Smith come back up from the paddocks yet?"

"No," she said with a shake of her head.

"No matter," said Maggie. "Young Jessie here wants to learn how to make bread an' such. Do ye mind teaching her?"

"Not at all, Mrs Smith."

"Good. Ye'll watch ye tongue, an' Jessie here will get up early to help ye with breakfast."

"Aye, Mrs Smith," said Eliza giving Jessie a conspiratorial smile.

"Now, I think we'll take tea on the veranda while we wait for Joe an' the boys," said Maggie as she watched Jessie carefully address her envelope.

"Aye, Mrs Smith. Ye make yer way out there and I'll fetch ye a pot of tea." She gave Jessie one last look before departing.

***

Jessie and Maggie had no sooner settled themselves on the veranda when Grandpa Joe and her brothers arrived.

"I'll take ye down to your Uncle Joseph's farm next week with me," said Joe stepping onto the veranda. "He's got a good lot of hogs."

"Can we ride?" said young George staring at Grandpa Joe. His eyes were alight with excitement. "I reckon I could ride all the way."

Joe laughed and grinned at him. "What about William? I don't think he could ride all the way to Pitt Town."

"What are ye planning?" said Maggie frowning at her husband. "I hope you're not set on some mad scheme?"

Joe smiled and placed an affectionate kiss on her forehead. "Nothing of the sort. I'm taking the boys to Pitt Town with me tis all."

Maggie looked thoughtful as she ran her eyes over her grandsons. "Ye can take George with ye, but William's too little."

"No I'm not," said an indignant William. "I can go, can't I Grandpa Joe?"

Joe rubbed his hand over his chin and looked at him. "Grandma's right. Ye can go next time when we take the dray."

"Ooh," said William slumping onto the veranda. He put his head in his arms. "It's not fair."

Jessie - who had been sitting quietly listening had to agree with William. It wasn't fair. How come George got to go to Uncle Joseph's and they didn't? Not that she was particularly fond of hogs or anything; but it was annoying to be left out. "Can I come?"

Grandpa Joe swung around and looked at her like he'd only just noticed she was there. “Well, lass I didn’t think you’d want to.”

“It’s just for us menfolk,” said George scowling.

Jessie poked her tongue at out her elder brother. He was such a pompous know it all.

“Perhaps next time. We’ll take the dray and ye and William can both come,” said Grandpa Joe.

"But only if yer manners improve,” said Maggie frowning at her.

Jessie felt her face redden and she lowered her lashes. She hadn’t intended for Grandma to see that.

“Jessie, run along an’ see where Eliza’s got to,” said Maggie looking up the veranda towards the kitchen. “Bring some milk for yourself an’ yer brothers as well.”

“Yes, Grandma,” said Jessie slipping from her chair. She walked along the veranda, glad to escape her grandmother’s scrutiny. Who cared if George got to go to Pitt Town? Not her. She’d be learning how to bake bread, and that was more exciting than some stupid hogs. She pushed all thoughts of

Pitt Town and Uncle Joseph from her mind as she made her way to the kitchen.

***

Chapter Five

MacDonald River July 1833

Jessie settled into life with her Grandma as though she'd always lived there. It would've been perfect if George had been left behind with Sophia instead of Mary. Other than that, she was loving life on the MacDonald River.

"Ye need to stretch that dough, Jess," said Eliza eyeing her critically.

Jessie sucked in another large lungful of air and pulled the dough before folding it and pushing it away from her. She turned it and repeated the process. She found kneading quite rhythmic, but she was already perspiring and panting slightly. Just a few more minutes and she thought it would be done. She stretched it again and felt it cling slightly to her palm.

The door to the kitchen opened and one of the farm-hands poked his head in the door. Jessie looked up and smiled. She thought his name was John. There were three farm hands – convicts all of them - or at least she thought they were. They rarely came up to the house and she'd never spoken to any of them.

Eliza swung around and glared at him. "What do ye think your bloody doing? Ye knows very well you're not to come in here."

He grinned, showing his uneven white teeth. "Calm down, Liza. Have ye seen the boss?"

"No I haven't, now bugger off."

He chuckled as he closed the door.

"How's that dough going?" said Eliza.

Jessie suppressed a giggle. "I think it's done."She wiped her hand across her brow and stepped aside so Eliza could inspect it.

Eliza pushed it and pressed it before smiling. "Aye, it's done. Put it by the oven to prove then ye can go."

Jessie put the dough in a bowl beside the oven and covered it with a cloth. She sighed as she removed her flour-covered apron and hung it on the peg by the door. "Do you want me to come back in an hour or so?"

"Aye, ye can do the vegetables for supper," said Eliza. "And ye can ask Mrs Smith if she'd like tea."

"Alright," said Jessie over her shoulder as she headed out the door.

A weak wintery sun was peeking out between the clouds, and a blustery wind was whistling around the veranda rafters. Jessie shivered as she hurried through the nearest door and into the house.

She wandered through the dining room and spied her grandmother through the glass doors sitting in the parlour. She had a letter in her hands and William was sitting on the rug on the floor. She opened the door and went into the parlour, closing it softly behind her.

"Jessie," said Maggie looking up from her letter. "Come and join us. I was just telling William about his cousins."

Jessie raised her brows and looked enquiringly. "Which ones?"

Maggie laughed as she folded her letter and slipped it into the envelope. "Good question - Mary's young ones." She put the letter on the side table and tapped it with her finger. "Unfortunately they can't come an' visit right now. Her little one's not well."

Jessie hoped her face was conveying some concern, but in reality, she wasn't anxious to meet a whole lot of little children or her Aunt Mary. She liked things the way they were. She sat down opposite Maggie and folded her hands in her lap. "I hope they get better soon."

"Aye, as do I," said Maggie. "Now, Aunt Mary's letter wasn't the only one I got. Yer Papa's written to say he's coming to visit."

Jessie's heart sank and she swallowed. Oh no – did this mean mother Sophia had arrived? She did her best to look both surprised and delighted with the news.

"When?" said William looking up from his slate.

"He'll probably get here next Friday," said Maggie smiling happily. "Twill be so lovely to see him again. Maybe we can convince him to stay for a few days this time. Wouldn't that be good?"

"Aye," said William jumping to his feet. "Will mother Sophia be with him?"

Jessie glanced sideways at her young brother. He sounded excited at the news, and she wondered if he perhaps liked Sophia. Surely not. She held her breath while she waited for her grandmother's answer.

"Well, I don't know," she said with a frown. "Your Papa didn't mention her, so I'd say not."

Jessie let out the breath she'd been holding – no mention of Sophia – thank goodness. "Oh, I almost forgot. Eliza wants to know if you'd like tea?"

"What a splendid idea. Aye," said Maggie getting to her feet. "William, run along an' tell Eliza we'll have milk an' tea for everyone."

"Aye, Grandma." William picked up his slate and put it on the side table before heading out the door.

"Come, Jessie. Let's go an' find Grandpa Joe an' George. They won't be far away."

***

Friday came, and as the day progressed so did Jessie's anxiety. Surely mother Sophia wouldn't have arrived so soon. It had been three months, but Jessie wanted it to last forever. She loved the hours spent with her Grandmother. She had such interesting stories to tell and had a way of making everything fun. Jessie hadn't felt so safe and secure since before her Mamma had died.

She closed her eyes tight as she tried to bring her mother's face to the forefront of her mind. A blurry image of a young woman with honey-blond hair swam in front of her eyes for a brief second, and then it was gone. She couldn't remember her face – it was always a blur. She sighed and snapped her book shut.

"Papa's here," said William slamming her bedroom door open and grinning at her. "Come on."

She put her book down and slid from the bed. "Is he alone?"

"No, Mary and mother Sophia are here too," he exclaimed with excitement. "Come on."

Without waiting for her he raced back down the hallway towards the front of the house. Jessie blew out her breath and looked around her small haven. It was over. They'd surely be leaving for Pitt Town tomorrow, and her life would be turned upside down once again. She slowly made her way along the hall to the front door. It was standing wide open, and she could see her father helping mother Sophia down from the spring cart. She groaned.

If anything Sophia looked more smug than usual. Jessie noted the new dress and matching bonnet with her blonde hair swept up under it. Her father looked happier than he had the last time she'd seen him. While she might loathe Sophia's return, her father clearly did not.

"Jessie." Mary came racing up to her and grabbed her in a tight hug. "Oh, how I've missed you." She let her go and planted a kiss on her cheek. "You must tell me all about your stay here with Grandma. Was she as wonderful as I remember?"

"Yes," said Jessie grinning at her sister. "And I don't want to leave."

"I don't blame you, but you'll like Pitt Town."

Jessie's brows arched as she opened her eyes in surprise. "What, you've been there already?"

"Yes, we arrived two days ago. The house Papa has rented for us is small but really nice."

Of course, it made perfect sense that they hadn't come up from Sydney today. She just hadn't stopped to think about it. "I suppose we're leaving in the morning then."

Mary shook her head and stepped aside to allow her father and Sophia into the house. "No. Papa intends to stay a few days. Where's Grandma?"

"Here," said Maggie arriving on the scene. She held her gnarled hand against her bosom, which was heaving considerably. "I was out back – oh George tis good to see ye again." She grabbed her son in a tight hug and kissed his cheek. "An' this must be Sophia." She let him go and drew Sophia into an equally tight embrace. "I'm ever so pleased to finally meet ye."

"Likewise," said Sophia in her silky voice. "I'm only sorry it's taken us so long to come and visit."

"Well no matter, you're here now," said Maggie before turning her attention to her granddaughters. "Mary, I remember ye well. Come an' give me a hug."

"Hello, Grandma," said Mary beaming at her grandmother. "I remember you from when you visited us."

"Good," said Maggie squeezing Mary and then letting her go. "Joe won't be but a moment, come, Sophia let's get ye settled. I hope ye'll be staying a day or two?"

"Aye, Ma," said George placing a kiss on Sophia's cheek. "I'll get the bags."

Jessie watched Maggie and Sophia disappear down the hallway, before looping her arm in Mary's. "Come, you can stay in my room with me."

"Alright, but I need to get my bag."

"Don't worry love, I'll get it," said Grandpa Joe appearing in the doorway.

"Thank you," said Mary smiling happily.

Jessie waited until they were safely ensconced in her room, with the door closed, before assaulting Mary with her questions.

"So how was it? You and mother Sophia, just the two of you in Launceston?"

Mary rolled her eyes and flopped down on the bed. “You got the better deal, Jess. She’s had me working all day, packing crates and clearing out the house. At least Charlotte was there.”

Jessie stretched out on the bed beside her. “How’s Charlotte?”

“Happy. At least she says so. Anyway, Tom and her have the house now, and everything we left behind,” said Mary rolling onto her side. “Sophia didn’t want any of Mamma’s things, so we left them all.”

“What, nothing?”

“Nothing,” she said with a sigh. “The lovely china and her best linen, all Charlotte’s now. And the furniture. She sold some of it including Mamma’s favourite chair. I don’t think Papa will be happy about that.”

Jessie scoffed. “Didn’t you see the way he looks at her? It wouldn’t matter what she did Papa wouldn’t care.”

“I don’t know. Anyway, we’ll have to get the house in order when we get to Pitt Town, and I’m sure Papa will expect us to help her.”

"And you can bet she'll be bloody bossing us," said Jessie scowling.

Mary stared at her with her mouth agape and then dissolved into a fit of giggles. "Where did you learn language like that?"

Jessie felt her cheeks redden and leapt from the bed as the door opened and Grandpa Joe came in carrying Mary's bag. She hoped he hadn't heard her or she'd be in trouble with Grandma.

"Ah. Are ye going to stay in here with Jessie are ye?" he said dropping the bag on the floor beside the bed.

"Yes," said Mary slipping from the bed. "Is that alright?"

"Aye, of course, it is. Once yer settled ye best come down to the parlour. Ye Grandma's arranged some tea and cake for ye."

"Yes Grandpa Joe, we'll be there in a minute," said Jessie.

He smiled and gave her a wink before stepping from the room and closing the door. Jessie groaned inwardly– he'd probably heard her swearing. She didn't think he'd tell Grandma, but she'd have to be more careful in the future.

***

Chapter Six

Pitt Town, 1834

Mary was right about one thing – Jessie liked Pitt Town. But that was all she liked. Sophia was more unbearable than she remembered, and her father was so busy with the new business she rarely saw him. She'd been living in Pitt Town for six months, and in that time everything had changed. She hated it and yearned to return to the MacDonald River, and her Grandmother.

Jessie watched as Mary wrapped her cloak around her shoulders. A single lamp was burning in their shared room, but it was casting enough light for her to see her sister. She was sneaking out again, and Jessie wanted to stop her but knew it was a waste of time.

She sat up and stared at her. "You're sneaking out again aren't you?"

"Shhh," said Mary putting her finger to her lips.

"You have to stop this, Mary. What if Papa finds out?"

"He won't as long as you don't tell him," she whispered. "Now go to sleep, I'll see you in the morning."

She lifted the sash window and climbed out. Poking her head back through it she grinned at Jessie. "I love you, Jess. Promise you'll cover for me?"

Jessie sighed and nodded. "For God's sake don't get caught."

"I won't." She blew Jessie a kiss before quietly closing the window and she was gone.

Jessie lay back down under the covers and tried to push all thoughts of Mary and her midnight escapade from her mind. She had no luck in doing so. She lay awake staring at the ceiling while imagining all manner of things.

She knew Mary was meeting Charles Kelly – a lovers tryst. She didn't quite understand what that meant, but Mary would return in a few hours, flushed and smiling. She imagined them lying in each other's arms, probably in a barn somewhere, or else under a tree. Did they kiss? She wondered what that might feel like - pressing your lips against another's. She pressed her lips against her bare arm and imagined it was a man's lips – but she felt nothing. She knew there must be more to it than that, but she'd only ever heard whispers.

She rolled over and buried her head under the covers. She should've asked Charlotte about men and such things; she would've told her she was sure. She had no intention of ever asking Sophia – she almost shuddered at the thought. Did Mary know about such things? Maybe.

The bedroom door swung open and Sophia's face, lit by the candle she was carrying, loomed before her. She looked at Mary's empty bed and then at Jessie. "Where is she?"

Jessie swallowed as her heart started hammering in her chest. Bloody hell! "P...Privy," she stammered. "She's gone to the privy."

"Really?" Sophia's crisp blue eyes shone like ice in the candlelight as she surveyed her.

Jessie maintained her gaze and hoped her thoughts would not betray her. "Yes, she hasn't been gone long."

"Hmph," she said putting the candle down on the nightstand. She crossed to the window and twisted the fastener into the closed position. "Make sure you keep this locked at night, anyone could come in." She swept the curtain across and glared at Jessie.

"Yes, we will. I thought it was locked."

"I'm watching you, my girl," she said picking up her candle.

With one final glare, she swept from the room and Jessie sighed with relief. Damn Mary, she would get them both into trouble. She was tired of covering for her and intended to tell her so. She waited a few minutes before creeping from her bed and unlocking the window. It would serve Mary right if she locked her out.

***

The inevitable happened. Barely a month later Mary's midnight escapades were discovered. Their father dragged them both into the sitting room to answer questions. Jessie shivered in her thin nightgown while Mary dissolved into a puddle of tears. Jessie didn't want to make eye contact with Sophia who was looking as smug as could be in the corner.

"I'm sorry Papa," sobbed Mary. "He's promised to marry me and I love him."

George ran his fingers through his dark hair as he stared from one daughter to the other. "And ye knew about this, Jess?"

Jessie swallowed. It was too late to try and deny anything, and the best she could hope for was that Mary would defend her. "Yes, Papa, but Mary made me promise not to tell." That at least was the truth.

"Is that true?"

Mary glanced sideways at Jessie before sucking in a breath. "Yes, Papa."

"Go to your room, Jess."

Jessie longed to hug Mary to show her that she wasn't alone in this, but that would have to wait. She gave Mary one final look, which she hoped portrayed her thoughts before hurrying from the room.

She left the door ajar and climbed into bed and wrapped herself in the quilt. There was no way she could go to sleep, not until she knew what was going to happen to Mary. She shivered, not just from the cold, and strained to hear the voices wafting down the hallway. She couldn't make out what they were saying, but she could hear her father's raised voice and Sophia's silky one interjecting. Poor Mary.

She must've dozed off because she awoke with a start as her head snapped back. All was quiet but there was no sign of Mary. Panic gripped her and her heart started hammering. What if they sent Mary away? What would she do without her? She was about to get out of bed and investigate when the door was pushed open and Mary entered.

"Mary," said Jessie diving out of bed and rushing to her side. "Are you alright?"

"Yes," she said hugging Jessie close. "I'm alright, but Papa is so mad."

Jessie clung to her sister and squeezed her. "I'm so sorry, Mary. I didn't know what else to say."

"It's alright," she said pushing her from her. "It's not your fault, it's mine."

"Come, come into my bed with me," said Jessie.

The two of them climbed into Jessie's bed and snuggled down under the covers. “What’s Papa going to do?” asked Jessie, almost afraid to hear the reply.

Mary sighed. “Well, tomorrow he’s going to see Charles and I expect I’ll be married as soon as he can arrange it.”

“Well, that’s what you want isn’t it?”

“I guess so, but I didn’t want it like this. I wanted Charles to ask for my hand, not be forced into it.”

Jessie thought about that. She thought she understood what she meant, but perhaps she should’ve thought about that before she went sneaking out. “Well, it’s not too bad then is it?”

“Not for me, no, but Sophia has convinced Papa to send you away.”

“What? Why? I didn’t do anything.”

Mary sighed. “You didn’t tell them about me, and Sophia says that’s worse.”

“I hate her,” said Jessie blinking back the hot tears that pricked her eyes. “That's so unfair.”

“I know, I’m sorry,” said Mary rolling over and putting her arm around her. “It’s all my fault and I’m sorry, but you’ll like it. They’re sending you to Grandma’s.”

"What!" Jessie searched her sister's face for any sign that she was lying. She half expected her to burst out laughing at her, but she didn't.

"You must act surprised when they tell you."

"You're serious? I'm to go to Grandma's?"

"Yes, I promise that's what Papa said."

A wide grin spread across Jessie's face as she thought about returning to the MacDonald River and her Grandmother. "It's almost too good to be true."

"Yes, but I'll miss you. I think that's why you're being sent away – to punish me."

"Well, I promise to enjoy your punishment," said Jessie squeezing her. "I do hope you get to marry your Mr Kelly though."

"So do I."

***

A week later George pulled the spring cart up out the front of his mother's house. Jessie breathed in the fresh air and craned her neck to see the river.

"You'll behave yourself, Jess," said George pulling on the brake. "I won't be coming back to get you until things are sorted between Mary and Mr Kelly. You understand?"

"Yes, Papa." She did her best to hide her excitement at being back at her Grandma's. It wouldn't do any good for her father to think this was going to be enjoyable.

He placed his hand on her leg. "I know this isn't your fault."

She looked at him. He appeared to be a man in charge of his life and his family, and yet she knew it was Sophia who ran things. Did he not realise that she knew that? "Thank you, Papa."

"You're a good lass. Now come on let's get you settled."

She jumped down from the cart and grabbed her small bag. She'd packed her few clothes and a book to read - enough for a short stay. She didn't think she'd be staying more than a couple of weeks at best.

The front door opened and Maggie peered out. She then flung the door open wide and came out onto the veranda. “Good Lord, is that ye George? An’ Jessie.”

“Ma, it’s good to see ye,” said George stepping onto the veranda and engulfing his mother in a warm hug.

“Likewise, but this is most unexpected,” she said placing a kiss on his cheek.

“Aye, well it’s a long story,” said George straightening. “I’m hoping ye won’t mind taking care of Jess for a few weeks. I’ve got to deal with an important matter.”

She eyed him quizzically, but he didn’t elaborate any further. “I’ve got to get straight back to Pitt Town, so I won’t be staying.”

“What? Ye can’t be serious?”

“I’m afraid so Ma. I promise I’ll stay when I return to pick up Jessie in a couple of weeks.” He stepped off the veranda and climbed onto the driver’s seat. “Thank ye.”

Jessie watched as he clicked the horse into a trot and headed back down the dusty road. A moment later he’d turned the corner and was gone. She picked up her bag and looked at Grandma. She was staring after her father with a look of confusion on her face.

"I hope ye can tell me what's going on?"

Jessie sighed. "Yes."

"Good. Come on we'll get ye settled."

Jessie followed her down the hallway to the bedroom she'd stayed in the last time she was there. Maggie opened the door and waited for Jessie to enter.

"While ye put your things away, ye can tell me what's going on," said Maggie easing herself into a chair.

Jessie put her bag on the bed and opened it. "Mary's been sneaking out at night to meet a man named Charles Kelly."

"Ah uh. An' she got caught did she?"

"Yes," said Jessie opening the wardrobe and reaching for a hangar. "She made me promise not to tell, and mother Sophia said that was worse than Mary sneaking out."

Maggie scoffed. "Is that why you're here an' not Mary?"

"I think so."

Maggie shook her head. “What did yer father have to say about it?”

Jessie paused and looked at her Grandmother. “He just said I was to stay with you until he got things sorted.” She hung her pinafore in the wardrobe and turned to face her. “I think he intends Mary to marry him.”

Maggie sighed. “Aye, I expect you’re right. I don’t know Mary but ye do. Does she love this Charles Kelly?”

Jessie shrugged. “She says she does.”

“Well, then it seems clear to me all except for one thing.”

“And what’s that?”

“Why yer father sent ye to me an’ not Mary. It would’ve made sense to send her here until things calmed down a bit. She’s too young to be getting married.”

“She’s fourteen.”

“Aye. Like I said, too young.”

“How old were you Grandma?”

“What when I was married?”

“No,” said Jessie blushing. “I mean when you went with a man.”

Maggie sighed and eyed her young granddaughter. “How old are ye?”

"Nearly eleven."

"Too young to be asking such things."

Jessie sat down on the edge of the bed and looked earnestly at her. "I've got no one else I can ask. I won't ask mother Sophia, and I don't think Mary knows about such things."

"Oh, I'd say she does," said Maggie rolling her eyes.

"Please, Grandma."

Maggie looked at Jessie thoughtfully. "I don't know that my story is one ye should be hearing."

"But I love your stories. Please…I'd really like to know."

She sighed in resignation. "Alright, but don't ye go telling yer father I told ye."

"I won't, I promise."

***

Chapter Seven

Maggie - Sydney, July 1791

I shivered, as much from the cold as from sheer fear. We'd just been brought off the ship and lined up on the docks, and all I could see were soldiers and men. I didn't take in the landscape or the township of Sydney, I was too focused on what was going to happen next. There were a hundred or more of us and a handful of children, and we all clung to our small bundles and one another.

The soldiers ushered us from the docks and up the street. After months at sea, it was so strange to walk on solid ground, and my legs felt like they belonged to someone else. My thoughts turned to William. I'd met him on board ship - well I'd become his wife so to speak. He promised he'd look after me and now I wondered how he'd know where to find me. I glanced around for any sign of him, but he'd no doubt still be on board the Mary Ann.

They took us to a sort of compound, and the surgeon inspected us before we were taken to some huts - eight women to a hut. We were told we'd be taking care of our own supper and that provisions would be unloaded from the ship for us. We'd be assigned to work the following day. I imagined I'd never see William again – but I was wrong. A week later he came for me.

"Maggie, I'm sorry it's taken so long to come for ye," said William throwing his arm around my waist."I've arranged a small house for us down at the rocks. It ain't much, but it will suit us nicely."

"An' I can come an' live with ye?"

"Aye, it's all arranged."

I'd never been so relieved in my life. We were to be together and maybe we'd even get permission to marry. William had promised me. A month later I realised I was with child, and the following April our son William was born. We were like a regular family. William worked down at the docks and I took care of our son and several other children while their mother's worked.

It wasn't like it is now. Food was always scarce and convicts were treated harshly, but I was protected from most of that. I thought we were happy, at least I was for the most part, but two years later everything fell apart.

"What are ye doing?" I asked. William was throwing everything he owned into a bag. "Are ye going somewhere?"

"Aye," he said slinging it over his shoulder. "I'm going back to England."

"What?" I stared at him as I tried to make sense of his words. What did he mean he was going back to England?

"I've signed on as crew, and I'm leaving. Goodbye Maggie," he said kissing the top of our son's head.

"When will ye be back?"

He paused in the doorway and turned back to face me. "I'm not coming back."

I was shocked, I didn't know what to say or do, and he just walked out. When my mind finally started to think I chased after him. "Wait, come back." He was already several doors down by the time I caught up to him. I grabbed him by the arm and screamed at him. "Ye can't do this."

"Don't make a scene, Maggie. Go home."

"Why? I thought ye loved me. Ye said ye did."

He pulled my hand from his arm and shoved me aside. "Go home."

"Ye can't," I screamed at him. "Ye can't leave me." I grabbed hold of his jacket and tried my best to stop him.

My head snapped as he slapped my face hard with the back of his hand. I stumbled backwards and fell, landing on my backside in the dirt. My face was already throbbing and I put my hand over what I imagined was a red welt forming on my face.

"Go home," he snarled at me.

The last I saw of him he was hurrying down to the docks, and I was left to take care of our son and myself. I had no idea where to start as I made my way back to our humble house.

"I had to find myself another protector, an' quickly if I hoped to survive."

"But you did survive, didn't you Grandma," said Jessie staring wide-eyed at her.

"Aye, I did," she replied with a sad look on her face. "My dear sweet baby

William didn't though. He died a few months later."

"Oh, Grandma I'm so sorry."

"Sometimes life deals ye a rough hand, Jess," said Maggie eyeing her young granddaughter. "Ye young ones shouldn't be in such a hurry to be running off."

Jessie lowered her eyes and looked at her hands folded on her lap. It wasn't the story she'd been expecting, but maybe Grandma was right. Mary shouldn't have been sneaking out to see Charles Kelly.

"Grandma, if you love someone, isn't that different?"

"It is. But sometimes ye just think yer in love, an' it turns out ye weren't," said Maggie flatly. "Now if yer finished unpacking, ye can go an' tell Eliza ye'll be here for supper. An' ye can also tell her we're expecting visitors on Monday."

"Visitors? Who?" said Jessie jumping to her feet.

"Yer Aunt Mary an' her two little ones. Now run along."

"Yes, Grandma."

Without waiting for Maggie she raced out of the bedroom and headed for the kitchen. She was excited at the prospect of seeing Eliza again and showing her how much her cooking had improved. She opened the door to the kitchen and hurried inside.

"Eliz....." Her name died on her lips as she stared at the scene before her.

Eliza was bent over the kitchen table, with her skirts hoicked up around her waist. John, one of the farm hands, was thrusting and grunting between her thighs. He looked at Jessie, alarm clear on his face, but he didn't stop what he was doing. Eliza squealed and shoved him from her as she straightened and pushed her skirts down. John turned his back to Jessie, and it looked to her like he was fumbling with his breeches.

"Bloody hell," said Eliza to John pushing him towards the door. "Get out."

Jessie stepped aside as he stumbled out the door. She stared opened mouthed at Eliza, who was buttoning her bodice and panting. She glanced sideways at Jessie, before sucking in a deep breath.

"Ye won't be telling anyone what ye just saw."

Jessie shook her head.

"Coz if ye do, your Grandmother will no doubt send me back to Parramatta. Ye understand?"

She nodded. "I promise I won't tell."

"Good," said Eliza straightening the chairs which had been shoved aside. "I must say, apart from being rudely interrupted, tis nice to see ye. How long are ye staying?"

"I don't know. A couple of weeks I suppose. My sister Mary got caught sneaking out at night, and Papa sent me here."

Eliza shook her head. "Well, that makes no sense at all. Sit, and tell me from the start."

Jessie sat on one of the kitchen chairs, and told Eliza about Mary and Charles Kelly – well at least the bits she thought she knew. "I asked Grandma about men and such, and she didn't really tell me what I wanted to know. Will you?"

"I will not," said Eliza swinging around from the bench and staring at her. "Although, I reckon what ye just saw ought to tell ye everything ye need to know." She laughed as she poured hot water into the teapot.

Jessie stared at her back. So that's what they were doing. She thought so, but she still didn't quite understand what was going on. "So you and John - you were making love?"

"I suppose ye could call it that," said Eliza putting two cups and saucers on a tray. "I'd say there weren't much love involved."

"Don't you love him?"

"God no," said Eliza staring at her. She sighed and slid into the chair beside Jessie. "Alright, what do ye want to know?"

"Everything," said Jessie putting her elbows on the table and leaning her chin on her hands. "And don't leave anything out."

***

October 1834

Monday dawned bright and sunny, with the promise of being a warm day with a lazy breeze. Jessie dressed with care – well, not that she had much choice in the way of dresses, but she donned a rather nice blue pinafore that had belonged to Mary. The lace was a little shabby around the neck, but she didn't think anyone would notice. She pulled her hair back into a braid and tied it with a matching ribbon. All in all, she thought she looked neat and tidy, and the blue brought out the colour of her eyes.

After breakfast, she dusted and swept the parlour and helped Maggie make up beds for their guests.

"How old are Aunt Mary's children?" she asked as she tucked in the sheet on the last bed. "They're only little aren't they?"

Maggie straightened and looked thoughtful. "Aye, little Maggie would be five an' half an' Willie's three."

"And will her husband be coming too?"

"No, no he'll be working," said Maggie tossing a blanket on the bed. "An' I expect they'll only be staying for a few days. Mary's just coming to be nosy an' to check on me an' Joe."

"Well that's nice isn't it?" Jessie spread out the quilt and added a pillow to the bed before standing back to assess it. It would be cosy and do fine for one of the children.

"Hrmph," said Maggie surveying the room. "I think we're done. Thank ye, Jess."

Jessie smiled at her grandmother as they left the room. She was a funny old thing sometimes. Why would she care that Mary was coming to check on her and Grandpa Joe? Jessie couldn't see how that could be a bad thing.

With the chores done, Jessie and Maggie settled themselves on the front veranda to wait for their guests to arrive. Joe joined them for their midday meal which they ate outside.

"I got a letter from the commissioner this morning," said Joe leaning back in his chair.

Maggie raised her brows and looked at him. "What about?"

"Eliza."

Jessie felt her heartbeat quicken and she licked her lips. She'd kept her promise and hadn't mentioned a word about what she saw in the kitchen. Surely they wouldn't be sending her back to Parramatta? Not that Jessie totally understood what that meant, but she knew Eliza didn't want to go back - that was for sure.

"She'll be free at the end of the month," said Joe

"Well, I don't want to lose her. We can afford to keep her, can't we?" said Maggie putting her cup down.

"Aye, of course, we can," he said rubbing his chin. "I'll have to talk to her though. She may not want to stay."

"Yes she does," blurted Jessie before she'd even thought about what she saying.

Maggie and Joe both turned their heads and stared at her.

"Ah, I mean…she told me so," she stammered.

"She told ye she wanted to stay here? Even after she was free?" said Maggie looking from Joe to Jessie with a crease in her brow.

Jessie felt her face redden and she swallowed. No - Eliz hadn't said that - well not in so many words. She couldn't tell Grandma and Grandpa Joe why Eliza and she had talked about her being sent back to Parramatta. She certainly couldn't tell them about the conversation they'd had after that either. She felt her cheeks redden further at the thought. The best thing to do was to stick to her story.

"Yes," said Jessie nodding in affirmation. It was a small lie and she didn't think she'd be found out.

"Ah well that's wonderful news," said Maggie beaming. "I was worried she'd want to leave as soon as she could."

"As was I," said Joe nodding.

"Under the circumstance, Jessie, ye should be the one to tell her she'll be free at the end of the month," said Maggie. "An' ye can also tell her how happy we are that she's staying on with us."

Jessie couldn't think of any way she could argue that point, and anyway, perhaps it was best that she told Eliza. She could explain to her that she hadn't meant to lie.

"Alright, Grandma," she said slipping from her chair. She gathered the dirty dishes from their midday meal and smiled. "I'll go tell her now."

***

Chapter Eight

MacDonald River, October 1834

Jessie's heart was fluttering with nerves as she opened the kitchen door. Eliza was sitting at the table eating her midday meal, and Jessie smiled as she walked passed her and put the dirty dishes on the bench.

"Thank ye," said Eliza between mouthfuls of soup.

"You're welcome," said Jessie leaning against the bench. She sucked in a breath and slowly let it out. "I have to talk to you about something, and promise you won't be mad at me?"

"Well I can't promise that can I?" said Eliza with a furrowed brow. "Ye haven't told your Grandmother I hope?"

"Not exactly."

Eliza rolled her eyes and pulled the chair out beside her. "Sit and tell me what the hell you've done."

"Well, Grandpa Joe got a letter about you," said Jessie sitting down beside her.

"And, your sentence is ending at the end of the month. You'll be free."

Eliza dropped her spoon and stared open-mouthed at Jessie. "I knew it was soon, but really, the end of the month? Well, that's only a couple of weeks away."

"Yes," said Jessie with a nod. "The thing is, Grandpa Joe and Grandma were wondering if you'd stay once your time was up?"

"I bet they bloody were," said Eliza pushing her empty bowl aside. "I still can't quite imagine being free in a few weeks. It's a bit overwhelming, to be honest."

"Hmm, I'm sure it is. The thing is, I may have told them that you wanted to stay," said Jessie. Without giving Eliza a chance to interject, she hurried on. "I didn't mean to. It just came out and then I had to say that you'd told me you wanted to stay. Otherwise, I would've had to tell them about what I saw and how you were worried they'd send you back to Parramatta."

"Bloody hell," said Eliza staring at her. "But ye didn't tell them about John did ye?"

"No."

"Thank God." She got to her feet and added her dirty bowl to the pile of dishes.

"You do want to stay don't you?"

"Not really," she said shaking her head. "There's nothing for me here. I want a life, ye know, a husband and a family. I can't get that here."

"What about John?"

Eliza scoffed as she sat back down beside Jessie. "I already told ye, I don't love him or nothing."

Jessie pressed her lips together as she pondered the situation. She truly hadn't meant to make life difficult for Eliza, but if she didn't stay, what would she tell Grandma? "What will you do?"

"I can't see that I can do anything other than stay, at least for the time being," she said frowning. "But, if ye dare say another bloody word about me I swear I'll have ye scrubbing the privy for a week. Ye understand me?"

Jessie nodded and swallowed. She was sure she meant it. "I'm truly sorry."

Eliza gave her a lop-sided smile and squeezed her arm. "I know ye didn't mean to. I'll stay for a wee bit, and then I'll leave. Ye can tell your Grandma I'm staying."

"Thank you, Eliza. I'll go tell her now, and then I'll come back and help you prepare supper."

"Good. Have our visitors not arrived yet?"

"No not yet," said Jessie getting her feet under her.

She heaved a sigh of relief as she stepped out of the kitchen and closed the door. Eliza was angry with her, but she'd taken it quite well. The best bit was Grandma would never find out she'd told a little lie.

***

It was mid-afternoon before a spring cart loaded with bags, Aunt Mary and her two children arrived. Jessie was surprised to see that she was very obviously expecting a baby. Grandma hadn't mentioned that. She waited on the veranda while Grandma and Grandpa Joe helped with the bags and the children.

"Oh what a marvellous surprise," said Mary beaming at Jessie. "I never expected to meet you. I'm your Aunt Mary."

"Hello, Aunt Mary."

"My, our side of the family didn't get a look in," said Mary turning to Maggie. "She's not like George at all."

"No," said Maggie smiling. "Jessie's like her mother. Ye never met her did ye?"

"No," she said stepping onto the veranda.

If Aunt Mary was surprised that she didn't look at all like her father, then Jessie was equally surprised that she looked so like him. They had the same pitch-black hair and long thin noses. She even walked a little like her father.

"And this is little Maggie and Willie. Come and say hello to your cousin, Jessie," said Mary ushering her two children forward so Jessie could see them.

Jessie did her best to smile politely. She didn't particularly like little children and always found them to be noisy and quarrelsome. A bit like her younger brother William - he was always a nuisance.

"How long are ye staying?" said Joe stepping onto the veranda loaded with bags.

"Oh just a few days," said Mary. "Here give me one of those, Papa. You look like a pack horse."

He smiled as he relinquished one of the smaller ones. "Well, tis good to see ye. But I wish ye'd waited. When's the little one due?"

She smiled as she ran he hand over her stomach. "Not for another couple of months at least, Papa. You needn't worry."

"Jessie, why don't ye show Maggie and Willie to their rooms, an' then run an' tell Eliza our guests have arrived," said Maggie.

"Alright." She groaned inwardly but hoped her smile hid her true feelings. "Come with me and I'll show you."

Willie looked dubiously at her before Mary urged him to go. Jessie headed inside and down the hallway to the end. She could hear their little footsteps behind her and she smiled. While she may not, particularly like little children, these two were her cousins, and that was kind of interesting. She opened the door near the end of the hall and beckoned them to enter.

“This will be your room,” she said following them inside. “I hope you like it.”

Little Maggie looked around and smiled. “It’s nice.”

“Good. Well, if you wait here, Grandpa will be along with your things in a minute.”

Jessie headed back down the hallway and ran into Maggie and Aunt Mary.

“Jessie, be a sweetheart an’ take Mary’s bag to her room,” said Maggie taking the bag from Mary and handing it to Jessie. “Then go an’ tell Eliza Mary an’ I will take tea on the back veranda. Bring some milk for the children too. Will ye join us?”

“Yes.” She nodded before heading back down the hall to the room where Aunt Mary would be staying. She put her bag down on the rug and looked around. It was a lovely room, but not as nice as the one she was staying in. She smiled as she left and closed the door.

***

Jessie thoroughly enjoyed Aunt Mary's visit. She didn't change her opinion of young children, but Aunt Mary had proved to be just about as interesting as Grandma. She told her about her other Aunt and Uncles. Uncle William had three children, whereas Uncle Joseph wasn't' married, nor was Aunt Sarah. She hadn't said much about her youngest Uncle Henry. Jessie wondered if that was where the most interesting family story was. Grandma was rather tight-lipped as well.

The day after Aunt Mary departed her father arrived unexpectedly. Well, she thought it was unexpected. She knew he'd come back for her, but had been hoping for a longer stay. He had young George and William with him, which did nothing to improve Jessie's mood. At least he'd left mother Sophia at home. But what about Mary?

"Thank ye for taking care of Jessie, Ma," said George seating himself in the most comfortable chair in the parlour.

"Yer welcome, but I hope you've got five minutes to explain to me what happened," said Maggie sipping her sherry.

"Aye," he said glancing around. "Perhaps when the children are abed."

Jessie had no intention of being sent to bed without first finding out what had happened to Mary. It was unfair enough that she'd been packed off to Grandma's – but she felt a pang of guilt when she thought of Mary. She hadn't given her sister a thought in the two weeks she'd been here. She tried to look disinterested, while every sense was on alert for her grandmother's reply.

She nodded but said nothing. And then her father got into a boring conversation with Grandpa Joe about his spring cart. Jessie stared at the fire and sighed. They'd probably be going home to Pitt Town tomorrow and to mother Sophia. She wished she could stay here. She thought it would suit her father and mother Sophia if she did. She glanced sideways at her father – he was talking about wheels and hubs – his favourite subject.

Half an hour later Jessie was nearly asleep from utter boredom.

"I think it's time ye were all abed," said George looking around at his children. "Say your goodnights and be off."

"Goodnight," said William standing up and stretching.

He gave his father and grandparents a hug and a kiss and waited for young George and Jessie to do the same. Jessie reluctantly got to her feet and said her goodnights, before following her brothers from the room. She closed the door, leaving it slightly ajar – not enough that anyone would notice.

She followed her brothers down the hall and bid them goodnight at her bedroom door. She slipped inside and waited. As soon as she heard their door clunk closed, she crept out into the hallway. There was no sign of them, and so she tiptoed back towards the parlour. She could hear the rumble of her father's voice but she couldn't make out what he was saying. She positioned herself beside the parlour door and put her ear to it.

"so after several days of crying and tantrums I conceded," said George with a sigh. "What else could I do?"

"Hrmm," said Grandpa Joe. "Daughters can be troublesome."

"Ye have naught to complain about with our girls," said Maggie. "So what did ye decide about the wedding?"

"Sooner rather than later," said George. "I'd sooner not risk a scandal, and I'm sure they'll be one if I don't get her married soon. Reverend Cartwright's agreed to marry them on Sunday after church. It'll be a simple ceremony, but they'll be wed."

Jessie pressed her back to the wall. Sunday! Oh my God, she couldn't believe Mary was getting married this Sunday. She felt hot tears prick her eyes and she swallowed. She'd probably move away and she'd never see her again.

She heard her grandmother asking if they could go to the wedding. She didn't wait to hear her reply, as she hurried back to her room and shut the door. She threw herself on the bed and buried her face in the pillow and let her tears go. It was so unfair. Now she was losing her other sister, and she'd be stuck with know-it-all George and bloody William.

***

Chapter Nine

Mrs Charles Kelly

Mary's wedding reminded Jessie of Charlotte's. The day was very similar, and apart from Grandma sitting beside her, it was just as horrid. She sat and waited while Mary and her new husband filed out of the church. She'd probably never see Mary again, or at least not very often. They were moving in with Charles' family in Wollombi – wherever that was.

"Ye don't look too pleased for yer sister," said Maggie nudging Jessie in the ribs.

She glanced at her grandmother and shrugged. "Should I be?"

"Hrmm, perhaps not," said Maggie squeezing her hand. "But tis the way of the world. It won't be too many more years afore yer get married yerself. Although, I hope yer not going to be in such a hurry."

"I don't know," said Jessie looking at her grandmother like she hadn't given it a thought before. Of course, she had. Grandma was right it was the way of things. “When did you fall in love? Were you young like Mary?”

“No,” said Maggie with a shake of her head. “No, I was much older.”

“Was it William Morrison? You know you told me about him.”

“No. Actually, if ye must know his name was William Smith, and he was yer father’s Papa.”

“Really?” said Jessie gaping at her. She’d imagined her falling in love with Morrison. She lived with him and had a baby with him. Jessie couldn’t imagine doing that with anyone she didn’t love. She felt her cheeks redden at the thought of doing ‘that’.

“Oh, he was so young an’ handsome, with pitch-black hair like yer father, an’ the bluest eyes.”

Jessie stared at her enraptured as she imagined her unknown grandfather. “Tell me about him. How did you fall in love?”

“Oh that bit was easy,” said Maggie with a laugh. “He was so handsome, with a welsh accent that I could listen to all day. I fell in love with him the first moment I saw him. It wasn’t long after William left me an’ returned to England. We moved in together right away, an' before I knew it I was expecting yer Aunt Charlotte."

"Did he marry you?"

Maggie sighed and looked sideways at Jessie. "No. We never married." She sounded wistful and stared off into the distance. "Not long after yer father was born, I lost him."

A crease marred Jessie's forehead as she tried to work out what she meant. Did he leave her too? "What happened, Grandma?"

She sighed and squeezed Jessie's hand. "He was killed in an accident building the new bridge."

Jessie couldn't help but notice her Grandma's eyes welling with unshed tears. She squeezed her hand and smiled. "I'm so sorry, Grandma. You must've been so sad."

"Aye, I was," she said reaching into her reticule and retrieving a handkerchief. She dabbed her eyes and smiled ruefully.

"Are ye two coming?" said George stopping at the end of their row and staring at them. Sophia was hanging on his arm and she glared down at Jessie.

"Are ye alright, Ma?"

"Oh, aye. I always shed a tear at weddings."

"Well, come along then. Mary and Charles will want to be going. They've got a three-day journey ahead of them."

"Of course," said Maggie getting to her feet.

Jessie slid along the pew and waited for her grandmother. The church was empty apart from them and all at once she became anxious to leave. She had to see Mary before she left, and Grandma was taking her time. She tried to swallow the broiling feeling in the pit of her stomach.

"I'll meet you outside," said Jessie pulling her shawl around her shoulders as she prepared to leave.

"You'll wait right there," said Sophia grabbing her arm. "Where are your manners girl? You'll wait for your grandmother and your father."

Her fingers dug into her soft flesh and it took all of Jessie's self-control not to pull out of her grasp and run. Sophia finally released her and pinned her with an icy stare. Jessie swallowed the ache in her throat – she'd be damned if she'd let her see her tears.

"Come, take my arm, Jessie," said Maggie looping her arm in Jessie's. "I'm feeling a little unsteady."

"Yes, Grandma."

As they walked slowly from the church Maggie patted Jessie's arm and looked knowingly at her. Jessie pressed her lips together in an effort to not let her tears fall. How odd that a kind look from her grandmother could make her want to cry even more.

***

The only bright spot in Jessie's world was her Grandma. She stayed for a few days after the wedding and Sophia was far more civil when she was there. But a cloud had descended upon Jessie that had nothing to do with her stepmother.

"Come, Jessie," said Maggie urging her to join her in the garden. "It's a beautiful day."

Jessie groaned but allowed herself to be led outside. It was a lovely day, and perhaps a walk in the garden would lift her spirits.

"I hate to ye so sad, Jess," said Maggie seating herself under a small gum tree. "Come, join me," she said patting the seat beside her.

Jessie sighed and sat beside her. "I'm sorry to be so dreary, but once you leave I'll be all alone."

"What nonsense. You've got George an' William haven't ye?"

Jessie rolled her eyes. "You don't know them very well. George is a pompous know-it-all and William's a pest."

A wry smile spread across Maggie's face. "Perhaps. But, George is yer older brother, an' I'm sure he'd help ye if ye let him."

Jessie eyed her grandmother and shook her head. She didn't think so. George was so full of his own importance that he barely even noticed her. He certainly wouldn't see that she was sad and needed a hug or anything. No - Mary would – but she was gone. "It's going to be just awful without Mary."

Maggie nodded and patted her arm. "Aye, it won't be easy I'm sure, but tis not the end of the world. I remember when

William was killed I thought I'd die too. But I didn't."

Jessie tilted her head to the side and looked at her grandmother. She'd had so much loss in her life and yet here she was, smiling and optimistic. Could she be like Grandma? She didn't think so. It wasn't the same, and she wasn't old enough to do whatever she liked. That would be different. She could go back to Launceston and visit Charlotte, or go to Wollombi – wherever that was. She smiled and nodded. "So what did you do after William died?"

"Well, I was lucky my sentence expired an' I was a free woman, an' then I met Patrick Shannon," she said. "Ye never know who ye'll meet that'll make a difference to yer life."

Jessie stared at her wide-eyed. "I thought you met Grandpa Joe?"

"No, not then I didn't." She paused and looked off into the distance. "I wasn't really looking for a new man, it just happened – life's like that. Charlotte was four and yer father had just turned two. I was on Government rations, but otherwise, I was managing alright. Then I met Patrick. He was still a convict – I think he had another two or three years left of his sentence. I wouldn't say it was love or anything between us, but he was prepared to support me and the children an' so we moved in together. He never said he loved me an' he never offered to marry me. I didn't want any of that either. I'd had enough heartbreak. Anyway, it wasn't long before I realised I was having his baby. I had a son, James – ye remember I told ye about him – he's a whaler. It seems Patrick an' I wanted different things because everything changed after James was born. He hung around for a bit an' then he left one morning an' he never came back."

"I never saw him again," she said wistfully. "Don't misunderstand me, I didn't miss him, but it was hard to take care of myself an' three children on my own."

Jessie looked at her hands folded on her lap. Grandma made her feel ungrateful and petulant. She didn't think she was any of those things, but there was a little pang of guilt tugging at her. She swallowed. "Am I being a child?"

Maggie laughed and wrapped her arm around her shoulders. "Ye are a child, an' don't be in a hurry to grow up. There's plenty of time for that," she said squeezing her. "I only wanted ye to see that yer situation isn't that bad. Ye could try an' make the best of it."

"I will, I promise." She felt better talking to Grandma. She'd made friends with Hannah Fulton at school, and maybe she could be that person like Grandma said – the person you meet who makes a difference in your life. "I feel much better."

Maggie smiled and let her go. "Good."

***

Two days later Maggie left and Jessie settled down to life without either of her sisters for company. She was determined to make the best of it. Her efforts were short-lived, however. No sooner had she arrived home from school the following day than Sophia pounced on her.

"You can get to and help me prepare supper, and then you can bring in the laundry."

Jessie groaned inwardly but smiled passively. Maybe she could get her chores done quickly and still meet Hannah. They'd made plans to go down to the creek to catch tadpoles. Not that she particularly liked the slimy things, but they were going to take them to school the next day.

She set to peeling and chopping the vegetables that Sophia wanted for supper. She liked being in the kitchen and cooking in general. She'd learnt so much from Eliza, and although she hadn't cooked an entire meal from start to finish by herself, she was confident she could do it. She put the chopped carrots in the pot and set to shelling the peas. She sat with a bowl between her knees and nibbled on the small sweet ones.

"Enough eating and more shelling," said Sophia glaring at her. "There won't be enough for supper if you don't stop eating them."

"Sorry," said Jessie looking up at her stepmother briefly. She was only eating the really small ones, that wouldn't end up in the pot for supper, but she was doing her best not to argue or antagonise Sophia. She didn't think she was succeeding. She sighed – would it matter what she did? Probably not.

Ten minutes later Sophia inspected her bowl of peas and nodded with satisfaction. "That'll be enough. Go and bring in the washing," she said taking the bowl. "And make sure you fold everything neatly."

"Yes, mother Sophia."

She sighed as she headed out the back door to the washhouse. She grabbed the large wicker washing basket and went down the yard to the clothesline. She groaned and dropped the basket on the ground. The lines were loaded with washing, and wouldn't be taken in and folded in five minutes. She pressed her lips together. It would only take a few minutes to go and find Hannah and tell her to go ahead without her.

She slipped up the sideway of the house, unseen, and headed for the creek. She took a shortcut through some vacant land that backed onto the creek and made her way along the bank. She saw Hannah as she rounded the corner and waved to her. Hannah waved back and a smile spread across Jessie's face. It was so good to see her.

"Where's your jar?" said Hannah frowning at her when she finally arrived at their meeting spot.

"I didn't have a chance to get one. Mother Sophia had me doing chores, and I'm supposed to be bringing in the washing," said Jessie panting. "I can't go with you." She saw the disappointment on Hannah's face immediately. "I'm sorry."

"Oh it's not your fault," said Hannah brushing her apology aside. "But I don't want to do this alone." She tucked a strand of dark curly hair behind her ear and frowned. "How about I come and help you with your chores, and then we can do it together?"

"Really? You'd do that?"

Hannah smiled and it made crinkles at the corners of her eyes. "Aye. What are friends for?"

Jessie hugged her as a warm feeling of happiness flowed through her. She was right. Hannah was that one person that Grandma had talked about. "Thank you."

***

Chapter Ten

The River is Unforgiving

Having a friend made life bearable – but only just. Sophia gave Jessie no time to herself, and as the months passed, she became more and more disgruntled. It didn't seem to matter what she did, Sophia found fault. George and William didn't come under her scrutiny like Jessie did, and that only helped to build her resentment towards her brothers.

Her father either didn't appear to notice or gave his support to his wife. Jessie longed to return to the MacDonald River and her grandmother. She swallowed her frustration as she finished drying the last of the dishes from supper. Her father's dinner was sitting over a small pot of simmering water – he was late home. That was unusual in itself – he was never late. Jessie wondered if he'd gone to the pub. Would he dare?

"There you are," said Sophia marching into the kitchen.

Where else would she be? She knew perfectly well she'd be in the kitchen drying the dishes from supper. She raised her brows and looked enquiringly at her stepmother, but said nothing.

"Your father's not come home."

Jessie's shoulders slumped. What was she supposed to do about that? Surely Sophia wasn't going to blame her for her father's tardiness. "No," she said putting the plates in the dresser.

Sophia paced up and down the kitchen. "I don't know what could be keeping him."

Jessie wondered why she was even having this conversation. What did she expect her to do about it?

"I want you to go to his shop and see what's amiss."

"What? Now?" It was already dark out and Jessie wasn't keen on the idea of wandering around the streets alone in the dark.

"Don't you dare take that tone with me," said Sophia glaring at her. "Yes, I mean now. Get going."

Without saying another word, Jessie removed her apron and hung it on the hook. She hurried to her room and grabbed her cloak. So many different emotions were flitting through her that she didn't know which one was going to win. She was angry, frustrated and so tired of being humiliated by Sophia. She sucked in a deep breath as she stepped out into the cool night air. Why wasn't George being sent to find Papa? He was the eldest. It wasn't fair, it never was, and she hated Sophia right now.

She was at the gate when the front door opened and closed. She turned around and was surprised to see George hurrying towards her.

"What are you doing?" he said coming to her side.

"Mother Sophia wants me to go and fetch Papa. What do you care?" Jessie thought she saw concern flit across her brother's face. She looked at him – puzzled.

"Well, I'm coming with you. You shouldn't be out here alone."

"What about mother Sophia? She won't be happy at you sneaking out," said Jessie. She almost wished he'd take the huff and go back inside, but the other half of her was curious. Did he really care about her?

"Humph, I don't care what she says," he said shoving his hands in his pockets. "Come on."

The two of them started walking down the street together towards their father's wheelwright shop. Jessie glanced sideways at him – he wasn't behaving like his usual pompous self.

"How come you're coming with me - really?" She couldn't hide the disbelief in her voice.

George sighed. "I know I haven't been the best brother, but that doesn't mean I don't see things," he said. "And, it's a bit odd that Papa hasn't come home tonight."

Jessie nodded. She had to agree with him on both counts. He was acting weird though. She shrugged as they turned the corner. The moonlight was casting long shadows, and Jessie was so glad George had accompanied her. She wasn't scared of the dark exactly, but she did find the night a bit creepy.

Her father's shop was situated halfway down the street, and from this distance, it looked to be in darkness. That wasn't surprising – but where was her father?

"It doesn't look like he's here," said George as they approached the front doors. He grabbed hold of the handles and pulled. "It's locked."

There was no lamplight shining through the window, but Jessie stood on tiptoes and peered inside anyway. It was dark and she couldn't see a thing. "Let's go round the back."

"Alright."

They made their way around to the rear yard and climbed over the fence. Jessie peered around for any sign of their father while George tried the rear door. She wasn't sure what she was looking for exactly. Her father might be injured or stuck under a wheel or something, but there was no sign of him.

"It's locked," said George rattling the rear doors.

Jessie sighed. Where was he?

"Come on, let's go home." George gave the doors one final shove before turning to face his sister.

"We can't," said Jessie staring at him. "Mother Sophia will be so angry if I go home without him."

"I'll deal with her."

Jessie scoffed as she climbed back over the fence. "Sure you will because you always stand up for me." Her voice was dripping with disdain.

"Look, I'm sorry," said George climbing the fence. He grabbed her by the arm. "I don't know how to make her stop, but from now on I'm going to do something."

Jessie shook her arm loose. "You're a pompous jackass, George. Far too concerned with yourself to help me." She turned her back and headed for the street.

"You're not so perfect yourself," said George catching up to her. "You think your Grandma's little favourite," he said scowling at her.

She swung around and stared at him. "Grandma's little favourite?"

"Yeah, you know it's true."

Jessie stopped and stared at him. "Are you jealous? Of me?" she said raising her eyebrows. "You've got to be kidding."

"No."

They continued to walk back home in silence. For one moment Jessie had thought that maybe, just maybe, her pompous brother might care. But no – as usual, George was all about George. He was jealous, whether he denied it or not, she knew it.

They walked down the sideway of the house to the back door. George put his hand on her arm as she reached for the doorknob. "Let me tell mother Sophia that we couldn't find Papa."

"Suit yourself," said Jessie with a shrug.

They found mother Sophia sitting in the parlour with her mending in her lap. William looked at them expectantly, but Jessie ignored him.

"Well, where's your father?" said Sophia putting her mending aside.

"We couldn't find him," said George

"What do you mean?" she said scowling at them both. "Get back out there and don't come back until you do."

"No," said George straightening his shoulders. "Papa's shop's locked and in darkness, and he's not there."

Jessie swallowed and licked her lips. She would never have dared to say no. She had to admit that right now George was standing up for her like he said he would.

Sophia rose from her chair and glared at them both. "You snivelling spoilt brats think you can speak to me like that? You will do as I say."

Jessie took a step backwards as her eyes flicked from Sophia to George. Her heart was hammering and her stomach felt like the bottom had just fallen out of it.

"Papa will come home when he's ready," said George standing his ground. "We're going to bed. Come, William."

Jessie stared open-mouthed as Sophia screwed up her face and screamed. She pulled back her arm ready to strike George, but he sidestepped and she staggered towards Jessie. Their eyes locked and Jessie stared into her enraged face. She felt like she'd been paralysed and was rooted to the spot. The slap across her face quickly brought her to her senses and she grabbed her stinging cheek. The look of rage was still on Sophia's face, and Jessie knew she'd hit her again. She took several steps backwards towards the door, not taking her eyes off her stepmother.

"Stop," said George stepping between Sophia and his sister. "Leave her alone."

"Get out of my way," said Sophia gripping George by the shoulders as she tried to push him aside.

He held his ground and glared at her. "Go - get out of here, Jess."

George flung Sophia from him and she staggered towards Jessie again. Jessie didn't need to be told twice. She turned and ran from the room and along the hall to the front door. She stepped out into the cold night air and sucked in several lungfuls of air. She was overwhelmed by the events of the evening and felt hot tears fill her eyes. She couldn't stop them and a small sob escaped her lips. Where was she going to go? She couldn't possibly head for Grandma's in the middle of the night, and Aunt Mary had moved from Pitt Town earlier in the year. Hannah's - God what would Mrs Fulton think about her coming in such a state? She didn't know, but she had nowhere else to go.

***

Jessie opened her eyes and looked around. She wasn't in her own room, and then the events of the previous night came flooding back. She was at Hannah's house. She sighed and rolled over.

Mrs Fulton hadn't asked too many questions and had made up a trundle bed for her in Hannah's room. Hannah, on the other hand, wanted to know every minute detail and was very curious about her father. Where had he gone? Jessie stretched and yawned. She hoped her father had come home last night, and that he wouldn't be too angry with her for running off to Hannah's for the night. She had to get home and explain.

It was only a short walk around the corner to home, and Jessie debated on whether to go straight there or go to her father's shop. He might be getting an early start today. It didn't take her long to decide that would not be a good idea. It would be better to delay the inevitable conversation with her father – he would not be in a good mood this morning. No doubt mother Sophia had already told him how rude George and she had been, and he'd be angry and disappointed.

As she neared her home she couldn't help but notice several carts parked out the front. She quickened her pace and hurried down the side of the house to the back door. As soon as she entered, she could hear voices coming from the parlour. Her heart started hammering in her chest as she walked up the hallway. She knew something was very wrong and it scared her.

"Jess."

She stopped and turned to face George who looked pale and serious.

"What's going on?"

He shook his head and blinked back tears. "It's Papa, they found him."

Jessie stared at him and waited for him to tell her more. She could feel her chest rising and falling as her breathing quickened. "Is he hurt?"

"No," he said blowing out his breath. "They found his body in the river this morning. He's dead."

Without warning, he threw himself at her and wrapped her in a tight hug. She felt his whole body heaving as tears wracked him. Her tears mingled with his as they clung to one another. Oh my God, he was dead. It didn't seem real to her. How could this happen? And what was going to happen to them now?

"What about mother Sophia?" she said pulling out of his grasp.

He wiped his eyes with the back of his hand. "She's really upset. The doctor's with her now."

"Do they know what happened to Papa? Did he drown?"

He shook his head. "I don't know. The police came and spoke to mother Sophia, but I don't know what they said. She told me to go away. And then the doctor came and Mrs Cartwright and Mr Bowman." He swallowed. "Someone should write and tell Grandma."

Jessie nodded. Mother Sophia should be the one to do that, but she wondered if she would. She sucked in a breath. "I'll do it. I'll write to Grandma."

***

Chapter Eleven

Arrangements for Jessie

It was a grey overcast day, which matched Jessie's mood perfectly. Her father's coffin was sitting beside the open grave – which looked like a monster with its mouth agape waiting for its favourite meal. She shuddered and looked away. The Reverend Cartwright was saying some final words, which washed over her not leaving any meaning behind.

And then they lowered her father into the grave and the tears she'd been holding back let go. A sob escaped her lips as Grandma's gnarled hand slipped into the crook of her elbow. No words were necessary between them. Her grandmother's small solid form standing beside her was comfort enough.

Maggie pressed a small clump of earth into Jessie's hand and urged her towards the grave. They stood on the edge peering down. It struck Jessie that burials were an odd custom. She wondered when the ritual had started – probably eons ago.

The thud of a small clod of dirt hitting the wooden coffin brought Jessie back to the present. She swallowed as she peered into the grave, and then she threw her small clump of earth in. It landed with a muffled thud and spread smaller clumps across the top of the coffin. That was that. There was nothing else to be done, and she turned and walked away with her grandmother on her arm.

Maggie was breathing heavily and Jessie stopped and peered at her. "Are you alright, Grandma?"

Tears clung to her eyelashes and she appeared to be trying not to cry. She nodded and patted Jessie's arm. "Aye. We shouldn't have come. Burials are no place for womenfolk."

Jessie agreed but she couldn't have stayed away. She had to see her father buried and say her farewell to him. She heard great thuds behind them as the men began filling in the grave. She shuddered at every thud and wished they'd waited until they'd gone.

"Are you alright?" said George walking up behind them. "Grandpa Joe will take us home if you're ready."

"We're ready," said Jessie with a sigh.

"Come on then," said Grandpa Joe taking Maggie's arm. "Let's get ye away from here."

Jessie was silent and lost in her own thoughts for the short journey home. Sophia hadn't joined them for the burial – she said it was too much. Actually, Jessie agreed with her. It was too much. But, what filled her thoughts now were concerns for the future. What was going to happen to them? Sophia hated her and disliked George and William almost as much. She may even hate George more after what had happened the night her father drowned.

She thought Grandma and Grandpa Joe would take the three of them to live with them. She'd be more than happy with that arrangement and hoped mother Sophia would send them with Grandma when she returned to the MacDonald River.

***

Grandma and Grandpa Joe returned home two days later – alone. Sophia said she had things that needed to be finalised, and then she would take them to the MacDonald River herself. Then she'd disappeared for a week, no doubt making arrangements for herself. Jessie delighted in having a whole week without her stepmother harassing her. She packed her clothes and belongings in readiness to depart. She was sure they'd be leaving for the MacDonald River as soon as Sophia returned.

When she finally came home Sophia was subdued and withdrawn. Jessie presumed she was missing her father and perhaps her arrangements hadn't gone to plan. She waited, hoping her stepmother would tell them when they were leaving, but the days passed, and she said nothing.

"We must be going soon," said George in a low whisper. "I'm going to ask her."

Jessie glanced around and looked over her shoulder. "She'll take us – she said she would," said Jessie. "But she'll only get cross if you ask."

George shrugged. "I don't care."

"I'll ask her," said William eyeing his siblings. "She likes me best."

Jessie looked at William and then at George, who gave her a slight nod. She had to agree with William's assessment – she did like him best. "Alright, go and ask her."

George and Jessie followed William down the hall to the parlour. They waited in the hall within hearing while William approached their stepmother.

"Mother Sophia, I was wondering when are we going to Grandma's?"

Jessie expected Sophia to rebuke William for being so cheeky, but she didn't.

"Soon" Jessie heard her sigh. "If you must know, I'm waiting for an important letter," she went on, "and then we'll go."

"Alright," said William. "Should I pack my things?"

"Go away and stop bothering me."

Without another word William retreated and joined Jessie and George in the hallway.

"What sort of important letter do you think she's waiting for?" said Jessie as soon as they were out of earshot.

"Who knows," said George with a shrug. "Probably something to do with Papa."

Jessie thought he was probably right. At any rate, she hoped her important mail would arrive soon and they would be off to Grandma's. Her life had changed so much in the past few years. First leaving Launceston, then meeting her grandmother – who she loved with all her heart. Now her father was dead and she was going to live with her. She was sad her father had died, but it wasn't all bad. She was going to escape Sophia and live on the MacDonald River. She couldn't help the small smile that crept across her face at the thought.

***

Another week passed before Sophia's important letter arrived. The very next day she bundled them into the spring cart with their meagre belongings. It was an uneventful trip up to Wiseman's Ferry and across the river to Grandma's. The closer they got to their destination the more Jessie's excitement grew. She just knew that life from now on was going to be so much better than it had been in Pitt Town.

It was just after midday, when Sophia pulled the cart up out the front of the homestead and Jessie, breathed a sigh. She was so glad to be back here.

"You boys grab your things and go tell your grandmother we're here," said Sophia as she climbed down and stretched.

Jessie jumped down and stamped her feet up and down to get them working again. They were so cramped after so many hours in the cart.

"You stay here," said Sophia glaring at her.

Grandpa Joe came walking along the veranda and smiled. "Ah, you're here at last. We were beginning to wonder if you'd changed ye mind."

Sophia smiled. "I had some business to attend to."

"I expect ye did," said Joe. "Will ye be staying a day or two?"

"No," she said with a shake of her head. "I have other matters to attend to. We won't be staying."

Jessie glanced at her, puzzled by her use of 'we', but before she could say anything, Grandpa Joe did. "What do ye mean?"

The front door opened and Maggie came hurrying out, with George and William. "Oh, we were worried ye'd got lost."

Sophia smiled at Maggie before turning her attention back to Joe. "Jessie and I won't be staying."

Jessie stared at her stepmother, her confusion clear on her face. What did she mean she wasn't staying? Of course, she was. She gaped at her for a moment before finding her voice. "I'm staying."

"Well, of course, ye are," said Maggie coming to stand beside Joe. "Whatever do ye mean, Sophia?"

"I mean I've made other arrangements for Jessie."

"Well, there's no need," said Joe looking at her intently. "We're more than happy to have Jessie stay with us."

"Perhaps, but that's not what's best for her," she said in a matter-of-fact tone.

"I've found Jessie an excellent position that will hold her in good stead for the future."

"She's not yet thirteen," said Maggie gaping at her. "What sort of position?"

Sophia puffed out her chest and drew in a breath. "If you must know, I've arranged for her to go and work for the Reverend Sharpe."

"Well I won't go," said Jessie scowling at Sophia. "I'm staying here."

"You'll do as you're told," said Sophia glaring at her. "Now, get back in the cart and we'll be on our way."

"I will not."

"Just a minute," said Joe stepping down from the veranda. "Ye cannot force the lass."

"I'm her legal guardian, and I most certainly can," said Sophia straightening to her full height. "The arrangements are made and she'll do as she's told."

Jessie was on the verge of tears. The wonderful life she'd imagined was evaporating before her eyes. She looked at Grandpa Joe who was glaring at Sophia. Surely he would stop her.

"What have ye done?" he said.

"I have done what needed to be done," she said grabbing Jessie by the arm. She shoved her towards the cart. "Get in."

Jessie's eyes pleaded with Grandpa Joe to stop her, but it didn't look like he could. She looked around at her brothers, who looked stunned. She didn't appear to have any choice, so she reluctantly climbed back into the cart.

"You've indentured the girl haven't ye?" said Joe glaring at Sophia.

Sophia climbed onto the driver's seat and collected the reins in her hands. "She'll work for the Reverend until she's sixteen or married. And, one day you'll all thank me."

She clicked her tongue and urged the horse forward. Jessie stared at her family as the horse broke into a trot, and they disappeared around the next corner. She was numb. She could never have imagined that Sophia was capable of such cruelty. She'd sold her.

***

Chapter Twelve

Milkmaid Reach

They travelled in silence for the most part. Jessie was lost in her own misery. She hated Sophia like she'd never hated anyone before. But how did she expect to make her stay with the Reverend? She'd run away as soon as she could. It seemed odd that Sophia hadn't considered this. She noticed a sign as they turned off the Main North Road onto a narrow track marked 'Pathway to Mr Sharpes'.

Sophia glanced sideways at her as they passed a rocky outcrop. "I've told Mr Sharpe all about you, and he'll expect you to be compliant," she said slowing the horse to walk. "And I expect nothing less of you either."

Jessie glared at her but remained tight-lipped. She had no intention of telling Sophia what she planned. Let her think she was going meekly to Mr Sharpes. She'd already worked out she couldn't return to Grandma's – that would be the first place they'd look for her. No, she'd find her way to Wollombi. She knew it was a three-day journey from Pitt Town, but far less from here. She turned her gaze back to the path ahead and ignored Sophia. She could feel her eyes boring into her and she was sorely tempted to poke her tongue out at her.

"You have no idea how it pleases me that Mr Sharpe agreed to our arrangement," said Sophia in her silky voice. "You've been the bane of my life ever since I married your father, and now I never have to see your face again."

Jessie felt tears prick her eyes and swallowed the ache in her throat. She wouldn't give her the satisfaction of seeing her tears. She stared steadfastly ahead, her jaw clenched and her hands balled into tight fists on her lap.

Sophia let out a soft laugh filled with malice, and Jessie's tears rolled down her cheeks. She couldn't wait to escape her stepmother's clutches, and hoped she'd never see her face again either. This torture would end and she would be free of her. Surely Reverend Sharpe would be a kind man if nothing else – after all he was a minister, a man of God.

“You’re such a pathetic little creature,” said Sophia clicking the horse into a trot as the path widened. “I can only imagine what a simpering dolt your mother must’ve been. Why your father loved her is beyond me.”

Jessie felt the anger rising from the pit of her stomach. She was breathing heavily through her flared nostrils as she wiped her tears away with the back of her hand. Jealousy, that’s what this was all about. Sophia couldn’t compete with her mother even though she was dead, her father loved her still. That thought gave her comfort, and she pressed her lips together. Sophia wanted her to react, wanted her to lash out at her, but no. It took all her self-control to sit rigidly looking ahead down the path, hoping to see the Reverend’s cottage around the next corner.

They travelled for another fifteen minutes in silence until they came to the end of the path. A small cottage was perched high on the edge of the river. It was a stone and timber house situated in a small clearing surrounded by tall gums. A wooden jetty was jutting out into a shallow inlet with a small row boat tied to it.

Jessie jumped down from the cart and stretched. She grabbed her bag and cloak from the back of the cart and ignoring Sophia walked up the dirt path to the front door. She rapped loudly and waited. She heard Sophia's footsteps thudding softly on the path behind her. Her back stiffened and she swallowed.

A few moments later the door was opened by a woman with straw blonde hair pulled back into a tight bun. She peered at them for a moment, before a warm smile spread across her face.

"You must be Mrs Smith and Jessie. We've been expecting you for several days now," she said gesturing to them to enter. "Please won't you come in. My husband's not home at present, but he won't long."

Jessie immediately felt her body relax. She hadn't expected that Reverend Sharpe had a wife, and was pleasantly surprised. Not that it would make any difference to her plans.

"Thank you," said Sophia pushing past Jessie and following Mrs Sharpe into the humble cottage. "I'm afraid I can't stay, I have other matters to attend to."

"Oh," said Mrs Sharpe focusing her astute eyes on Sophia. "Well, no matter. I can get Jessie settled, but my husband will be disappointed that he missed you."

"As am I," she said in a dismissive tone. "I presume he received the necessary papers for Jessie?"

"Yes, I believe he did," said Mrs Sharpe. "He would've liked to discuss them with you."

"There is naught to discuss," said Sophia turning around and heading for the door. "Keep a close eye on her – she's a troublesome one."

Without waiting for a reply she walked out the door and up the path. She climbed onto the driver's seat without even a backward glance over her shoulder.

Mrs Sharpe stared after her and appeared to be rooted to the spot for a moment. "Well, she's a strange one." She closed the door and turned to face Jessie.

"And just what are we going to do with you? Hrmm."

Jessie swallowed the nervous flutter in her stomach and pressed her lips together. Just what were they planning to do with her?

"Oh relax my dear," she said smiling. "Come and I'll show you to your room."

The cottage consisted of one main room, which was both a dining room and parlour. Several doors led off from the parlour, and Mrs Sharpe opened the one beside the fireplace and entered. Jessie followed her into a small neat room, with a bed, tallboy and washstand. It was simply furnished but cosy and inviting.

"This will be your room," she said turning and looking at Jessie expectantly.

"Thank you, it's lovely."

Mrs Sharpe sighed. "It's simple but serviceable. Once you've put your things away come and join me so we can get acquainted."

Jessie waited for Mrs Sharpe to leave before dropping her bag and tossing her cloak on the bed. She flopped herself down on the bed as well. She sighed as she looked around the small room. Well, one thing was certain, she'd never set eyes on her stepmother again. She got off the bed and opened her bag and began unpacking her few clothes and putting them away. She wasn't sure how long she'd stay before she put her plan into action.

It was further back to the main road than she'd anticipated, but she thought she could walk it in a few hours. She just wasn't sure how she'd get to Mary's without any money to pay for a lift. Maybe she could steal a few shillings from Mrs Sharpe. No – not steal - borrow. She'd send the money back once she got to Mary's. Her plan was unclear and she blew out her breath as she put the last of her things in the tallboy and tucked her bag under the bed. She'd have to wait and see what opportunities there might be for her to escape.

She walked out into the main room, where Mrs Sharpe was sitting with her mending on her lap. She indicated to a chair beside the fire. Jessie smiled, in what she hoped wasn't a grimace, and sat down.

"Now that you're settled we can have a little chat," she said looking up from her mending. "I understand from what my husband said that you're recently orphaned. I am sorry."

Orphaned? Jessie must have looked surprised because Mrs Sharpe put her mending aside and looked at her puzzled.

"You are an orphan aren't you?"

Jessie continued to look rather surprised while she thought about it. "I suppose so," she finally said. "My father died recently."

Mrs Sharpe nodded and went back to her mending. "I'm so sorry you've lost your father. But, Mrs Smith has made arrangements for you. That was most kind of her."

Jessie sucked in a deep breath and resisted the urge to retort. Most kind of her! She'd sold her down the river and she couldn't understand why Mrs Sharpe didn't see that.

"I'm so pleased to have you come and work for us," she went on, appearing not to notice that Jessie hadn't made any comment. "We did have a convict servant for a while, but she didn't work out. We also have Ed, he mainly accompanies Mr Sharpe when he does his rounds, and he does a few odd chores." She stabbed the needle in and out and glanced up at Jessie. "I believe you can cook?"

"Yes – well sort of. I can bake bread and prepare vegetables and such," she said. "I haven't cooked a meal from start to finish, but I suppose I could do it."

Mrs Sharpe looked up from her sewing and smiled. "That won't be necessary. I'll need your assistance in the kitchen, and I think you can do the dusting and sweeping. Do you garden?"

"No."

"No matter. It's not difficult to pull a few weeds and tend to the vegetable patch. I'll show you."

Jessie nodded. She wasn't too concerned about the chores that Mrs Sharpe was rattling off - she wasn't staying. As soon as she could she'd be going to her sister's – it was just a matter of time.

Mrs Sharpe smiled warmly and leant forward in her chair. "Are you hungry? Come, we'll get you something to eat."

***

The thud of horse hooves on packed earth announced the arrival of Reverend Sharpe. Jessie almost held her breath as her anxiety grew. What would happen to her she didn't know. Grandpa Joe had said something about her being indentured – not that she knew what that meant, but she thought it was an agreement of sorts. Would the Reverend and Mrs Sharpe send the constable after her if she ran away? Everything was whirling around in her mind and she wiped her sweaty palms in the folds of her skirt.

The door opened and Mr Sharpe walked into the room. He looked tired and worn. He removed his travelling cloak before turning his attention to the room's inhabitants.

"Tom, do sit down you look exhausted," said Mrs Sharpe going to her husband's side. She placed an affectionate kiss on his cheek. "Jessie arrived this afternoon."

"Ah, at last," he said turning to face Jessie.

She leapt to her feet and gave a tremulous smile.

"I hope you had a pleasant trip," he said reaching into his pocket and retrieving his pipe. "We've been expecting you for a few days, and I'm very happy to see you've arrived safely." He pulled out his tobacco pouch and stuffed his pipe with tobacco.

"Thank you," said Jessie swallowing a nervous flutter.

"Where's Mrs Smith?" he said lighting his pipe and drawing on it. He blew out a puff of smoke and looked expectantly at his wife.

"She didn't stay," said Mrs Sharpe with a sigh. "She simply dropped the girl off and left. A rather odd woman if you ask me."

"Well, that's unfortunate I was hoping to speak with her."

"Hrmm," said Mrs Sharpe returning to her seat by the fire. "I doubt it would've been enlightening."

"Well, no matter," he said returning his attention to Jessie. "Has Mrs Sharpe explained your duties to you?"

"Yes."

"Good, good. I may also like you to accompany me sometimes when I visit the sick."

"Alright," she said nodding. It made little difference – she wasn't staying.

"Now, we'll be providing your board and lodgings, as well as a modest stipend for your services of course. However, you won't have much need for money." He drew on his pipe and blew another puff of smoke into the room. "And so, I propose we keep a portion of your wages which we'll put aside for your future."

Jessie stared open-mouthed at him. "You're going to pay me?"

He chuckled. "Well of course, what else would you expect?"

"I…I don't know," she stammered. Sophia hadn't mentioned that. She wasn't sure what she'd expected but it certainly wasn't this. "Thank you."

"Well, I hope the arrangement works to both our benefits young lass."

***

Chapter Thirteen

Decisions, Decisions

Jessie awoke the following morning with no clear plan of what she was going to do. She lay there staring at the timber-lined ceiling as she weighed up her options. She'd been so focused on running away that she hadn't considered what the Sharpes might offer her for staying. She was sure of one thing – Sophia would never have made such an arrangement if she thought it would benefit her. She suppressed a giggle. What Sophia had planned as some awful punishment, might turn out to be quite the opposite.

She finally climbed out of bed without making any decisions whatsoever. She dressed in her pinafore and pulled her apron over her head. One thing was certain – there would be chores to do this morning.

She made her way out through the parlour. There was no sign of Mr or Mrs Sharpe in the dining room so she made her way out to the kitchen. She opened the door and went inside. It was a small kitchen with a cast-iron stove on one wall, a long bench and a small table in the middle. Mrs Sharpe was sitting at the table with a piece of parchment spread out in front of her. She looked up and smiled.

"I thought to let you sleep for as long as you wanted this morning," she said folding the parchment and tucking it into her pocket. "There's porridge on the stove – help yourself."

"Thank you." Jessie lifted the lid and breathed in the aroma of boiled oats. She got a bowl from the dresser and scooped a serving into her bowl.

"I thought you might help me in the garden this morning."

"Oh, of course, I'd be happy to," said Jessie seating herself at the table.

Mrs Sharpe smiled and nodded. "And then I'd like your help to make soup for supper. Perhaps you could bake us some fresh bread?"

"Hmm," said Jessie nodding as she swallowed a mouthful of porridge.

"Wonderful," said Mrs Sharpe rising from the table. "Come and join me in the garden when you're done with breakfast."

"I will."

As soon as Mrs Sharpe left the room Jessie slumped in her chair. She didn't mind helping in the garden – or whatever – but she felt like she was betraying herself. She sighed as she swallowed another mouthful of porridge. She was so confused.

She finished breakfast and headed out to the rear garden to find Mrs Sharpe. The rear yard led down to the river which was lined with tall weepy gum trees, all wearing their drab green livery. She spied her immediately – kneeling beside a plot overgrown with weeds. She was pulling them out and tossing them into a pail.

Jessie made her way toward her.

"Oh good you're here," she said looking up from her work. "Come, this whole plot needs weeding." She reached into the pocket of her apron and withdrew a pair of gloves. "Here, wear these. It'll protect your fingernails and help you to grip the weeds."

"Thank you," said Jessie slipping on the gloves and kneeling down on the other side of the plot. It was thick with weeds, but she grabbed the first one tightly around the stem and pulled it as hard as she could. It snapped off leaving the root behind.

"No-no-no. Like this." Mrs Sharpe came around and knelt beside her. "You need to grab them way down low and wiggle them a bit to loosen them," she said grabbing a weed and demonstrating her method. "Then pull gently." The weed came out of the ground with the root covered in dirt which she shook off before tossing it into her pail. "See. Now you try."

Jessie nodded and grabbed hold of another weed and this time successfully pulled the whole thing out. She grinned as she shook off the dirt.

"That's the way," said Mrs Sharpe pulling another weed. "Sometimes they're a bit tough and you have to dig around the roots. I've got a little spade here just for that purpose."

Jessie and Mrs Sharpe spent the best part of the morning weeding the plot. Mrs Sharpe chatted about all manner of things, and Jessie found herself being drawn to her. She appeared to be interested in Jessie's life and asked her all manner of questions about her family. Jessie noticed she didn't mention her own, and she wondered why the Reverend and she didn't have any children. However, she kept her thoughts to herself.

"So you have a grandmother?" Mrs Sharpe raised her brows and squinted at her. "We thought you had no family, or very little."

Jessie sat back on her haunches and shook her head. "I'm sure that's what my stepmother wanted you to think."

"She's a strange one I'll give you that," she said tossing another weed into the pail. "Still, is there some reason you didn't want to go and live with your grandmother?"

Jessie sucked in a breath and swallowed the unexpected tears that pricked her eyes. She looked down at her apron and did her best to regain her composure. The last thing she wanted to do was to burst into tears. After several deep breaths, she looked up. Mrs Sharpe put her hand on her arm and smiled. It lit up her whole face all the way to her eyes which looked at Jessie with sympathy and concern.

"You don't have to tell me if you don't want to."

Did she want to? Her confusion over her situation wasn't abating but in an instant, she decided to trust Mrs Sharpe. Maybe she would have some helpful advice. "It's not that I didn't want to, I did," she said shaking her head. "And Grandma and Grandpa Joe wanted me, but Sophia wouldn't have it. She said coming to work for you and Reverend Sharpe was a good opportunity for me."

Mrs Sharpe shrugged and nodded. "Well, she's right about that. When you leave us in a couple of years you'll leave with good housekeeping skills and an excellent reference. You'll be able to secure yourself a good position I'm sure."

Jessie wasn't sure if any of that was important to her or not. She smiled and hoped that would suffice for an answer. Mrs Sharpe gave her a reassuring pat on her arm and went back to her weeding. Jessie really didn't know what she wanted and Mrs

Sharpe wasn't helping to lessen her confusion.

***

Milkmaid Reach, June 1836

The next few weeks just flew by. Mrs Sharpe kept Jessie busy with all manner of household chores and cooking. Sunday was the only exception, and then she was expected to attend church with the Reverend and his wife. She quite enjoyed her mornings at church and they were generally invited to one of the parishioner's homes for their midday meal. Jessie was delegated to the kitchen with any other servants, but she didn't mind that either.

Sunday afternoon was the only time she had to herself. After tending to her mending and other personal care she had very little time to do anything else. Any thoughts of when she might leave had been pushed aside.

"Jessie. Jess are you there?"

"Yes Reverend," said Jessie hurrying from her room into the parlour.

He smiled as she came to a halt in front of him. “Sorry to disturb you,” he said looking apologetic. “I was hoping you might join me tomorrow when I visit Mrs Clarke. Mrs Sharpe has other matters to attend to.”

“Of course.”

“Good, we’ll leave at nine,” he said scratching his chin. “Do you ride?”

“Ah…yes.”

“Excellent, you can ride Mrs Sharpe's mare, Cammy.” He turned to leave and hesitated as he reached into his pocket. “Ah, I meant to give you this” He held out five shillings in the palm of his hand.

“Thank you,” said Jessie taking the money and closing her fingers around it.

“Good. Well, be ready at nine, hrm?”

“Yes.”

She waited for him to leave before hurrying back to her room. She opened the top drawer and pulled out a tightly knotted handkerchief. She pried the knot apart and added her five shillings to her growing stash. She counted them before knotting the handkerchief and tucking it safely back in her drawer. Fifteen shillings. What could she buy with that?

The household was a flurry of activity the following morning. Ed was driving Mrs Sharpe into town to run a few errands but had saddled the horses for the Reverend and Jessie. Mrs Sharpe tucked a flask of soup into Jessie's saddle bag and a canteen of water.

"Be gentle with her, Jess," she said stroking her horse with affection. "Just watch her when you're crossing the creek – she's shy of the gurgle and babble of the water."

"I will," said Jessie eyeing the horse with some trepidation.

She hadn't ridden in an age and had been alarmed to discover she'd be riding side-saddle. She slipped her boot into Ed's waiting cupped hands and hoisted herself into the saddle. She looped her knee around the pummel and was surprised had how secure she felt. She gathered the reins and waited for the Reverend to mount.

"Do take care, Tom," said Mrs Sharpe kissing her husband on the cheek. "And do give Mrs Clarke my apologies. I hope it's nothing serious."

"I'll pass on your felicitations my dear," he said mounting his large bay,

Biscuit. "I pray she's just been too busy to attend church."

Mrs Sharpe frowned and shook her head. "Really, Tom the poor woman lives alone. We can show her some common care and concern."

"Of course, Elli, I didn't mean anything by it. Expect us home in time for supper."

He clicked his tongue and with a soft nudge of his heels, they were off. Cammy trotted sedately along behind Biscuit, and Jessie focused all her attention on remaining seated in her saddle. The mare had a gentle gait and Jessie found it quite easy to get into rhythm with the horse.

"Are you alright?" called Reverend Sharpe swivelling around in the saddle to see her.

"Yes."

"Well, come and ride alongside."

She gave Cammy a gentle nudge with her boot and she quickened her pace. She slowed her gait when they came alongside Biscuit and the Reverend.

"Ah, that's better," he said smiling. "You ride well I must say."

It was difficult to hear what he was saying above the clop of the hooves on the compacted earth. Jessie smiled and nodded and returned her attention to staying upright. Any conversation was going to be impossible unless they slowed to a walk.

They continued in relative silence until they came to the creek crossing. Recent rains had flooded the causeway and Jessie eyed it with trepidation. Mrs Sharpe had mentioned that Cammy didn't like the burble of the creek, and she was already prancing on the spot in agitation. Jessie reined her in gently and stroked her neck.

"Shh, it'll be alright," she whispered to the skittish mare.

"It doesn't look too deep," said the Reverend urging his mount forward and into the stream.

Jessie watched as the water rose above Biscuit's knees, and skimmed the Reverend's boots. He reached the other side with ease and turned to face her.

"Come," he called to her. "Just ease her into it, she'll be fine."

She swallowed and gripped the reins firmly in both hands as she urged Cammy forward. She sidestepped as soon as the chilly water reached her knees, but Jessie managed to direct her back into the middle of the causeway. She held her breath as the mare pranced her way across the creek. She let it out with a sigh of relief when they drew even with Reverend.

"Well done," he said turning his mount around. "It's not far now."

Jessie nudged Cammy with the heel of her boot urging her into a trot to keep up with Biscuit. As she settled back into the rhythm of her horse, she wondered why Mrs Clarke chose to live all the way out here alone. She prayed nothing had befallen the poor woman. What if they found her dead or something? She swallowed and pushed such horrid thoughts aside. Surely the Reverend wouldn't have asked her to join him if he thought that.

***

Chapter Fourteen

Mrs Clarke

True to his word, a short time later Reverend Sharpe turned off the well-worn track onto an overgrown driveway. It meandered through the gum trees and finally ended at a ramshackle house. It looked like it had started out as a one-room slab hut, but had been added onto in a rather haphazard way. Parts of it were timber slats while other bits were made of tin and other bits appeared to be wattle and daub. It was a most peculiar house in Jessie's opinion.

Mr Sharpe came to a halt near the front door and dismounted. He tied Biscuit to the railing and gestured to Jessie. "Can you dismount on your own?"

"Yes," she said unhooking her leg and slipping from the saddle. She wasn't so sure she could mount Cammy again without assistance. She tied her to the railing and waited for the Reverend.

He walked up to the front door and knocked, and they waited. It was quiet except for the screech of a cocky overhead – there was no thud of footsteps coming to answer the door. After a short pause, he knocked again, before pushing the door open with his foot.

"Mrs Clarke? Are you there?"

There was no answer. Jessie followed Mr Sharpe into the house. It was dimly lit, with only a small amount of light coming in through one window. However, it was enough to see a sparsely furnished sitting room, which to Jessie's surprise was very neat and tidy. A newspaper was neatly folded on the sideboard, and a basket of knitting sat by the fire. Plump cushions decorated the two armchairs, and a rather colourful rug covered almost the entire floor.

"Mrs Clarke, it's Reverend Sharpe. Are you there?" he called again.

Jessie held her breath and strained to listen for a reply. She half expected to hear a weak call for help to come from somewhere, but all was quiet. Reverend Sharpe frowned and also appeared to be listening intently.

"That's odd," he mumbled as he pushed open another door. "Mrs Clarke."

Jessie peered around Mr Sharpe into what was obviously Mrs Clarke's bedroom. The bed was made and everything was as neat and tidy as the sitting room. Still, there was no sign of its occupier.

A thorough search of the rest of the house didn't reveal Mrs Clarke.

"Perhaps she's gone visiting or something," said Jessie as they walked out of the house and closed the door.

"No," said Reverend Sharpe with a shake of his head. "She's a recluse and apart from Church doesn't generally go anywhere. Certainly not visiting." He glanced around the yard. "Ah," he said as though he'd just discovered something.

Jessie followed him around the side of the house, and finally spied what she thought he'd seen. A small barn, or rather a lean too which looked even more ramshackle than the house. It had two doors on the front and one of them was standing wide open. Several loud curses could be heard emitting from within even before they reached the open door.

"I think we've found her," said Reverend Sharpe with a chuckle.

Jessie grinned as she followed the Reverend into the barn.

"Damn thing," said Mrs Clarke before banging the wheel of her cart with a hammer. She sat back on her haunches and ran her fingers through her hair.

Jessie stopped and stared. Mrs Clarke was an elderly white-haired woman, and she was sitting on the floor of her barn surrounded by a variety of tools. Her hair was sticking out in all directions and she had what looked like grease smeared across her face. She was not at all what Jessie had expected.

"Mrs Clarke I'm so glad we've found you," said Reverend Sharpe.

Mrs Clarke looked up in surprise. "Reverend what are ye doing here?" She grabbed hold of the wheel of her buggy and hauled herself to her feet.

"We were worried about you when you didn't come to church yesterday."

She scoffed. "Good Lord don't tell me you've come all the way out here because of that," she said wiping her hands on her apron. "Quite unnecessary, Reverend."

"Well, I would disagree. What seems to be the problem?"

"My damn buggy," she said kicking it. "The linchpin's broke an' I can't get the damn thing out to replace it."

"Perhaps I can do it." Without waiting for a reply he removed his jacket and slung it over the front seat of the buggy.

"You'll do no such thing," she said staring at him. "An' who's this?"

"This is Jessie. She's recently come to work for us." He ignored Mrs Clarke's protests and knelt beside the wheel for a closer look. "Hrm it's quite stuck isn't it? I need something to grip it with," he said looking around at the selection of tools.

"I'll thank ye to go fetch Bill Young, he'll fix as quick as winking." She said it with finality and then turned her back on the Reverend. "So where ye from?"

Jessie was momentarily startled. She hadn't expected to be called into the conversation. "Oh...I suppose I'm from Launceston."

"What…Van Diemen's Land ye mean? Not England?" She peered at Jessie with an expectant look on her face.

Jessie swallowed and licked her lips. “Van Diemen’s Land.”

“Were ye born there?”

“I’ll go and see if Mr Young can come and have a look at it,” said Reverend Sharpe getting to his feet. “Jessie, you wait here with Mrs Clarke,” he said grabbing his jacket. “I won’t be long.”

“Good. I do thank ye Reverend,” said Mrs Clarke following him to the door. “Take ye time.”

He nodded and slipped through the open door. As soon as he was gone Mrs Clarke turned her sharp brown eyes back onto Jessie. “So, now what were we saying?”

“You were asking where I was born,” said Jessie. “I was born in Van Diemen’s Land.”

“Ah, so you’re a currency lass. Well no mind,” she said in a matter-of-fact tone. “You’re fortunate to have been taken in by Mr and Mrs Sharpe. They’re the kindest people.”

Jessie stared at the old woman. She’d never been called a ‘currency lass’ before – not even by Sophia. She sucked in several breaths in quick succession.

"Oh, don't be offended," said Mrs Clarke with a wave of her hand. "I didn't mean anything by it."

Jessie swallowed. "I didn't expect someone like you would think less of me."

"Someone like me?" she said with raised brows. "An' just who do ye think I am? I'm not currency that's for sure," she said in an affronted tone.

"I'm sorry…I didn't mean…"

"Hrmph."

She gave Jessie a scathing look before walking from the barn. Jessie stood rooted to the spot. She hadn't meant to offend her, and she wasn't sure what she should do – stay in the barn or follow Mrs Clarke.

"Come," she heard Mrs Clarke call to her.

She sucked in a breath and slowly let it out before exiting the barn. She followed Mrs Clarke at a respectful distance back to the house.

"Did Mrs Sharpe happen to send something along in ye saddlebags?"

"Yes," said Jessie hurrying to catch up to her. "Soup"

"Oh," she said looking over her shoulder at Jessie. "Well, it's better than nothing I suppose. Next time see if ye can't get her to bake some biscuits or something."

"I'll do that. Shall I fetch the soup?"

"Aye."

Half an hour later the two were happily slurping soup in awkward silence. Jessie eyed Mrs Clarke warily. She wasn't sure if she was still angry with her. She tried to think of something to say to break the silence, but she failed miserably. It was Mrs Clarke who finally broke the silence between them.

"I was born in Bristol," said Mrs Clarke resting her spoon on the side of the bowl. "My husband was in the army, that's how we came here."

"Oh," said Jessie eyeing her with interest. "My grandfather was a soldier too."

"Was he now? Do ye know what regiment he was in?"

Jessie thought for a moment. She wasn't exactly sure if she remembered right or not. Her father used to talk about him all the time. Jessie always thought he must've really liked him.

“I think it was the 73rd? Would that be right?”

“Oh aye, Macquarie’s regiment,” said Mrs Clarke nodding enthusiastically. “Same as my husband, John.”

“Really?”

“Did your grandfather join the veterans? Do ye know?”

“I don’t know,” said Jessie staring off into space while she thought about what had happened to him. He’d died before she was born, but there’d been talk about him. “I think he went away and never came back.”

“Oh, he must’ve gone to Ceylon then,” said Mrs Clarke taking another spoonful of soup.

“Maybe.”

“Oh, not maybe. The 73rd were sent to fight in Ceylon. My John transferred to the veterans so he could stay here with me,” she said slurping the last of her soup. “If your grandfather went away an’ never came back then he must’ve died over there.”

Jessie had never known him, but somehow he now seemed like a real person. “Maybe your husband knew my grandfather. His name was Theophilus. Theophilus

Feutrill." Jessie remembered his name without difficulty. It had always seemed like such an odd name to her and she rather liked saying Theophilus.

Mrs Clarke shook her head. "I can't say that it's familiar. Anyway, I presume he was in Van Diemen's Land. My John never left New South Wales."

"Oh," said Jessie spooning the last of her soup into her mouth.

"Ye know I've not spoken to anyone about my husband in many years. But I've enjoyed our conversation young Jessie. Thank ye."

"You're welcome. And I hope you'll forgive me for earlier."

"Nonsense," she said with a wave of her hand. "There's naught to forgive."

There was a soft knock on the door, which opened a moment later revealing Reverend Sharpe. He smiled and removed his hat as he entered the small kitchen.

"It's all arranged. Bill Young will come by in the morning and see to your buggy."

"Thank ye, Reverend. I so appreciate your help. Would ye like some soup? I think we've left enough for ye."

"No, no. I enjoyed some repast at the Young's," he said. "If you're ready to go, Jessie, we might start for home before the weather turns."

"I'm ready to go," said Jessie getting to her feet. "Thank you so much for your hospitality, Mrs Clarke. I've really enjoyed our visit."

"As have I."

Reverend Sharpe looked from Jessie to Mrs Clarke with a perplexed expression on his face. "Well, that's splendid."

Jessie smiled to herself as they left the kitchen and mounted the horses. She expected the Reverend would want to know how she had softened Mrs Clarke. Actually, she wasn't too sure how it happened – just something in common with her dead husband. She really was a nice old thing.

***

Chapter Fifteen

The Agreement

Over the next few weeks, Jessie discarded all thoughts of leaving. She was enjoying her life with the Sharpes, and even more, her stash of money – which was growing every week.

"Can you chop those carrots for me," said Mrs Sharpe gesturing with her chin. "And then I'll need some herbs from the garden. Rosemary? What do you think?"

"Yes," said Jessie grabbing the three carrots. "I think rosemary would go well with the lamb, or maybe some thyme if it hasn't died back. It wasn't looking very healthy last time I looked."

"Hrm, just the rosemary I think."

"Alright," said Jessie slicing and chopping the carrots with enthusiasm.

She always felt at home in the kitchen, and Mrs Sharpe had taught her quite a bit about cooking. They were making a sort of lamb stew out of a flank old Mr Barnett had sent home with the Reverend.

She finished chopping the carrots and added them to the pot. The stew was looking good. “I’ll just go get the rosemary.”

“Thank you.”

She headed out of the kitchen and down towards the vegetable patch. A large rosemary bush was growing just beyond. She snipped off a few sprigs of the fragrant herb and breathed in the aroma before making her way back to the kitchen. She shivered in the chill afternoon air. Winter was well and truly upon them and although a weak wintery sun was shining, the air was frigid. She opened the kitchen door and was immediately engulfed by the warmth from the stove. She sighed and closed the door behind her.

She ran her fingers down the stalk, removing the fine leaves before adding them to the pot. She breathed in the alluring smell of the stew and smiled. “Hmm, it smells good already.”

“Oh it’ll be a while yet,” said Mrs Sharpe stirring it with her wooden spoon. “But, yes it’s going to be delicious.”

Jessie smiled. “Will the Reverend be home for supper?”

“Yes, I expect so,” she said frowning. “He may be a little late. You never know with the river. Come, let’s leave this to cook.”

The Reverend had gone downriver with Ed to visit Mr Pullman. He lived on the other side of Wiseman’s Ferry, and according to Mrs Sharpe always kept the Reverend for as long as he could. He was often late home after visiting Mr Pullman.

The two settled themselves in the sitting room. Mrs Sharpe with her mending and Jessie with the polishing cloth and the canteen of cutlery.

“I was thinking,” said Mrs Sharpe with her needle poised. “We should take a trip into town, the two of us.”

“Really?”

‘Yes. I think you need some new dresses and petticoats,” she said. “I’ve noticed you don’t have much to choose from.”

Jessie felt her cheeks warm and flush. She had hardly any clothes, and what she did have were hand-me-downs from Mary. She just didn’t think anyone had noticed.

"The local draper has a good choice of fabrics and I've got plenty of patterns. Although I think we ought to get at least one outfit made by Mrs Moore. She's a wonderful seamstress."

"I don't think I'd have enough money for that," said Jessie alarmed. While she'd love a new dress and she definitely needed petticoats, she only had one pound and ten shillings. She didn't think that would be enough.

"Don't worry," said Mrs Sharpe waving her hand in the air. "We've put some money aside for you for just such a purpose."

She stared at Mrs Sharpe for a moment before she remembered the Reverend saying that when she first arrived. She couldn't help the wide smile that spread across her face. "I'd love that."

"Then it's settled. We'll go tomorrow."

***

Tomorrow dawned wet and cold, not at all a day for travelling into town. Jessie's disappointment however was short-lived when Mrs Sharpe gave her the day off to do as she pleased.

“Go read your book or perhaps you should write to your grandmother?”

Jessie felt a twinge of guilt which quickly amplified into remorse. She hadn’t given Grandma a thought in weeks. Considering the situation the last time she saw her, she knew she’d be worried. She pressed her lips together. “Yes, I should definitely write to Grandma.”

“Excellent. Do be sure and tell her how happy and settled you are. We don’t want her worrying unnecessarily.”

“I will,” said Jessie full of every intention of doing just that. “May I use some of Mr Sharpe's parchment and a quill?”

“Of course, go ahead he won’t mind. Use his desk if you like.”

The Reverend had a small study off the main sitting room. It was cluttered with papers and books, but he generally kept the middle of the desk clear of paperwork. Jessie sat down and breathed in the earthy leather smells coming from the books. It was such a manly smell, and that combined with the scent of stale smoke left her in no doubt she was invading the Reverend's private space.

Several prepared quills were sitting neatly in a jar on the desk alongside a small ink pot, but she couldn't see any parchment lying about. She didn't like to rummage through the pile of paperwork, but after several more minutes of scouring the study, she was left with little choice. She sat back down and stared at the piles of papers. It wasn't likely that he'd keep unused parchment amongst his correspondence. She slid open the top drawer and peered in. Nothing but odds and sods – she opened the next drawer down. It appeared to hold his registrar's notes.

She closed the drawer and turned her attention to the ones on the other side. Once again the top drawer held an assortment of smoking paraphernalia, a small paring knife and what looked like a collection of gum nuts. How very odd. She smiled as she closed it and slid open the last drawer. It contained numerous papers and tucked underneath them was what looked like clean parchment.

She pulled out the pile of papers and retrieved a page of parchment. One should do – it wouldn't be a long letter. Jessie thought her writing had improved but she wasn't a keen letter writer. As she was putting the papers back they slipped from her fingers and fluttered to the floor.

"Damn."

She got down on her hands and knees and gathered them into a neat pile. She had no idea if they'd been in any particular order, but hoped not. As she was collecting them together her name jumped off the page at her. She sat back down and put the papers back in the drawer, all except the one with her name on it. She licked her lips and glanced at the open study door. Would Mrs Sharpe come along and notice her snooping? She hoped not as she quickly ran her eyes over the page in front of her.

She soon realised this was the agreement Sophia had made with the Reverend. She swallowed as she began at the top to read the whole thing. A minute or two later she dropped it on the desk in front of her and sat back in the chair. So, Sophia had sold her into servitude until she was either married or turned sixteen. Several emotions were bubbling away trying to reach the surface. Tears burned her eyes, but they weren't out of sadness or despair – they were full of sheer fury. She could feel her blood pumping through her veins as her heart raced and her temples pulsed.

She did her best to swallow the ache that stretched across her throat. She'd known, of course, known that her stepmother had hated her and had wanted rid of her. But seeing her signature on the bottom of the page brought it into sharp focus. It was large and flamboyant and Jessie imagined she'd signed with a flourish, glad to be paying her one final unkindness.

But then it occurred to her that she hadn't – she'd tried but she hadn't. Jessie's anger subsided as quickly as it had come. She sucked in a lungful of air and slowly let it out. No, Sophia hadn't won – Jessie had. A small smile crept at the corners of her mouth. She was actually happy here with Reverend Sharpe and his wife.

"Did you find everything?" said Mrs Sharpe stepping into the study. She eyed Jessie with a raised brow.

Jessie looked up in alarm, and then her eyes went to the agreement which was sitting on the desk in front of her. Her surprise and guilt must've been obvious.

"Is everything alright?" Mrs Sharpe walked over and looked at the document sitting on the desk. She reached down and picked up the agreement. "I see you found this."

"I…I," said Jessie swallowing. "I dropped some papers…I'm sorry…and that fell out."

Mrs Sharpe walked slowly around the other side of the desk and sat down. She read the paper while Jessie sat holding her breath. A minute or more ticked by. Jessie didn't know whether to say something or wait.

"Well, I think you knew what it said, didn't you?" said Mrs Sharpe looking at her squarely.

"Sort of."

"It doesn't matter, Jessie. Tom and I will never hold you to it," she said tossing it distastefully onto the nearest pile of papers. "It was unnecessary and you're free to go if you wish. But I think you like it here, and we love having you."

"I do."

"Then let's not speak of it again. How's the letter writing going?"

Jessie felt her cheeks flush with warmth. "I haven't started."

"Well the day's your own," she said rising to her feet. "However, if you get it written today then you can post it when we're in town tomorrow."

She swept from the room and Jessie let out a long breath. That hadn't gone how she'd expected. Mrs Sharpe's words kept on rolling around in her mind – 'Tom and I will never hold you to it' – leaving her with a feeling of warmth and happiness.

***

Chapter Sixteen

Doing God's Work

Winter finally came to an end and the busy season in the garden arrived. Mrs Sharpe had Jessie working non-stop, digging, weeding and planting. For the most part, she enjoyed her solitary time in the garden. The days were getting warmer and she looked forward to summer at Milkmaid Reach. She imagined herself paddling in the river on a hot Sunday afternoon. How delightful that would be.

She finished planting the last of the seeds and sat back on her haunches. The vegetable garden was looking well tended with neat rows of planted seeds. Jessie's heart swelled with a sense of achievement. She was surprised at how much she enjoyed watching things grow and flourish.

She put her tools into her pail and went to put them away in the small lean-to-shed at the bottom of the garden. She hung her outdoor apron on the hook and headed for the house. Her stomach gave a rather loud grumble as she poked her head into the kitchen.

"You're just in time," said Mrs Sharpe handing her a plate of buttered bread. "Take this through to the dining room, and set the table for supper. Mr Sharpe's home already." A small crease marred her otherwise smooth forehead. "I wasn't expecting him until after sundown."

"Alright," said Jessie taking the plate and heading for the house. She had no idea why Mrs Sharpe wasn't expecting the Reverend. He didn't go out every day, but on days when he went to check on his parishioners, he would arrive home in time for supper. It was only when he visited Mr Pullman that he'd come home late.

She found Mr Sharpe sitting in a comfortable armchair in the sitting room. "Good evening."

He looked up with a surprised look. "Ah, Jess – good evening."

She thought he looked more weary than usual. "Did you have a good day?"She put the bread on the table and opened the dresser door. She removed three bowls.

"Aye."

She shrugged as she placed them on the table and went to fetch the cutlery. He seemed distracted, but it could just be her imagination. More than likely he was tired after a busy day. She'd gone with him on the river with Ed on a couple of occasions. She'd loved it, but it was a long day. She didn't know how Ed did it – rowing all the way. She supposed it would be easier when going with the current. She was still lost in thought when Mrs Sharpe arrived carrying a large tureen.

"What are you doing girl?"

"Oh sorry," said Jessie coming back to the present. She slid open the drawer and retrieved three spoons which she quickly put on the table. She closed the drawer and waited for the Sharpes to seat themselves at the table before joining them. She always ate with them, unlike Ed. Of course, he was a convict whereas she was a free woman. Well, sort of free. She lowered her head and waited for the Reverend to recite grace, and tried to keep her mind from wandering. Was she free? She wasn't sure, and the opportunity to ask further questions had well and truly passed.

"Amen," said Mr Sharpe raising his head.

Jessie raised her head and smiled.

Mrs Sharpe filled the Reverend's bowl first and then Jessie's, before finally ladling the hot soup into her own.

"How was your day?" she asked placing the ladle back in the tureen. "Bread?" She pushed the plate closer to her husband and waited for him to take a slice.

It was only then that Jessie realised she hadn't put out any plates. "Oh, sorry," she said diving from her chair. She grabbed three small plates from the dresser and put them on the table beside the bowls of steaming soup.

"Thank you, my dear," said Mr Sharpe placing his bread down on the plate. "My day was weary, to say the least, however, it was pleasant enough on the river."

"Well I'm glad to hear it," said Mrs Sharpe taking a slice of bread. "And how was Mr Burnett? Much recovered I hope?"

"Indeed. His leg has healed well I think, and he was in fine spirits."

"Wonderful."

Jessie dipped her spoon into the soup and took a mouthful. It was delicious. Mrs Sharpe really knew how to make the most wonderful soup. This one was her salt pork soup with a variety of vegetables. She could taste the rosemary. It was an easy enough recipe although Jessie had never made it by herself. Mrs Sharpe was always there supervising in the kitchen. Still, she thought she could do it by herself.

"We have plenty of time before we'd need to go," said Mr Sharpe putting his spoon down with a clatter. He reached out and squeezed his wife's hand. "I feel this could be God's calling."

It was only then that Jessie realised she'd missed half the conversation. She looked from Mr Sharpe to Mrs Sharpe and back again and wondered what was going on. She waited, hoping more of the conversation would make the situation clear.

"You know I do love it here," said Mrs Sharpe looking wistful. "But if you think this is what God wants you to do, then you must do it."

"What about you Jessie?" said Mr Sharpe looking expectantly at her. "Of course we expect you to accompany us."

"Ah," she said glancing from one to the other. "I'm sorry, I must've been daydreaming."

"Mr Sharpe was just saying that he's been asked to take up a new position," said Mrs Sharpe looking at her husband with obvious affection. "On Norfolk Island."

Jessie's eyes widened at the mention of Norfolk Island. "Isn't that a prison?" From what she'd heard – which wasn't very much – it was where the worst convicts were sent.

"Well, aye I suppose you could describe it as such," said Mr Sharpe rubbing his chin.

"So when would we have to leave?" said Mrs Sharpe reaching for another slice of bread.

"After Christmas I expect. As you're in agreement, I'll write and accept the position, and then arrangements will be made for us. These things tend to take time."

"Jessie will of course accompany us, but what about Ed?" said Mrs Sharpe.

"He's been a fine and loyal servant, and I don't think he deserves anything less than a recommendation from us," said Mr Sharpe dipping his spoon into his soup. "I'll write to the Commissioner and recommend he be given his ticket."

Mrs Sharpe smiled. "That would be most appropriate."

"Um...I wonder if I could ask a favour?" said Jessie licking her lips.

"Hrm? What's that?" said Mr Sharpe casting his gaze in her direction.

She felt a flutter in the pit of her stomach but breathed in and ploughed on. "Would it be possible for me to visit my grandmother before we leave? I wouldn't feel right just going off without saying goodbye to her."

"Of course."

"I think that's a fine idea," said Mrs Sharpe smiling with a look of satisfaction. "Perhaps Jessie could go ahead of us? What do you think?" She scooped another spoonful of soup into her mouth and waited expectantly for her husband to answer.

"I'm sure something could be arranged," said Mr Sharpe shaking his head.

"We'll make final arrangements when we get closer to the time. It's a bit difficult to imagine how we can make that work right now."

"I understand," said Jessie nodding. "Thank you."

***

Later that night Jessie snuggled under the covers and stared at the ceiling. Thoughts of Norfolk Island were going around and around in her mind. What would it be like? Did the convicts just wander about or were they kept locked up? She couldn't imagine so many men being stuffed in together all the time. They must go out and work or something. She rolled over and found a more comfortable position. Her life was taking yet another turn, and she couldn't quite dispel the knot that had formed in the pit of her stomach.

She was up early the next morning, and it was as though the conversation of the night before hadn't happened. Her day was just the same, and neither, Mr nor Mrs Sharpe made any reference to their move to

Norfolk Island. Jessie on the other hand could think of little else.

It was three weeks later that the first mention of their move was talked about again. The Reverend had asked both Mrs Sharpe and Jessie to join him in the sitting room after supper. Jessie finished her kitchen chores before joining her employers.

“Sit down, Jess,” said Mr Sharpe as soon as she entered the sitting room.

She nodded and perched herself on the edge of a dining chair. She folded her hands in her lap and waited patiently.

“I was just telling Mrs Sharpe that I have received my instructions,” said Mr Sharpe puffing on his pipe. “We’re expected on Norfolk Island in early April. That gives us plenty of time to pack and make our arrangements.”

Jessie nodded.

“We’ll be limited in what we can take with us.”

Mrs Sharpe leant forward and smiled. “One chest for you and me, Jess which should be ample.”

Jessie nodded again. She could hardly fill a whole chest with her meagre belongings. Still, it was good to know she wouldn't have to decide what to leave behind.

"I'll be taking an extra chest with my books and papers and such," went on Mr Sharpe. "Now, I was thinking you could go and visit your grandmother at the end of March, or thereabouts. We'll come by and pick you up on our way to Sydney. You can take Cammy if you think you can manage her."

"I think I could manage her," she said nodding. "I'm just not sure I could find my way."

The closest settlement to Milkmaid Reach was Wiseman's Ferry, and she knew she had to take a road from there to get to her grandmother's. She just wasn't confident she could find that on her own.

"Good gracious, Jess," said Mrs Sharpe sitting back in her chair. "We wouldn't send you off on your own. Ed will accompany you."

"Aye," put in Mr Sharpe. "Ed should have his ticket by then, and I'll instruct him to sell the mare once you're safely at your grandmother's."

“Alright. Thank you.”

“You’re welcome,” he said blowing a puff of smoke into the air. “I’d like to assure your grandmother myself that I’ll be taking full responsibility for your safety on Norfolk Island.”

Jessie nodded. She didn’t think Grandma would care one way or the other, but if it would make the Reverend feel better then it made no difference to her. Both Grandma and Grandpa Joe had been convicts, and Jessie didn’t think for one moment that they'd worry about her living amongst them.

***

Chapter Seventeen

Selling and Packing

Christmas came and went, and slowly life on the river began to show signs of change. Mr Sharpe put the house up for sale complete with all the furniture and even some household items.

Jessie had been hard at work cleaning everything within an inch of its life. The dresser and sideboards were freshly polished, and the whole house had been tidied and cleaned. Several people had come to look, but no one had yet made an offer to buy it. Jessie wondered if they'd sell it before they had to leave. She was going to miss Milkmaid Reach, but for the very first time in her life, she was looking forward to moving. Norfolk Island had sparked her imagination and she was anxious to get there.

Her thirteenth birthday arrived without fanfare and went unnoticed. She hadn't expected the Sharpes to mark the occasion, but she couldn't help the feeling of disappointment that none of her family had remembered. It seemed she was out of sight and out of mind. She held her small bundle of letters to her breast. It was all she had of her grandmother and sisters – a few short letters. She sighed as she tucked them back into the drawer – perhaps if she wrote more they would as well. She screwed up her face as she slid the drawer closed – she really didn't like writing letters.

The next month flew by and Jessie was relieved when Mr and Mrs Watson decided to purchase the house. She was very thankful that Mrs Sharpe wasn't so insistent on the house being kept in a constant state of spotlessness. However, with that came a renewed fervour to pack and sell unwanted items.

"What do you think, Jess? Should we sell this dinner set? We can't take it with us." said Mrs Sharpe eyeing a set of flowery crockery.

Jessie groaned inwardly. "We could leave it for Mrs Watson."

They'd been going through the house room by room, cupboard by cupboard, and the fate of every item had to be decided upon. 'What should we do with this?' had become Mrs Sharpe's catch cry. Jessie would've been happy to just leave it all for the new owners, but Mrs Sharpe insisted that everything be packed and either sold or crammed into a sea trunk.

"No, pack it into one of those chests and Mr Sharpe can take it into town."

Jessie nodded. "Alright."

Every night Jessie climbed into bed – exhausted. The packing never seemed to end, and there was still the Reverend's study to go through. She settled down under the covers and sighed. Images of what she fancied Norfolk Island would be like floated in her mind. They'd be living in a small settlement with other civil officers and their families. According to the Reverend, they'd be quite separate from the prison and its inmates. Maybe there might be someone she could befriend. She was missing her sister Mary and the companionship of her friend Hannah. She rolled over and pulled her knees up around her chin. Why was the future always so uncertain?

***

The packing took another three weeks, and when it finally came to an end Jessie heaved a massive sigh of relief. She hoped to never have to do that again. She'd packed the bulk of her clothes and her few personal items into a large sea trunk. It was already half full of things that Mrs Sharpe had decided she couldn't live without. Jessie kept several outfits aside that would do her until she was reunited with the rest of her wardrobe on Norfolk Island. She closed her bag and looked around her small bedroom. She was going to miss waking up here every morning, but she felt a flutter of excitement when she thought about the future. She took one last look at herself in the mirror. She'd braided her honey-blonde hair and tucked it up under her bonnet. Her blue eyes gazed steadily back at her – what was that look – confidence?

"Are you ready, Jess?" called Mrs Sharpe from the sitting room. "Ed has the horses saddled and he's ready to go."

"Coming." She smiled at herself in the mirror showing her even white teeth. "You've grown up Jessie Smith," she said to her image as she cocked her head to the side.

She looked down at herself – her small rounded breasts were noticeable and respectfully covered by her new jacket. Her skirt ballooned over her shapely hips accentuating her budding figure. She liked what she saw.

She wrapped her hand-me-down cloak around her shoulders and grabbed her bag. She'd grown so much in the last six months that her cloak was now noticeably short. She'd planned to buy a new one on her last trip to town, but she hadn't had enough money. She gave the room one last look before stepping into the sitting room.

Mrs Sharpe smiled. "Now don't forget we'll be coming by to pick you up next Monday. We can't be late getting to Sydney, so do be ready."

"I'll be ready," said Jessie with a nod.

"Good. Well enjoy your few days with your grandmother, and safe travels my dear."

"Thank you."

She opened the door and walked out into the front yard. Ed was there with Biscuit and Cammy saddled and ready to go.

“Here give me ye bag,” he said holding out his hand for it.

Jessie handed it over and he secured it to Cammy’s saddle, before cupping his hands and looking at her. She put her boot in his hand and he hoisted her into the saddle.

“Thank you.” She hooked her leg around the pummel and gathered the reins.

Ed nodded before mounting Biscuit. Jessie watched him as he settled himself in the saddle. He was a man of few words. They’d hardly spoken in the ten months she’d lived at Milkmaids Reach. However, she felt quite safe and protected in his company. He’d never been anything but polite and the Reverend had even recommended him for a ticket of leave – which he now had.

She clicked her tongue and gave Cammy a nudge with her boot as Biscuit started down the road. Unlike the Reverend, Ed didn’t encourage her to ride alongside – he clearly had no intention of starting a conversation. As they rounded the first corner Jessie urged Cammy into a trot to match Biscuit’s gait. She sighed as she settled herself firmly in the saddle. It was going to be a long ride if Ed wasn't going to engage in chatter.

Jessie pulled her thin cloak around herself as the cool autumn air hit her. It was a sunny day at least but there was little warmth in it. The ride to Wiseman's Ferry was always enjoyable, as the track wound its way through the gum trees. Now and again Jessie caught a glimpse of the river sparkling in the sunshine. From Wiseman's Ferry, they followed the main road until they came to the track that led to Grandma's house. Jessie surprised herself by recognising it immediately.

She felt her heartbeat quicken as they set off on the final leg of their journey. She was so looking forward to spending a few days with her grandmother, but she was also excited about seeing her brother, George again. That thought had rather surprised her. A wide smile spread across her face – he'd tried his best to protect her and their relationship had shifted because of it.

A flutter of nerves went through her when she caught her first glimpse of the house. She gazed up at the sky and estimated the time to be close to noon – they'd made good time. She pressed her lips together as they approached the house – had Grandma received her letter telling her to expect her? She hoped so.

She reined Cammy to a halt and waited for Ed. He grasped her firmly around the waist as she dismounted, easing her effortlessly to the ground. "Thank you," she murmured as he released her.

He untied her bag and handed it to her. "I'm not staying," he said looking at the house. "I've got things to do."

"Well, thank you for bringing me," she said. "And good luck."

"Aye, ye too."

He tethered Cammy to Biscuit's saddle and mounted with ease. He tipped his hat in her direction before nudging Biscuit in the side with his heels.

"Jess." George came bounding down from the veranda.

Jesse gave Ed one last look before turning her attention to her brother. She gaped at him – he'd changed so much. He'd grown at least five inches and was sporting a thin wispy moustache. He looked like he'd outgrown his body – he was all arms and legs as he grabbed her in a crushing hug.

"It's so good to see you." He let her go and held her at arm's length. "Are you alright? We were so worried when Sophia took you away."

"I'm fine," she said grinning at him. "What about you? My how you've changed."

"You too," he said picking up her bag and slinging his arm around her waist. "Come, Grandma will be so happy to see you."

The front door opened as they stepped onto the veranda and Maggie's smiling face peered out. "Is that ye Jessie?"

"Yes Grandma," she said racing towards her and throwing herself into her open arms. "How I've missed you."

"Oh my sweet girl," she said holding her face between her gnarled hands. "Are ye alright?"

"Yes, yes I'm fine."

She kissed both her cheeks before letting her go. Jessie couldn't help but notice unshed tears clinging to her eyelashes. "I'm truly fine, Grandma. Mr and Mrs Sharpe are the kindest most generous employers."

"It does my heart good to hear it," she said leaning against the open door. "Come, ye must be starving. George, take your sister's bag down to her room, an' then go an' fetch Grandpa Joe."

"Aye, Grandma."

William came running down the hallway and as soon as he spied his grandmother, he slowed to a sedate walk. "Jessie."

Jessie smiled at her youngest sibling. "William tis good to see you."

"Ye too," he said casting his eyes downward.

"Come, give me a hug," she said holding her arms open wide.

"William, go an' tell Alice we'll have luncheon in the dining room," said Maggie as soon as they'd parted. "Come, Jessie, I want to hear all about the Sharpes."

Jessie followed Maggie down the hall and through the sitting room to the dining room. She couldn't help but notice her grandmother was running her fingers along first the wall, and then the furniture they passed. She waited until they'd settled themselves in the dining room before she mentioned it.

"Are you alright Grandma?"

"Aye, why wouldn't I be?" she said in a dismissive tone as she seated herself. She patted the chair beside her. "Sit, an' tell me all about yer new life."

Jessie removed her cloak and hung it on the back of the chair before sitting down. "Well, it's been rather wonderful. Mrs Sharpe's taught me so much about running a house and gardening and cooking."

"An' you're happy with them?"

"Yes, very. I'm sure it's not what mother Sophia had in mind when she sent me there. They pay me and I'm saving my money, and they're most kind," said Jessie smiling reassuringly. "They treat me like a daughter."

Maggie sat back in her chair with a sigh. "I'm so pleased to hear it. An' now you're off to Norfolk Island? My, my."

"Yes, I'm looking forward to it. They're picking me up on Monday, so you'll get to meet them."

Maggie patted her arm and smiled. "We've all been so worried about ye. But, I can see that you're happy."

"I am."

"Jessie lass," said Grandpa Joe arriving in the dining room.

Jessie leapt to her feet and was soon wrapped in Grandpa Joe's bear-like arms.

"It's so good to see ye lass."

"I've missed you too Grandpa Joe."

She sat back down and grinned as she looked around the room. George and William had arrived on Grandpa Joe's heels and were settling themselves at the table.

"Where's that girl?" said Maggie looking exasperated.

"She'll be along in a moment I'm sure," said Grandpa Joe patting Maggie on the shoulder as he seated himself at the end of the table.

"Where's Eliza?" said Jessie raising her brows.

"She left," said Maggie with a frown. "We didn't want her to go, but she'd had enough of being out here I think. She went to Wilberforce."

A young woman came hurrying into the dining room carrying a large tureen. She almost dropped it onto the middle of the table and wiped her brow with the back of her hand. Her dark hair had escaped her cap and was hanging down in long tendrils. She looked quite flustered as she turned on her heel and hurried out of the room.

"Should I go and help her?" said Jessie staring after her.

"No, no, she'll be fine," said Maggie shaking her head. "Ye can serve the soup though if ye like."

"Alright."

Lunch was a hectic affair with everyone wanting to hear all about Jessie's new life. She still had half a bowl of soup to eat when everyone else had finished theirs. Not that she minded. She was discovering that she had lots of stories to tell about her time at Milkmaid Reach.

"Leave her be," said Maggie at last. "There's plenty of time to hear all about it."

Jessie smiled and nodded. She was grateful for the intervention.

***

Chapter Eighteen

Family Matters

Jessie awoke the next morning in the room she'd stayed in previously. She stretched and yawned and then buried herself back under the pink floral counterpane. It was such a luxury to have no particular reason to get out of bed, and she was in no hurry to meet the day.

A soft knock on the door was quickly followed by Maggie. Jessie popped her head up and smiled when she spied her grandmother.

"Stay there," said Maggie running her fingers along the bed as she made her way to a chintz-covered chair. She eased herself into it and sighed. "How are ye this morning?"

"Well, thank you, Grandma," said Jessie piling the pillows behind her and sitting up. "And you?"

"Fine thank ye. I thought we might find a moment to talk before ye meet the day."

Jessie nodded and settled herself against the pillows. "What did you want to talk about?"

"Oh, nothing really. I just wanted to be sure that ye were happy."

"I am. And I can't wait to get to Norfolk Island, it's going to be such an adventure."

Maggie chuckled. "It will be interesting I'm sure. Just be careful – all those men stuck there in that awful place. They'll eat a juicy little morsel like ye if ye aren't careful."

Jesse shrugged. "Reverend Sharpe says we'll be staying in the settlement, away from the prisoners. He says we'll be quite safe."

"I'm glad," she said with a sigh. "Have ye heard from your sister, Charlotte? Ye know she an' her husband have moved to Pitt Town?"

"No," she said staring wide-eyed. "I haven't written to Charlotte since Papa died. She wouldn't have known where to write me." She sighed as a pang of guilt stabbed at her. She really should've written to Charlotte more often, but she always found an excuse not to.

"Well, they've settled in Pitt Town with their two young ones. Maybe ye could visit on your way to Sydney? I'll give ye the address."

Jessie shook her head. "I won't have time. Did you say she has two children now?"

"Aye, she has Mary, an' her son George, named for yer father, was born last year. Ye really must write to her Jessie."

"I will. What about Mary? Have you heard from her?"

"Not recently. The last letter I got from her she said they'd moved to Maitland."

Jessie knew it was her fault her sisters didn't write to her. She hardly ever wrote letters and since she'd moved to Milkmaid Reach they wouldn't even know where to write to her. "I'll write to them both before I leave here and let them know I'll be on Norfolk Island."

"Good," said Maggie getting to her feet. "Well, I'm ready for breakfast. Won't ye join me?"

“Yes.”

She pushed back the covers and climbed out of bed and wrapped herself in her dressing gown. Maggie slipped her arm in hers as they headed for the kitchen. It was so good to be back here with her grandmother. She just couldn’t shake the feeling that something was wrong with Grandma, even though she’d insisted there wasn’t.

***

After breakfast, she dressed for the day and went to find George. If anything was going on, he’d surely know. She searched the house before stepping out onto the veranda to look for him. She spotted him immediately crossing the rear yard with a pitchfork over his shoulder.

“George. George,” she called.

He stopped and turned. A wide grin spread across his face when he saw her. “Good morning,” he said marching over to her.

“Good morning. I wonder if you might have a moment to spare?”

"Of course," he said pushing the pitchfork into the ground and looking at her with an expectant expression.

"It's Grandma. Is she alright?"

He sucked in a breath and looked left and right before his gaze rested on her face. "She hasn't told you then?"

"No. Told me what?"

"She's going blind. It started a few months ago and it's getting worse," he said in a low voice. "She wouldn't want you to worry, so don't tell her I told you."

"Blind? Well, that explains it. Oh dear."

"She's doing alright, Jess. She knows her way around the house, as long as no one moves anything."

"But you said it's getting worse?"

"Aye. She'll eventually go completely blind."

Jessie blew out her breath. Poor Grandma. Surely she'd need more help soon with all kinds of things. She wouldn't even be able to eat if she couldn't see. "Thank you for telling me, George, but I'll have to tell her you told me."

"She won't be happy," he said pulling his pitchfork from the ground. "But I can deal with that. Go ahead."

"Thank you, George."

Jessie went back inside the house to find Grandma. She found her in the sitting room relaxing in one of the many overstuffed chairs. She didn't appear to be doing anything – no book or letter in her hands, no mending or sewing in her lap. Jessie felt a surge of sadness tug at her heart – poor Grandma. What would life be like for her?

"How are ye Jess?" she said looking up and smiling.

"Fine, Grandma." She seated herself in one of the chairs next to her grandmother. "I've just been talking to George," she said deciding to dive straight into the matter at hand. "He told me your eyesight's been failing."

"Did he now? Well, he shouldn't have done that. I'm perfectly fine, an' I don't want ye to worry none."

"Grandma, you know that's not true. He said you're going blind, and I've noticed it. You hang on to furniture and run your fingers along the walls. Is it bad?"

"Aye, it's getting worse," she said with a sigh. "It's like I'm looking down a tunnel – all the bits on the side are fading into darkness."

"Oh, Grandma I'm so sorry."

"It's not that bad. I'll be fine," she said with a wave of her hand.

"Well, I think I should stay and not go to Norfolk Island. Mr and Mrs Sharpe will understand that you need me more."

"Nonsense. You'll do no such thing."

"Please let me stay and take care of you."

"No. At any rate, ye know perfectly well that ye aren't free to do that," said Maggie frowning. "Have ye forgotten? You're indentured until you're sixteen."

It was now Jessie's turn to wave her hand in the air, dismissing her grandmother's argument. "They won't hold me to that – Mrs Sharpe told me they won't."

"Hrmph. I won't have ye throwing away yer future for me. I've got Grandpa Joe, George an' William to take care of me. I don't need ye." She crossed her arms across her breasts and glared at her granddaughter. "An' that's final."

Jessie wasn't prepared to give up so easily. She was really looking forward to going to Norfolk Island, but how could she? Her poor grandmother needed her. "Please Grandma, don't be so stubborn. I could be like your personal maid. I can take care of you better than my brothers and Grandpa Joe. You know it's true."

"I don't need ye!" She got to her feet and walked across the room to the door without feeling her way. She turned to face Jessie with a satisfied look on her face. "See."

"Yes Grandma," said Jessie in a defeated tone. "I see."

"Good. Let that be the end of the matter." She gave Jessie one final withering stare before making her way down the hall.

Jessie leaned back in her chair and sighed. She wasn't going to get anywhere with her direct approach – that was obvious. Perhaps she could get around Grandpa Joe instead. She was determined not to end the matter there.

***

No opportunities presented themselves to talk to Grandpa Joe. He was busy most of the time, and Jessie didn't like to interrupt him. After another conversation with George, she decided to let it go. He assured her they could take care of her grandmother and that she should go to Norfolk Island.

She wrote letters to both her sisters and hoped they'd write back to her. She missed them both, particularly Mary. She tucked both letters into her bag – she'd arrange to post them when she got to Sydney. Her few days spent with her family flew by and she was full of mixed feelings when Monday arrived. She packed the last of her things and looked around the bedroom. She hoped she'd be back here again before too long.

She left her bag near the front door and went to find her grandmother. It was their last morning together, and she intended to spend every moment with Grandma. She found her sitting on the veranda with a rug wrapped around her knees. The sun was shining, but the chill of autumn was in the air.

"What are you doing out here?" said Jessie sitting beside her grandmother. "It's a bit cold."

"We can go in if ye like," she said smiling. "But, I like the crisp autumn air, it's invigorating."

Jessie smiled. "No, it's fine."

"Are ye all packed an' ready to go then?"

"Yes."

"It's been so lovely having ye for a few days," said Maggie eyeing her. "Is that the only cloak ye have?"

Jessie looked down at her hand-me-down cloak. It was thin and worn and too short but it was all she had. "Yes."

"Oh good Lord, we can't have ye going off like that." She got to her feet and folded her blanket and put it on the chair. "Come with me. I've got a cloak I hardly wear that should fit ye nicely."

Jessie followed her down the hall to her bedroom. She'd never been in Joe and Maggie's room before and was surprised at how large and airy it was. It was cluttered with furniture including two large wardrobes.

Maggie went over to one of them and opened it.

"Here, take that old thing off an' try this on," she said handing Jessie a brown woollen cloak.

She did as she was bid and wrapped herself in her grandmother's cloak. The wool was soft and supple under her fingers and the linen lining was smooth and crisp. She wondered if her grandmother had ever worn it – it was brand new and expensive.

"Oh it fits ye like a glove," said Maggie eyeing Jessie with a critical eye. "Turn around."

She turned around and smiled. "It's beautiful but I can't take this, Grandma. It's like new."

"Nonsense," said Maggie with a wave of her hand. "I want ye to have it." She walked over to her and placed a warm kiss on her cheek. "I've hardly given ye a thing in ye life, so please, make me happy an' take the cloak."

"Thank you. I love it."

Alice appeared in the doorway and knocked softly on the open door. "Excuse me. Mr and Mrs Sharpe have arrived to collect Miss Smith."

"Oh they're early," said Jessie with a disappointed look. She'd hoped to have a bit more time.

"Thank ye, Alice. We'll be there momentarily."

Alice disappeared back down the hallway and Maggie engulfed her granddaughter in a tight hug. "Promise me you'll take care, an' write me."

"I promise." Jessie wrapped her arms around her grandmother and breathed in the scent of lavender. She'd never noticed that before. "Promise me that you'll let George and Grandpa Joe take care of you."

They separated and Maggie wiped an errant tear aside. "I doubt I could stop them. Come, ye mustn't keep the Sharpes waiting."

***

Chapter Nineteen

The Brig Governor Phillip

After a quick bite to eat and farewell hugs and kisses, Jessie climbed into the cart beside Mrs Sharpe. They'd borrowed Mr Burnett's post chaise, which had seats for four and room in the back for their trunks and bags. Ed climbed onto the driver's seat and waited for Mr Sharpe, who was shaking hands with Grandpa Joe.

"Safe travels," said Grandpa Joe, "and take care of our girl."

"I promise I will," said Reverend Sharpe nodding. "Thank you for your kind hospitality."

He hoisted himself up onto the driver's seat and Ed wasted no time in urging the horses on. Jessie waved to her family as they headed down the road. She had such mixed feelings. On the one hand, she was so excited about what may lie ahead, but the other part of her wanted to stay. She settled herself and pulled her cloak around her shoulders as they rounded the first corner.

"I've missed you these past few days," said Mrs Sharpe squeezing her arm. "I hope you enjoyed your time with your grandmother?"

Jessie smiled. "I did."

"And I see you have a new cloak. It's lovely."

"It was a gift from my Grandma," she said running her fingers over the soft wool. "I love it."

Any further conversation was impossible. Ed urged the horses into a trot and the noise from the chaise and hoofs drowned out all other sounds. Jessie was glad the day was clear and dry even if the air was chilly.

The trip to Sydney took most of the day and they arrived on the outskirts late in the afternoon. Jessie noticed Mr Sharpe pull a hand-drawn map from his pocket and was giving Ed directions. They wound their way through the streets, getting ever closer to the harbour. Jessie spied the tall masts of the ship docked at the wharf as Ed turned off George Street. A shiver of excitement ran down her spine at the thought that she would soon be boarding that ship.

As if reading her mind, Mrs Sharpe turned and smiled and took Jessie's gloved hand in hers. “I think that’s our ship.”

“Yes my dear,” said Mr Sharpe swivelling around in his seat. “I believe that’s the Governor Phillip. It’s a fine ship to be sure.”

“It certainly is,” said Mrs Sharpe letting go of Jessie’s hand. “Will we be boarding tonight?”

“Aye, of course.” Mr Sharpe nodded before turning back around to face the front.

Jessie had only been on a ship once before, and that was when she came to Pitt Town with her brothers and father. Her father had only paid for one small cabin, and the four of them had been squashed in on two narrow bunks for the entire voyage to Sydney. It had been uncomfortable, and smelly and the food was horrid. She grimaced as she remembered – would it be very different on this ship? She hoped so.

Ed brought the post chaise to a halt opposite the wharf where the Governor Phillip was moored. It was a large ship with two masts and Jessie thought she saw at least one gun. She swallowed at the thought of the

Captain having to use that. Were there pirates in these waters? She had absolutely no idea and had only heard stories about pirates and their escapades in the Americas. Still, she wasn't too sure if they were out there or not.

"Ed, go and see if you can get someone to assist with our baggage," said Mr Sharpe folding his map and putting it back in his pocket.

"Aye," said Ed leaping down from the cart and marching across the dock.

Mr Sharpe got down and stretched before helping Mrs Sharpe to alight. Jessie climbed down and stretched her back and stamped her numb legs up and down. A chill breeze was blowing off the harbour which whipped her cloak around her legs. She shivered and pulled the hood over her head. She hoped Ed wouldn't be too long – they'd be chilled to the bone if they stayed here much longer.

Ed returned about ten minutes later with several soldiers in tow.

"Corporal Jones at your service, Mr Sharpe. The Captain extends his salutations."

"Thank you," said Mr Sharpe.

"Take those trunks on board," the Corporal commanded the soldiers. "Harris, take Mr Sharpe's baggage to his cabin."

The soldiers sprang into action, grabbing a trunk between them and heading for the ship. Private Harris loaded himself like a pack mule with their bags and hurried after the others.

"Ma'am," said Corporal Jones doffing his hat in Mrs Sharpe's direction. "If you're ready I'll escort you to your cabin."

"Thank you, Corporal," said Mrs Sharpe slipping her hand into the crook of her husband's arm. "Come, Jessie," she said over her shoulder.

"Coming." She followed the Sharpes across the dock to the waiting ship and stepped tentatively onto the gangplank. It was narrow and felt slippery under her foot. There was nothing to hold onto, but raised bits of wood attached to the top of the plank allowed her to get some grip. She almost held her breath until she stepped safely onto the deck.

She followed the Sharpes across the deck to the main hatchway and waited while they disappeared below. She followed a moment later and was relieved to be out of the relentless cold wind. Below deck was dimly lit, but Jessie had no trouble following the Sharpes along the narrow corridor. She thought they were heading towards the rear of the ship, but she couldn't be sure. Up ahead she heard Corporal Jones open a door and show the Sharpes into their cabin.

"Your cabin, Mr and Mrs Sharpe. It's one of our best."

"Thank you, Corporal," she heard Mr Sharpe reply.

She craned her neck, but she couldn't see passed Mrs Sharpe. She sighed and leaned against the timber bulkhead. A moment later, Mrs Sharpe disappeared into the cabin along with Mr Sharpe and the Corporal. She hurried along to the doorway and peered inside. It was a small cramped cabin with a large bunk and a small table and two chairs. Their bags had been dumped higgledy-piggledy in the corner like sacks of potatoes. Jessie imagined Private Harris had simply dropped them there without a second thought.

"This should serve us nicely," said Mr Sharpe gazing around the small space. "And our servant? Miss Smith?"

"Ah, I wasn't aware you were bringing a woman," he said looking at Jessie like she'd just appeared out of thin air.

"The Captain was informed," said Mr Sharpe.

The Reverend appeared to be quite unperturbed by the Corporal's lack of knowledge who was left stammering in the doorway.

"Perhaps, if I may suggest, Corporal, you should go and enquire." The Reverend raised his brows and gazed steadily at Corporal Jones.

"Aye," he finally said ducking his head as he exited the cabin.

"Wait here with us Jessie," said Mr Sharpe with a sigh. "I'm sure the good Corporal will have something sorted for you in short order."

Jessie suppressed a smile as the Corporal hurried back down the corridor.

He returned fifteen minutes later with Harris, who had a roll of canvas tucked under his arm. Jessie watched as he disappeared through the door opposite.

"I apologise for the oversight, Mr Sharpe," said Corporal Jones, "however, we aren't equipped to deal with a single young woman. She can't bunk down with the men and we don't have another cabin we can give her."

"Miss Smith is under my care and protection, Corporal, so I suggest you find a suitable solution," said Mr Sharpe pulling himself up to his full height.

"Aye, we have," he said nodding. "The best we can do is a hammock in the store room opposite your cabin. Harris is hanging it now."

"Thank you, Corporal," said Jessie interjecting. "That will be most suitable."

Mr Sharpe gave Jessie a stern look and frowned.

"I assure you, Miss Smith will be quite safe and comfortable," said Corporal Jones.

"Very well," said Reverend Sharpe with a sigh.

Harris appeared from across the narrow corridor. "All done, sir."

"Thank you, Harris," said Corporal Jones. "Mr Sharpe, the Captain extends an invitation to you and Mrs Sharpe to join him for supper this evening."

"Thank you. Please advise the Captain that we'd be honoured," said Mr Sharpe.

"Very well," said the Corporal, and with a doff of his hat he and Harris retreated.

Jessie waited until they disappeared up the hatchway before she went to investigate her quarters. They were exactly as the Corporal had described – a storeroom with barrels and boxes piled high in the corner. Harris had strung a hammock between two beams, and there was just enough room for Jessie to walk between it and the boxes. A small barrel looked like it had been deliberately placed to serve as a stool.

She'd never slept in a hammock before and wondered how one got into it. She'd find out later tonight.

"Well it's rather cramped," said Mrs Sharpe arriving on the scene with Jessie's bag over her arm. "But it's only for a few days. Will it be alright?"

"It'll be fine," said Jessie in a reassuring tone as she took her bag. "I'm just not sure about sleeping in a hammock." She laughed as she dropped her bag and pushed the hammock back and forth.

Mrs Sharpe eyed it dubiously. "Rather you than me my dear. I'm afraid it would only make my morning sickness worse."

Jessie stared at her. Did she just say she had morning sickness? Then a wide smile spread across her face. "Are you expecting a baby?"

Mrs Sharpe smiled shyly and ran her hand over her flat stomach. "I am."

"Well, that's wonderful news. Congratulations."

"Thank you," she said sighing. "I pray I can carry this child full term. We had a daughter, Elizabeth. She was born two years ago, but she came too soon and she died."

"I'm so sorry." Jessie had no idea they'd lost a child, although she'd often wondered why they didn't have any. She would add Mrs Sharpe and her baby to her prayers.

“Thank you.” She turned to leave and then looked back at Jessie. “It will mean more work for you.”

“That’s alright,” said Jessie with a laugh. “Although, I have no idea about babies.”

Mrs Sharpe laughed as well. “That makes two of us.”

***

Chapter Twenty

Norfolk Island, 1837

Their departure was delayed due to unfavourable weather, which allowed Jessie and Mrs Sharpe to get better acquainted with the ship. The Reverend accompanied them on their morning walk on the top deck. Soldier's wives and children and several other passengers also joined them. Their stroll on the deck this morning was short due to the inclement weather, but they were free to explore below decks. Jessie didn't think there was much to see - the crew's mess and various storerooms. Most of the ship was off-limits to them including the stern. Prisoners being sent to the island were housed there.

"We have sixteen prisoners on board," Private Harris informed them. "Ye needn't worry they're well secured and guarded."

Jessie was curious about the prisoners. Not just the ones on board, but the ones detained on the island. The Reverend had told her they were really bad men, and there was very little chance of them repenting or showing any remorse for their sins. She wasn't so sure. Didn't everyone deserve a second chance? She leaned against the railing and watched the men going about their business on the dock. Another ship had moored beside them early this morning and the docks were a hive of activity.

She shivered and pulled her cloak more firmly around herself. The cold breeze would drive her back down below soon.

Another five minutes and she gave into the cold and made her back down below. She knocked on the Sharpe's door and waited for a reply. A moment later she heard Mrs Sharpe call out to her to come in.

She poked her head into the cabin and smiled. Mrs Sharpe was lying down on the bunk propped up against some pillows.

"Can I get you anything?"

"No, I'm fine, thank you. Why don't you come in? Tom's gone to see the prisoners."

She went in and closed the door before perching herself on the edge of one of the chairs. "Are you feeling alright?"

"Yes, I'm fine. I'm just resting. Really, there isn't much to do is there?"

"No," said Jessie with a shake of her head. "Do you think we'll set sail today?"

"I have no idea," she said with a shrug. "We'll have to wait for favourable weather, whatever that is."

Jessie smiled. She had no idea what that was either. She presumed they'd have to wait until the wind and the tide were heading in the right direction. It seemed a bit haphazard to her.

She spent the remainder of the morning chatting with Mrs Sharpe. When the Reverend returned the three of them went to have their midday meal. This was a shared occasion with the soldiers and their families in a large mess. It had wooden tables with benches down the sides that were attached to the deck and couldn't be moved. At least the food was well-seasoned and quite palatable. She wouldn't have described it as delicious, but it certainly wasn't horrid.

The Governor Phillip spent the rest of the day tied firmly to the dock. The crew didn't make any preparations to depart until the next morning, and it was nearly midday before they finally set off for Norfolk Island. They spent most of the afternoon tacking back and forth up the harbour and finally broke free of the heads at sunset.

Getting into her hammock that night proved more challenging than it had when the ship had been docked. She ship was rolling from side to side in rhythm with the waves, and Jessie just had to time it right. She wrapped her blanket around herself, and as the ship swayed to the left she tossed herself at the hammock, bottom first. She landed in the hammock alright, but she didn't have enough time to get her balance before the ship rolled back the other way. She had no way of holding on as she'd wrapped her arms inside her blanket, and so she landed on the floor with a thump like a sack of potatoes.

She lay there for a moment – surprised and glad she hadn't embarrassed herself in front of anyone. She untangled herself from her blanket and wrapped it around herself again, this time leaving her arms free. As the ship rolled she launched herself at the hammock again, and this time managed to lie down before it tipped her out.

The hammock wrapped itself around her forming a safe cocoon. She groaned as she struggled to get her arms wrapped in the blanket, and by the time she'd tucked herself in she was breathing heavily. She'd be glad to sleep in a bed again.

It took eight days to reach Norfolk Island, and apart from a few gulls, it was like they were the only people on earth. No other sails were spotted, and Jessie's earlier concerns about pirates were completely unfounded. If anything, she was grateful it only took a week to reach the island – she found sea travel rather mundane and monotonous.

***

The Governor Phillip made anchor off the island early on the morning of the 21st of April. Jessie joined the Sharpes and the other passengers on the top deck as soon as breakfast was done. The day was overcast but mild, verging on warm. It was such a contrast to how chilly it had been in Sydney.

Her first glimpse of the island left her feeling anxious to disembark. Tall pines and other trees with dark green foliage she'd never seen before framed the small bay. Steep cliffs on either side of it were covered in creepers and other vines. They appeared to be clinging to the island, making the whole look most delightful. Two launches were lowered and the first of the soldiers and their families disembarked. Jessie watched as they were rowed ashore, anxious that they might be next.

They weren't. The prisoners were brought up from the hold in readiness to disembark next. Jessie had never been so close to prisoners before, and couldn't help staring. They were unkept and an odour of fear and of men who have been confined in close proximity assaulted her nostrils. She grimaced but she couldn't stop staring at them. Their shaved heads were covered in drab caps, but the most notable item were the chains - leg irons with what looked like a heavy chain joining them. It made it impossible for the men to run or even walk very fast. She swallowed as they passed her – were they all going to be like this? Chained and pitiful?

It was mid-morning before Jessie and Mr and Mrs Sharpe finally boarded the launch and were rowed ashore. According to Private Harris, they were landing at what they called 'Cascades'. It wasn't where the main settlement was established, but the safest place to land. They would have to make their way to Kingston on foot under the escort of Corporal Watkins. Jessie quickly discovered that was only a short walk of a couple of miles.

Kingston was located close to the beach, and Jessie thought it looked like a quaint settlement. There were a couple of large stone buildings, with many thatched cottages scattered about here and there. Overlooking the settlement was the Commandant's house. It was perched on a little eminence with what looked like a lovely garden surrounding it. Corporal Watkins pointed out several of the landmarks to Mr and Mrs Sharpe but Jessie wasn't paying a lot of attention to what he was saying. She was quite in awe of Kingston and its surrounds.

"The Catholic chaplain, Mr Atkins lives in that house opposite the barracks," said Corporal Watkins indicating to a small stone cottage with a flourishing garden. "The other parsonage is just up ahead. I think it's better situated of the two. It overlooks the bay."

"It looks delightful," said Mrs Sharpe taking her husband's arm. "I have to agree Corporal, it's much better situated."

The cottage looked like the others with a well-tended garden out the front. The Corporal opened the front door and stood aside while Mr and Mrs Sharpe went inside. Jessie followed last.

She stepped straight into a parlour, which was furnished with several chairs, and a dresser with a seagrass rug on the floor. A small fireplace shared the west wall with a solid-looking sideboard.

"The main bedroom's through there and two smaller rooms make up the rest of the house." Corporal Watkins waved his arms in the general direction as he said this. "Out the back, you'll find a washhouse and out-kitchen."

"Thank you, Corporal, this should be most serviceable," said Mr Sharpe as he poked his head into the main bedroom.

"You'll find the larder well stocked, and if ye need anything, the Commissariat Store will assist ye."

"Our trunks?" said Mr Sharpe looking quizzically at the Corporal.

"Ah, they'll bring them up for ye before too long. If there's nothing else, I'll leave ye to get settled."

Mrs Sharpe smiled as the Corporal left and gazed around the parlour. "Come, Jessie. Let's see what the rest of the house is like."

Jessie put her bag down by the front door and followed her as she inspected the other rooms. One was rather tiny but well-furnished. It had a single bed and a tall boy with a small half-size wardrobe.

"It's small, but I'm sure it'll serve you, Jessie. What do you think?"

"Yes," said Jessie nodding. It was rather small, but then she didn't have very many belongings, and it would soon feel like home.

Mr Sharpe joined them as they investigated the other room. It contained two single beds and other bedroom furniture.

"This will do nicely for my study," said Mr Sharpe. "I'll speak to someone about removing this furniture and installing a desk."

"I think you're forgetting something, Tom," said Mrs Sharpe smiling shyly at her husband. "We're in need of a nursery."

"Ah…quite right. I hadn't forgotten." He put his arm around her waist and kissed her cheek. "Perhaps the other room would better suit for my study, and Jessie could share with the nursery?"

"Yes, I think that would work," she said turning to face Jessie. "Would that suit you?"

"Of course."

"Then it's settled," said Mr Sharpe with a satisfied look. "I'll arrange for a desk to be brought down, and we'll rearrange the furniture to suit."

Their tour of the rest of the house didn't take long. The kitchen was rather basic, but Jessie thought they'd soon have it in order. Corporal Watkins was right about the larder being well-stocked. However, Jessie was most delighted about the back garden. There were four large vegetable plots and several fruit trees growing at the bottom of the yard. The kitchen garden would keep them well supplied she thought.

Their trunks arrived in the early afternoon, and Mrs Sharpe kept Jessie busy unpacking and sorting things for the rest of the day. She'd hoped to be able to have a look around Kingston, but that would have to wait.

All in all, Jessie was delighted with Norfolk Island. It was all that she had imagined and more. She felt like she was on the verge of a wonderful adventure.

***

Chapter Twenty One

Orange Vale and Beyond

A week later and still no opportunities for Jessie to explore Kingston had presented themselves. Mrs Sharpe insisted that the house be scrubbed from top to bottom, and the garden tended and brought up to scratch. Jessie had to agree that the house was dusty and had a neglected feel about it. However, the garden was soon brought into order, and Jessie had a feeling of satisfaction to see it flourishing in the sub-tropical climate. The weather was so different to what she was used to.

The Reverend went out every day to visit the sick in the hospital, the soldiers in the barracks and prisoners confined to gaol. Jessie looked forward to him coming home and sharing his tales from the day over supper. She wished Mrs Sharpe was feeling better so they could go out and about and meet their new neighbours. But, she continued to suffer from morning sickness, which actually lasted most of the day.

Several women had come calling, but they came to see Mrs Sharpe, not Jessie.

Jessie placed Mr Sharpe's supper on the table and went to fetch hers and Mrs Sharpe's. She returned as fast as she could and placed their plates of mutton and vegetables on the table. She didn't want to miss a word the Reverend had to say.

"The poor woman is most grievously afflicted," he said cutting into his mutton. "She laments her vile heart – but I did my best to assure her of God's forgiveness, even for the most lost of his lambs. I trust the poor woman will repent her sins."

"Has she sinned so badly?" said Mrs Sharpe staring wide-eyed at her husband.

Jessie was sitting on the edge of her seat, her entire attention focused on Mr Sharpe. What had the woman done? She was more than a little curious about the unknown woman.

The Reverend shook his head. "I know not. She keeps her own counsel with God."

Jessie groaned inwardly as she slumped in her chair – disappointed. What was the point of that? She could only hope

Mr Sharpe would somehow wheedle it out of her and then he'd share it with her and Mrs Sharpe. She glanced up in time to see the disappointment mirrored on Mrs Sharpe's face. Well, she wasn't the only curious one.

"You said she has an affliction. Is there anything we can do?" said Mrs Sharpe.

"No. She's under the care of the surgeon, but I fear it may be consumption and there's little hope of her recovery."

"The poor woman," said Mrs Sharpe taking a mouthful of her supper. She grimaced as she swallowed and pressed her lips together.

"How are you, my dear? Are you feeling any better?" he said putting his hand on her arm.

"No, I'm afraid not," she said shaking her head.

"I'm so sorry to hear it, Elli. I was going to invite you to join me tomorrow. I'm going out to Orange Vale, and I believe you'd enjoy the excursion."

"Under normal circumstances, I would I'm sure, but I'm afraid I'd only be a hindrance to you," she said smiling weakly. "Why don't you take Jessie? The poor thing's been stuck indoors with me since we arrived."

"Well, of course, if you'd like to join me I would welcome your company," he said turning his attention to Jessie.

She hastily swallowed a mouthful of her supper and felt a great lump of unchewed mutton make its way down her throat. She coughed but the damn thing wouldn't dislodge. She swallowed hard and finally felt it go down. "I'd love to," she said gasping.

***

Mr Sharpe and Jessie set off early the following morning for Orange Vale. Jessie breathed in the fresh sea air as they walked down the road. It was so good to be out and about, and the day was perfect for a walk. She quickly discovered it was only a short walk of about a mile and a half to Orange Vale, and her first glimpse of the little valley reminded her of a fairy glen she'd seen in a book once.

Towering pine trees covered the steep hills with a clear stream running through the middle of the valley. There was a well-arranged garden with fruit trees and creepers and vines, with guava and arrowroot growing in abundance. Small thatched cottages were scattered about the hillside like a whole lot of bee hives.

"That's the Commandant's garden," said Mr Sharpe as they wound their way down the valley. "I believe it's the only place on the island where they grow oranges."

"So the orange trees belong to the Commandant?"

"Well yes and no," he said smiling. "I understand the fruits and crops from the garden are shared with the civil establishment."

"Oh. That's us?"

"Aye, it is."

As they entered the perfect little glen Jessie noticed a number of prisoners working in a grove of trees with several soldiers standing guard. Others were tending the gardens and they all appeared to not notice their intrusion, except for one man. He looked up and then he started walking towards them. He didn't look very different from the others – he was dressed in a similar manner but he had an air of authority about him. It was like a small alarm bell had gone off in Jessie's head and she instinctively stepped behind the Reverend.

"Good morning to ye," he said removing his cap which showed his head wasn't shaved like the prisoners. His brown hair shone in the morning sun showing flecks of grey at his temples.

"A fine morning it is," said Mr Sharpe. "My name's Sharpe. I'm the new chaplain here, and this is my servant, Miss Smith."

Jessie murmured a greeting but remained close to the Reverend as she eyed the man with a mixture of curiosity and nervousness. His hazel eyes seemed to rest on her too long which only added to her feeling of uneasiness.

"Pleased to meet ye. I'm Overseer Price," he said putting his cap back on. "I wasn't expecting ye, but I have no complaint if ye wish to speak with the men."

"Thank you," said Reverend Sharpe with a wave of his hand. "No, I simply wish to acquaint myself with each of the settlements on the island"

"Well, you'll find Orange Vale has much to offer," said Price grinning. "We have a fine crop of coffee and the bananas are nearly ripe."

"It would seem you have many fine crops here."

"Aye. Feel free to inspect the garden and orchards." With a nod, he went back to his work. His commanding voice echoed around the glen as he ordered a group of men to get back to work.

Mr Sharpe and Jessie spent a most enjoyable morning inspecting the garden. Orange Vale was like an oasis and Jessie was enchanted. The Reverend stopped and spoke with several of the prisoners, while Jessie meandered through the Commandant's garden.

It seemed to her that the island was a place of contrasts. On the one hand, men were worked nearly to death here and punished harshly – she knew that. She'd heard of this place long before she came. And yet, here was this perfect little glen where she could forget this whole island was a prison full of dangerous men. None more so than the Overseer? She stopped and looked over her shoulder as a nervous shiver went down her spine. What was it about him that made her feel so wary? The man was unnerving.

It was nearing midday before they began the walk back to Kingston. Mr Sharpe was full of praise for Orange Vale and the coffee crop that was being harvested. They were nearly back at the main settlement when three soldiers on horseback came trotting down the road. The man in the lead had a large bushy beard and deep-set eyes which reflected the astute man behind them.

"Reverend this is most opportune," he said coming to a halt.

"Good morning, Major."

"I trust you enjoyed your visit to Orange Vale?"

"Indeed," said Mr Sharpe with a wide smile on his face. "I'm anxious to try your coffee."

"You won't be disappointed," said Major Anderson with a chuckle. "I'm riding out to Anson Bay tomorrow and I thought you might like to accompany me?"

"I would indeed."

"Excellent. I'll expect you at the house at nine."

"I'll be there."

"Until tomorrow. Good day." He tipped his hat before digging his heels into the horse's flank and continuing on his way. The Reverend and Jessie stood watching them trot down the road.

"That was the Commandant," said Reverend Sharpe.

"Oh," said Jessie taking another look at the disappearing trio. She hadn't expected to meet the Commandant, nor did she know what she'd expected him to be like. But Major Anderson appeared to be a completely reasonable man to her.

They arrived back in Kingston and were heading for home when the Reverend came to a halt. "Would you mind greatly going on without me? I should see if I can give Mrs Williamson some solace."

"Is that the woman you were telling us about?"

"Aye, she's in the barracks. Tell Mrs Sharpe I'll be along shortly."

"Alright."

It was only a short walk back to the house and Jessie rather enjoyed her few moments alone. She realised she hadn't been by herself since leaving Milkmaid Reach, and that seemed like a long time ago. She passed two women who were talking over a fence. She knew them by sight – they'd visited Mrs Sharpe the first week they were here. She thought one of them was the Superindent's wife. They didn't acknowledge her, and she didn't expect them to.

She removed her bonnet as she went in the front door and hurried through to her small bedroom. She donned her cap and tied on her apron. No doubt Mrs Sharpe would want her help in the kitchen to prepare the midday meal. She gave herself a cursory look in the mirror and smiled. There was some colour in her cheeks from her morning walk, and she thought she looked rather well.

She went out to the kitchen and was shocked to find Mrs Sharpe sitting on the floor. Her skirt was bloody and she was sobbing into her apron. Jessie stopped dead and stared as her mind tried to make sense of what she was seeing.

"Mrs Sharpe, what happened?" she said kneeling by her side. Her heart started beating faster at the sight of her blood-stained skirt – something awful had happened, and she knew even before Mrs Sharpe answered her.

"My baby," she said as another heartbreaking sob escaped her.

Jessie swallowed. "I'll go get help."

Without waiting for Mrs Sharpe's response she hurried from the kitchen. She closed the door and leant against it for a moment as she sucked in a large lungful of air. Poor Mrs Sharpe. She hoped the women she'd seen earlier would still be there, talking over the fence. Surely they'd know what to do – Jessie had no idea about such things.

She stepped out the front door and looked down the street. A sense of relief coursed through her at the sight of the two women who were still where she'd last seen them. She gathered her skirts in one hand and hurried towards them.

"Help. Excuse me," she called as she neared them. "Please help."

They both looked up at the sound of her voice with concern etched on their faces

– or was it alarm? "Help, please help. It's Mrs Sharpe."

"What's the matter?" said one of the women as she began walking towards her. "Is it one of the prisoners?"

"No. No. She's bleeding, she's lost her baby." An image of Mrs Sharpe sobbing on the kitchen floor materialised in her mind as she said the words out loud. She felt tears fill her eyes and she let out a sob. "I don't know what to do."

The woman nearest put her arm around her shoulders. "There child," she said patting her. "These things happen. Come, Hannah, we best go help poor Mrs Sharpe."

Jessie wiped her eyes with the corner of her apron as she led the two women back to the house. They found Mrs Sharpe on the kitchen floor exactly where Jessie had left her.

"We've come to help Mrs Sharpe," said the woman kneeling beside her. "It'll be alright. I'm Mrs Ackhurst."

Mrs Sharpe looked at her with tear-filled eyes. "Thank you," she managed to say between sobs.

"Hannah, go with the girl and fetch the bath," said Mrs Ackhurst getting to her feet. "I'll get some water on."

"Aye," said Hannah.

Jessie and Hannah returned minutes later hauling the tin bath between them. Mrs Ackhurst had helped Mrs Sharpe off the floor and she was now sitting on a chair. A bloody smear where she'd been sitting stained the floor, and Jessie averted her eyes. She wasn't normally squeamish where blood was concerned, but this was altogether different.

They spent the next hour filling the bath with enough water so Mrs Sharpe could get in.

"Go and fetch a clean nightgown and towels," said Mrs Ackhurst as she began helping Mrs Sharpe out of her bloody clothes.

Jessie didn't need to be told twice. She nodded and happily hurried from the kitchen. She tucked a wayward tendril of hair back under her cap as she entered the main bedroom. In a few moments, she'd found a clean nightgown, and she grabbed two towels from the closet in the sitting room. She was about to go back to the kitchen when the front door opened and Mr Sharpe walked in.

He looked at her and then at the things she was holding in her arms. “What are you doing?”

She swallowed. “Something’s happened…it’s Mrs Sharpe…she’s…”

“What?” His eyes seemed to bulge as he stared at her. “Tell me.”

“She’s lost the baby.” She sucked in a breath but she couldn’t stop the tears from filling her eyes. She swallowed. “I’m so sorry.”

“Where is she?”

“In the kitchen, with Mrs Ackhurst and a lady called Hannah. They’re bathing her. I’ve got to take these things for her.”

“Give them to me,” he said snatching them and hurrying out to the kitchen.

Jessie was glad to be relieved of them - she didn’t want to go back out there. She waited a few moments. She had no choice. Mrs Ackhurst might need her to do something else. She headed out to the kitchen, only to find Mr Sharpe sitting on the doorstep with his head in his hands.

She felt so ill-prepared to deal with someone else's grief. What could she say? She pressed her lips together and let out a sigh as she sat down beside him. There was nothing she could say that would make a difference, but she could be there. She put her hand on his arm and the two of them sat there, each lost in their thoughts.

***

Chapter Twenty Two

A Plan for Jessie

Aaron Price wasn't one to indulge in fanciful imaginings. Having spent the past eleven years as a prisoner on Norfolk Island, he'd learnt not to think about the future. At first, there'd been no hope of a future, but that had changed about eight years ago. His old bushranging mate Paddy had been murdered, and Lawrie was sent to Cockatoo Island. It was then that he decided he had to change – or he'd be next.

In his own mind, he'd become a snitch. At first, it sat uneasily on him, but soon enough he began to reap the rewards. He was given a position of trust and then a paid job as an Overseer. Now, he had his own cottage and as long as he kept on being a snitch, he'd earn his freedom one day. That was his plan, but now, he wondered if that couldn't be hurried along.

The image of the young woman with clear blue eyes swam before him. Sharpe had introduced her as his servant and that had given rise to Aaron imagining how she might be useful to him. The only women on the island, generally speaking, were the wives or daughters of the military or civil officers. None of whom would let him anywhere near them – but a servant, now that was different. He paused as he was pulling on his breeches. Was she free or a convict? He didn't think it would make any difference to his plans, but it might.

He fastened his breeches and straightened. It had been a long time since he'd thought about a woman. He idly ran his thumb over the place where a love heart was tattooed on his arm. He knew what it said – NS for AP. He hadn't thought about Nellie Skinner in a very long time. She'd been the love of his life and he'd been prepared to do anything so they could be together. He grimaced as he slipped into his shirt. It was best not to dwell on Nellie.

He'd formulated a rough plan on how he might get to speak to Miss Smith. He pulled on his boots and put on his cap. There was no time like the present. He stepped out into the fresh morning air and closed the door. Aaron took his time walking to

Kingston – not wanting to arrive too early and find the Reverend at home. As he neared the parsonage he was surprised to find he had a nervous feeling in the pit of his stomach. He breathed in as he knocked on the door and waited. Would she be the one to answer it?

A few moments later the door opened and there she was, staring at him.

"Good morning. If you're looking for the Reverend he's not here." She gazed coolly at him with one eyebrow arched upwards.

"Ah, good morning," he said removing his cap. "I was hoping to speak with the Reverend about a couple of men in solitary confinement. Would ye pass on a message for me?"

"Of course."

"Thank ye," he said with a smile. "There're two men who've been in solitary for a few days. I believe they'd benefit greatly from a visit from the Reverend and some kind words."

"Well, I'll tell him. What are their names?"

"Newport and Pollard. However, I would add that all the men in confinement would find solace in his words, I'm sure. They've had such little in the way of a kind word."

"I'll be sure to tell him," she said with a nod.

"Thank ye. Do ye remember my name? Overseer Price," he said putting his cap back on. "Aaron Price."

"I remember," she said pressing her lips together.

"Well, then good day, Miss Smith."

He turned and sauntered back down the path, and with a tip of his cap he set off along the road.

***

Jessie closed the door and leant against it. Her heart was hammering like a mad thing and she licked her lips. That was an encounter she hadn't expected and if she was honest with herself, most surprising. He seemed genuinely concerned for the men in confinement and had gone out of his way to seek some solace for them. Jessie had to admit that maybe her first impression of him had been wrong. She hadn't thought he was the sort of man that would concern himself with such things.

"Who was that Jessie?" called Mrs Sharpe from the bedroom.

Jessie went into the bedroom where Mrs Sharpe was resting. Jessie thought she was looking much better. She had some colour in her cheeks but her eyes were still dull and haunted.

"Mr Price. He's an Overseer," said Jessie standing at the end of the bed. "He wants Mr Sharpe to visit some men who are in solitary confinement."

"Oh."

Her disinterest was obvious and Jessie's heart wrenched at the sight of her. She wished there was something she could do to help her recover from her loss.

"I hear the Governor Phillip will sail in a day or two," she said perching herself on the end of the bed. "You'll be pleased to know I've written to my grandmother."

Her gaze rested on Jessie and she smiled weakly. "You're quite right. I am pleased to hear it."

"It will be strange though won't it? I mean, we'll be here all alone, separated from the rest of the world."

"I suppose so," she said with a wry smile. "There are plenty of people here to keep us company. Speaking of which, I really must go and thank Mrs Ackhurst."

"That's a great idea," said Jessie leaping to her feet. "We could take her some freshly baked bread. I've got some dough proving in the kitchen."

Mrs Sharpe nodded and swung her feet over the side of the bed. "Bread alone would be a very poor gift."

Jessie had to agree with her. A loaf of bread would hardly thank her for all she'd done. "What about if we made her some soup to go with it?"

"I think that would be perfect," she said getting to her feet. "Come, you can help."

They immediately set to work chopping vegetables and making soup. The simple activity seemed to lift Mrs Sharpe's spirits, and Jessie found herself smiling happily as she kneaded the bread dough.

Without warning, thoughts of Aaron Price invaded her mind. He was quite attractive she thought in a rugged sort of way. He was old enough to be her father, but still, he was not unattractive. And he had wrinkles that creased around his eyes when he smiled. There was something else though. She paused her kneading and looked into space. What was it about him? She couldn't quite put her finger on it.

"Are you done with that dough?" said Mrs Sharpe.

Jessie jumped and stared at Mrs Sharpe. She'd been so lost in thought she'd forgotten where she was. "Ah, not quite."

"Well do hurry up." A crease marred her brow as she looked at Jessie. "Are you alright?"

"Yes, I'm fine." She folded the dough and put it in the bread tin and ignored the inquisitive look on Mrs Sharpe's face. She had no intention of sharing her thoughts on Mr Price. Anyway, what would she say?

***

The rest of the week was busy. A visit with Mrs Ackhurst resulted in Mrs Sharpe being invited to join the lady's sewing circle on Wednesday afternoons. Mr Sharpe requested Jessie accompany him on his visits to the hospital. She hated going but couldn't think of a reasonable excuse not to. She didn't think she offered the poor afflicted men much comfort. She grimaced and screwed up her face at the horrible smells and sounds. Several of the men in there had been flogged, and the surgeon was applying ointment to their bloody backs and their cries echoed down the room. Jessie wanted to run and not look back.

She longed for Sunday afternoon when she could finally have a few hours to herself. The Reverend's sermon was droning on and she found it increasingly difficult to pay attention. It was odd that the Sunday service was held in the barracks. She wondered why no one had thought to build a church. Divine service was such a big deal on the island. Everyone was expected to attend. Those prisoners that could were required to attend on Sunday afternoons. The military and civil establishment on Sunday mornings. Well, Jessie was glad she didn't have to attend with the prisoners. The less she had to do with them the better in her opinion.

Finally, the Reverend's sermon ended and everyone stood for the final prayer. As soon as that was done, she could finally escape and enjoy a few hours to herself. She joined in the chorus of 'amen's' and began shuffling to the end of the row. She couldn't wait to escape. She was edging her way down the aisle when someone brushed up against her.

"Miss Smith, you're just the person I was looking for," said Aaron Price smiling broadly.

She swallowed as she stared up into his rather handsome face. "Really Mr Price? How can I help you?"

"Please, would ye mind stepping outside? It's so noisy in here."

She nodded as she began making her way to the exit. He was right about the noise. It was like everyone had started talking at once and the noise reverberated around the barracks making it impossible to hear anyone.

An unexpected shiver went down her spine when he put his hand on the small of her back and guided her out the door. She gasped and glanced sideways at him. He didn't appear to have noticed anything. She pressed her lips together and then breathed in a calming breath. As soon as they were outside he removed his hand from her back and smiled.

"I wanted to thank ye. The men in solitary really appreciated the Reverend's visit."

Jessie was shaken and still gasping for air. He appeared to be quite unaware that she was flustered and gulping in lungfuls of air. "Um…you're welcome."

"I'd like to repay your kindness," he said leaning casually against the barracks. "I thought ye might enjoy a stroll out to the bluff. It's a great lookout for spotting ships."

She arched one eyebrow upwards. "Are there likely to be any ships?" Her voice sounded quite calm to her ears but that's not at all how she felt.

"Ye never know," he said with a shrug. "There might be a passing whaler. Or ye might see an albatross."

She smiled and despite feeling quite out of her depth she found herself agreeing to accompany him.

‘I have a couple of things I have to do. Can I come by and pick ye up in an hour?”

“No.” She felt her stomach do a somersault at the thought. “I’ll meet you.”

“Where?”

Jessie looked around and pressed her lips together. Where? Not anywhere where Mr or Mrs Sharpe might see her. She had the distinct feeling they would not approve of Mr Price. “What about here?”

“Alright,” he said with a grin. “I’ll meet ye right here.”

She watched him walk down the road before going back inside the barracks. What had she just agreed to? Her stomach clenched at the thought of accompanying him – alone. What was she thinking? She swallowed. She couldn’t back out or he might come to the house and she didn’t want that. A sense of excitement and apprehension filled her and she wasn’t sure which one was going to win.

***

Chapter Twenty Three

Call me Aaron

An hour later Jessie stood outside the barracks - waiting. She'd spent the best part of that hour wondering why she'd ever agreed to meet him. A little voice in the back of her mind had whispered the answer in her ear. It was the first time in her life that any man, other than her father or brothers, had paid her the slightest bit of attention. She was both afraid of it and liked it – along with a bunch of other conflicting emotions. Was this what falling in love was like? She wasn't sure – but her heart fluttered at the thought.

She glanced down the road – there was no sign of him. What if he'd forgotten? She groaned at herself as a pang of disappointment went through her. What did she want? She remembered the day Mary had torn a flower apart, chanting he loves me, he loves me not. That's exactly how she felt. I want to go with him – no I don't want to go with him. She was confusing herself.

The door to the barracks opened and his head popped out. As soon as he saw her he grinned and came out to join her.

"I wasn't sure you'd come," he said closing the door behind him.

Jessie swallowed. She wasn't sure she should've come. She tried to give him a confident smile, but she wasn't sure if she succeeded. "Why wouldn't I? It's such a lovely afternoon for a stroll."

"It is."

He grinned and the creases around his eyes wrinkled. She rather thought it made him look even more attractive. She briefly wondered how old he was. Would he really be interested in her?

"Come on then," he said looking at her. "The lookout's on the other side of Longridge."

She hadn't been to Longridge. "Is it far?" She'd worn her sturdy boots and easily kept pace with him as they began walking.

He grinned again. "Nowhere is far. The island's no more than eight miles in any direction."

"Oh, I hadn't thought how big it might be."

They walked along in silence for a few hundred yards. “Do ye like it here?” he said glancing at her.

She nodded. “I do. Although, I must say I’m glad I don’t have anything to do with the prisoners. They’re treated so cruelly and I couldn’t bear to see that.”

He shrugged. “I suppose you’re right. Punishments are a lot harsher here than in Sydney, but ye have to remember most of them are incorrigible."

“Does that mean they should be flogged half to death?” she said staring at him. ”I visited the hospital with the Reverend last week and two men had been flogged to within an inch of their lives. It was horrible.”

“I’m sure it was,” he said in a gentler tone. “I suppose I’ve got used to seeing it.”

She didn’t think she could ever get used to seeing it. “How long have you been here, on the island?” she said, anxious to change the topic of conversation.

“Eleven years or thereabouts.”

Silence descended between them again as Jessie tried to work out what to say next. She had so many questions going around in her head, but should she ask him?

A few more minutes went by as they walked down the road before she decided to just do it.

"Are you still a prisoner or are you free?"

He grimaced. "I'm a prisoner. I've earned the trust of the Commandant, and I've a paid position, but I can't leave."

"Do you mind if I ask what you did to end up here?"

He glanced sideways at her and laughed. "I didn't murder anyone."

"Well, I'm glad to hear it."

They passed a gang of prisoners heading in the other direction. They were under the supervision of several soldiers, but still, Jessie tried not to look at the poor things. No doubt, they would be going to Kingston to listen to the Reverend's sermon. The thought crossed her mind that they only went because they had to.

"Come this way," he said indicating to a shady road that went down a steep incline. "Here, take my arm." He held his arm out, inviting her to take it.

She glanced at the rutted road and then at him. "Thank you."

She gripped his arm and steadied herself as they began slowly walking down. They were nearly at the bottom of the steepest part when some small stones slipped under her boot. If he hadn't grabbed her she would've fallen. She gripped his shoulders and gasped as his arms tightened around her. His face was mere inches from hers and her breathing quickened as his hazel eyes stared into hers. Was he going to kiss her? She swallowed and pursed her lips. The whole encounter lasted no more than a few seconds, and she was left feeling quite disappointed when he apologised and let her go.

"Are ye alright?" he asked.

She was perfectly alright and unharmed, but she felt like such an idiot. She felt her cheeks warm under his probing gaze. "Yes…thank you…I'm fine."

"Good. It's not much further."

They walked on in silence. Jessie thought he must have noticed her tilting her face up to his with pursed lips. He must think her such a child. She watched him with lowered lashes. He appeared to be quite unaware of her, whereas she was acutely aware of his male scent and the way his muscles rippled under his shirt. He was an intriguing man.

"Can I ask ye a question?" he said startling her out of her perusal of him.

"Oh, of course." She did her best to look disinterested and smiled benignly.

"How old are ye?"

Her eyebrows shot up. She hadn't expected him to ask that. She did her best to hide her surprise while she determined what to tell him. She was quite sure he'd lose interest if he knew she was only thirteen. But just how old did he think she was?

"I apologise if I've been too forward, Miss Smith."

"Oh no, not at all," she said waving his concerns aside with her hand. "I'm sixteen. I'll be seventeen in January." She watched his face to see how he might react but she couldn't read his thoughts at all. "What about you?" she added with boldness.

"Ah, well I'm somewhat older than ye," he said grinning. "I'm thirty. But, ye have to remember I've been here on the island a while. I was barely older than ye when I was sent here."

Jessie nodded. She wasn't sure what that had to do with it but didn't find his age enough to deter her interest in him. "You have been here a long time, Mr Price."

They turned a corner and there laid out before them was the ocean. A small lookout perched high on the cliffs gave an uninterrupted view of the horizon from east to west. The air was filled with salty sea spray and the squawk from several gulls hovering in mid-air above the cliffs.

"It's beautiful," said Jessie. She was quite taken by the vista. "Do you come here often?"

"No," he said shaking his head. "Although, there's someone out here every day looking for sails. I don't see any today."

"I suppose it'll be a few months before a ship comes."

"Aye, it will." He gazed out to sea for a few moments, before turning his attention back to her. "I was wondering…would ye mind calling me Aaron?"

Once more her eyebrows rose in surprise. She didn't think they were so well acquainted to be on first-name basis. She pressed her lips together. "I'm not sure that would be appropriate."

"Aye," he said nodding. "I thought ye might say that."

He looked out towards the horizon but before his eyes left her she glimpsed a lonely haunted look in them. She looked at him and wondered if maybe she should allow him to call her by her name. It was definitely not the norm but this island was far from civilised society.

He turned to face her. "I didn't mean to offend ye."

"You didn't," she assured him with a smile.

"It's just that I don't remember the last time anyone called me Aaron. And I thought ye might."

She could almost feel the sorrow emanating from him and her heart clenched. "Alright," she said swallowing. "I'll call you Aaron."

A wide smile lit up his face at her words. "Thank ye. May I call ye by your name as well?"

"Well, yes I suppose so," she said nodding. "But, not in front of the Reverend or Mrs Sharpe – I don't think they'd like it."

"I understand," he said in an assuring tone. "So, what's your name?"

"Uh…oh…it's Jessie."

"Well, Jessie – we best make our way back to Kingston." He held out his arm for her to take with a wide grin on his face.

Shyness overcame her as she took his arm and they began the walk back. She really didn't know enough about him for them to be sharing such intimacies, but he was so persuasive. Charming was the word she thought best described him. Yes, he was charming.

***

They parted company outside the barracks, and to Jessie's surprise, she was disappointed that he hadn't made arrangements for them to see each other again. She was sure he'd enjoyed their outing as much as she, but there was a reserve about him that she didn't understand.

She arrived back at the parsonage in time to help Mrs Sharpe with supper. It was her afternoon off and Mrs Sharpe wouldn't expect her to assist, but Jessie knew she still wasn't back to herself after losing the baby. She removed her bonnet and slipped her apron over her head before searching out her mistress.

She found her out in the garden kneeling beside the potato patch. She'd obviously been weeding as the pail beside her was full. She smiled and stretched her back, as she pressed her hands to her hips.

"Oh, you're back. Did you enjoy your afternoon?"

"I did," said Jessie inspecting the newly weeded bed. She was about to tell her that Aaron Price had accompanied her, but she thought better of it. "I had a lovely walk out to the bluff. It's just beautiful. Have you been out there?"

"No, I haven't." She got to her feet and removed her gloves before brushing the dirt from her skirt. "Did you go alone? I really wish you wouldn't," she said in a disapproving tone.

"I was perfectly safe. I only saw one group of prisoners who were well guarded."

Mrs Sharpe sighed and picked up the pail. "You're so young, Jess and you don't know the way of men. Please, promise you won't go out there by yourself again."

Jessie thought she knew the way of men well enough, but conceded she had no experience herself. "I promise."

It was an easy promise to keep, or so she thought. She didn't ever intend to go out there alone. But, it was a lovely secluded spot to go with someone. A pair of hazel eyes staring down at her came into sharp focus. She felt her cheeks warm at the thought of those eyes piercing hers. Would he ask out her again? She came out of her reverie to find Mrs Sharpe staring at her.

"I said, why are you wearing your apron? It's your afternoon off."

"Oh… uh…sorry. I thought I'd help you with supper."

"Well, that's most kind of you." She smiled and patted Jessie on the shoulder. "Come on then, let's go get it underway. Mr

Sharpe will be ravenous when he comes home."

***

Chapter Twenty Four

A Frustrating Afternoon

Jessie sighed as she left the barracks. Aaron Price had been invading her thoughts for the past week to the point where she could think of little else. She'd expected to see him today at divine service, but for some reason, he hadn't come. She glanced up and down the road. Soldiers and their families were still milling about, and it was only then she realised none of the Overseers had attended today. It gave her some solace – something must be going on.

She briefly thought she'd walk to Orange Vale in the hopes of seeing him, but quickly dismissed the idea. She wasn't quite that sure of herself. She wrapped her cloak around herself as she headed back to the parsonage. She had plenty to do at home. She'd caught her blue skirt on a nail last week and it needed mending, and her stockings also required her attention.

Jessie spent her afternoon off sewing and washing and generally taking care of a number of personal items. She'd done her best to push all thoughts of Aaron aside, but her frustration was not so easily squashed. By the time she sat down to supper with the Sharpes, she was feeling quite anxious.

"Any news to share?" asked Mrs Sharpe raising her brows and gazing at her husband. "I hear several prisoners tried to escape. That they'd made a makeshift boat."

Jessie looked from one to the other. So that's what was going on today.

"Aye, but they were quickly discovered and rounded up," said Mr Sharpe with a shake of his head. "I don't know why they persist."

"I expect they want out of this place," said Mrs Sharpe deftly slicing the pork on her plate. "You can't blame them."

"Perhaps not, but the punishment will be swift and I believe Major Anderson will want to make an example of them."

Jessie suppressed a shudder as she swallowed a mouthful of her supper. She didn't want to think about what sort of punishment would be inflicted on them. And she prayed the Reverend wouldn't ask her to attend upon them in the hospital afterwards.

"What other news?" said Mrs Sharpe pushing a stray strand of hair aside. "I don't think this is suitable supper conversation." She looked directly at Jessie and smiled.

Jessie did her best to smile serenely in return but was relieved that Mrs Sharpe had noticed her discomfort. She did her best not to think about the poor souls imprisoned on this island, but there were times when that was impossible.

"Ah, well some of the prisoners are putting on a play," said Mr Sharpe putting down his cutlery. "The Commandant hopes it will provide us with some entertainment and we're all invited to attend. You to Jessie."

"Oh, that should lift everyone's spirits," said Mrs Sharpe smiling and looking from her husband to Jessie. "Don't you think so, Jessie?"

"Yes."

Since the Governor Phillip had sailed they'd been left completely isolated from the rest of the world. The morale of the island's inhabitants had slowly but surely declined. Jessie could well imagine the Commandant wanting to lift everyone's spirits by providing some small entertainment.

However, she couldn't imagine what sort of play the prisoners would put on.

"What play are they performing, do you know?" asked Mrs Sharpe.

Mr Sharpe shook his head as he swallowed a mouthful of pork. "I believe it's some sort of pantomime. We'll have to wait and see."

"Oh, I can hardly wait. It's been such an age since we had any sort of social occasion. When are they doing it?" asked Mrs Sharpe.

The excitement in her voice was rather contagious, and Jessie looked to Mr Sharpe for his reply. She hoped it would be soon. Surely, Aaron would attend and she might find an opportunity to speak with him. She felt the blood thrum through her veins at the mere thought of seeing him again.

"Friday afternoon at the barracks. It will be quite the event I'm sure."

***

After a week that had dragged by like someone had adjusted the rate of time, Friday arrived. The excitement in the Sharpe household was almost palpable, and Jessie was taking extra care with her attire. She'd donned her best dress and with Mrs Sharpe's help had piled her honey-blonde hair on top of her head. A few wispy tendrils refused to be secured, but she thought they were rather flattering. She tied her bonnet with a large bow under her jaw and thought the whole effect was rather attractive. Would Aaron notice how pretty she looked? She certainly hoped so.

"Are you ready Jess?" called Mrs Sharpe from the parlour. "We'll be late if we don't hurry."

"Coming." She took one last glance at herself in the small polished mirror and smiled with satisfaction.

The three of them walked out of the house and joined the throng of people heading for the barracks. Jessie thought all of Kingston had turned out to watch the performance, she just hoped Aaron was among them.

"Reverend, oh Reverend," a short thin man accosted the Reverend almost as soon as they started walking down the road.

"Good day Doctor Harnett. My wife, Mrs Sharpe."

"Ma'am," he said tipping his hat. "I do apologise for bothering you, but one of my patients is in great need. Would you visit the hospital after the performance?"

"Of course. I'll come directly."

"Thank you."

He tipped his hat again and disappeared into the throng.

"He's a rather excited little man," said Mrs Sharpe putting her hand in the crook of her husband's elbow. "If you'd rather go now I don't mind."

"No, no. I'm sure he can wait."

The doors to the barracks had been propped wide open and the usual room used for divine service transformed into a theatre. A small stage had been erected up one end and chairs and makeshift benches were arranged in rows. Jessie thought there was enough room for at least two hundred people.

"Mrs Sharpe, how lovely to see you," said Mrs Ackhurst appearing in front of them. "Won't you join us down the front? My husband's already seated. Good afternoon Reverend."

“Good afternoon,” said Reverend Sharpe.

“We’d love to. Thank you Mrs Ackhurst,” said Mrs Sharpe smiling widely.

Jessie watched the three of them walk down the aisle to the front of the room. She hadn’t been invited to join them and hadn’t expected to be. She would find a seat towards the back of the room with the soldiers and their families. Or, perhaps right at the back where she had more chance of seeing Aaron – she gazed around – there was no sign of him.

She pushed her way through the people milling about and sat down on one of the benches. She had a good view of the door which she glued her eyes to. The minutes passed, and everyone found a seat, and still, there was no sign of him. Jessie could feel her anxiety rising from the pit of her stomach. She had the overwhelming desire to leave – to go in search of him. She licked her lips and sucked in a breath as she tried to remain calm.

An announcement from the stage indicated the panto had started. The actors were dressed in a mixed array of cobbled-together costumes – some of which were quite ridiculous. One of them was dressed as a woman – a fairy or something Jessie imagined. Her view of the stage was blocked by the many hats and people in front of her, but she could see enough to make out several of the characters. One dressed in wide pantaloons was obviously playing a fool, and the one in the big hat appeared to be the main character. She had yet to work out what panto they were re-enacting.

Her eyes darted back to the door. The players acted and sang and paraded about, and the audience laughed and joined in and Jessie saw none of it. Her eyes remained on the door and her mind fixed on seeing and speaking with Aaron. The overwhelming desire to leave grew until she thought she'd run from the place. As the play came to a close, she conceded that he wasn't coming, and disappointment flooded her. How was she ever going to see him again? It was infuriating and she swallowed the ache that stretched across her throat. She blinked back her tears of frustration - she wouldn't cry – not here.

Jessie waited until much of the crowd had cleared before making her way to the exit. She had no idea what she was going to do but positioned herself near the door where Mrs Sharpe would easily find her. She didn't have to wait long for her mistress.

"Oh, Jessie there you are," she said coming to stand beside her. "Mr Sharpe has gone to the hospital and Mrs Ackhurst has most kindly invited me to join her for afternoon tea. Why don't you take a few hours to yourself? I'll see you back at home in time to prepare supper."

"Alright, thank you," said Jessie.

What was she going to do? It was nice to have some time to herself, but it only fuelled her frustration. Now she had time to see Aaron and had no idea where she might find him. She watched Mrs Ackhurst and her mistress leave and leaned against the wall of the barracks and sighed. There was no point hanging around the barracks and she'd never see Aaron if she was at home. Taking her skirts in her hands she began walking down the road with no clear idea of where she was going.

"Is yer name Jessie?"

She stopped and turned and came face to face with a young freckle-faced boy. “Are ye Jessie?” he asked again.

“Yes.”

“Here,” he said shoving a note into her hand.

She was about to ask who it was from, but he’d already turned and was running back towards the barracks. She looked at the neat writing – *Miss Jessie Smith.* Her heart leapt. It must be from Aaron, who else would send her a note? Her breathing quickened as she unfolded it and read.

Meet me at Black Rock after supper tonight.
Aaron.

Relief flooded her as all her frustration and anxiety evaporated. Tonight – she would see him tonight. A wide smile spread across her face as she tucked the note into her pocket. She’d begun to think he didn’t want to see her again – but now everything had changed.

***

Chapter Twenty Five

Black Rock Interlude

Jessie spent the afternoon working in the garden formulating a plan. The Sharpes would ask too many questions if she told them she was going out after supper. She had the feeling they wouldn't approve of Aaron. He was a prisoner and much older than her and she didn't want to risk them interfering.

After supper, she feigned tiredness and begged to be excused.

"It's not like you, Jessie," said Mrs Sharpe pausing with her sewing needle in mid-air. "I do hope you aren't coming down with something." A crease marred her forehead as she studied her.

"I don't think so. It's just been a big day, what with the performance and all."

Mr Sharpe merely grunted but didn't enter into the conversation.

"It was a big day indeed," she said nodding. "Hopefully an early night will restore you. Good night."

"Good night then," said Jessie followed by a big yawn. "Oh, excuse me."

Mrs Sharpe smiled. "Good night, my dear."

As soon as Jessie was safely in her room she closed the door and leaned against it. The first part of her plan had gone perfectly. Now for the next part. She removed her apron and hung it on the hook before opening her small wardrobe and retrieving her cloak. She tossed it onto the bed while she opened the small window. She rarely opened it and was thankful that she'd pried it open this afternoon while no one was home. It had grated and complained loudly the first time she opened it. It now slid noiselessly open thanks to the soap she'd rubbed on the window frame. She grinned as she grabbed her cloak and climbed out.

It seemed like a lifetime ago that her sister Mary had done the very same thing – climbing out the window to meet Charles Kelly in the dead of night. Jessie felt a pang of guilt that she hadn't written to Mary which she quickly brushed aside. She'd think about that tomorrow.

It was a clear cloudless evening and there was still enough daylight for her to see. There was little chance of rain and so she decided to leave the window open. No one would check on her. She wrapped her cloak around herself and hurried down the side of the house and out into the street. Black Rock was only a short stroll along the beach. The soldiers were often down there fishing but she knew they wouldn't be there now.

She picked her way through the soft sand until she came to the firmer wetter sand and then walked along the edge of the sea towards the rocks. She couldn't see any sign of anyone and wondered if she was too early.

As she neared the rock she saw him leaning against it; he was almost indistinguishable from it in the diminishing light. Her heart did a little flip-flop and she quickened her step. As she approached he stepped out from the shadows and beckoned to her.

"I wasn't sure you'd come," he said grasping her hand. "There's a more private spot just up ahead."

She allowed him to lead her a little further along the rocks to a secluded nook.

Her heart was hammering in her chest and his nearness was making her breathless. The whole feeling was rather intoxicating and coupled with the musky scent emanating from him, Jessie had to resist the urge not to throw herself into his arms.

"Here," he said letting go of her hand and indicating to a blanket, neatly folded on a flat rock.

She smiled as she sat down. "Thank you."

He squatted down beside her. "I'm so glad ye came. I didn't know if ye would."

There had never been any doubt in her mind, but she wasn't sure if she should tell him about her frustration and desire to see him. "I enjoyed our last outing, and I thought I might have seen you last Sunday," she said folding her hands in her lap. "But that was not to be."

"Aye. I would've liked that as well. But I'm afraid I was busy chasing down some would-be escapees."

"I heard."

"I'm sorry to ask ye to come out tonight, but I could think of no other way to see ye." He quickly added, "I had to see ye."

His demeanour was intense as he stared into her clear blue eyes. Jessie thought she could drown in those hazel pools – what was it about him that she found so alluring? She felt her cheeks warm under his gaze and she lowered her eyes, fluttering her eyelashes as she did so.

"I'm glad you did," she murmured. "I wanted to see you too."

He seemed to relax at her words and he sat down beside her on the blanket. "I know I have to no right to ask anything of ye. I have nothing to offer ye except myself and the promise that one day I'll be free."

She nodded – uncertain as to what he was going to say next. He may not think he had anything to offer but she disagreed. He was stuck here on the island - he couldn't leave. He couldn't leave her like everyone else in her life had done. She swallowed and licked her lips while she waited for him to go on.

"I wonder if you'd allow me to call on ye?"

The alarm must've been visible on her face as her eyebrows shot up to her hairline. "No - you can't."

He looked perplexed as he stared at her. “But I thought...well, I thought ye enjoyed my company.”

“It’s not that I would not welcome it,” she said shaking her head. “It’s the Sharpes. I don’t believe they’d approve. I wouldn’t want to risk it.”

He grinned showing his even white teeth. “For a minute I thought ye were spurning me.” He laughed softly. “I can see that ye might be right about the Sharpes. What exactly do they hold over ye?”

“Nothing.” She was unsure of what he meant exactly. She was their servant that was all, but they’d become more than mere employers. “They’ve been very good to me, and I wouldn’t want to jeopardise that.”

“Are ye free, Jessie?”

“Yes.”

“Well, then there’s naught they could do to stop ye,” he said matter of factly. “But…if ye prefer to keep it from them, then I respect your decision.”

“Thank you. And I do prefer they not know…at least not yet.”

"Well, that'll make it a might more difficult for us to see one another, but we can meet like this if you're alright with it."

Now that her alarm was subsiding the realisation of what she was agreeing to hit her. She wanted it – but where would this ultimately lead? He was a prisoner. "I'm alright with it. There's just one thing," she said twisting the fabric of her skirt between her fingers. "You're a prisoner still. You're not free to…" She didn't know how to say it. Was she being presumptuous? Was he even thinking of asking her to marry him eventually? She felt her cheeks redden.

He raised his brows and looked at her puzzled. "Not free to what?"

She swallowed and licked her lips. "Marry."

He grinned and his shoulders slumped back into their relaxed position. "Aye, I'm not, but…I've worked hard for the position of trust I hold, and I'm confident that the Commandant would grant me permission if I was to ask him."

He took her hands in his. They were big and warm and calloused and Jessie sucked in a breath as a tingle went down her spine. “And I would ask him if ye wanted it.”

He leaned forward until his face was no more than an inch from hers. She could feel his warm breath and hear his heart beating. She held her breath. Was he going to kiss her? She resisted the urge to tilt her face towards his or to purse her lips – she had embarrassed herself once before and had no intention of doing so again.

She was taken by surprise when he placed his finger under her chin and gently forced her head back. “Do ye think ye might want it one day?”

He was looking straight into her eyes – and she felt like straight into her soul. Her breathing quickened and she licked her lips. “I…I might.”

“Tis enough for now,” he said removing his finger and sitting back on his haunches. “Come, I should get ye back afore you’re missed.”

Her heartbeat had quickened and her lips tingled in anticipation. She’d thought he was going to kiss her, but then he didn’t. She frowned and cast her eyes downward. Why hadn’t he? She thought he’d wanted to – she was sure she'd seen a flicker of desire in his eyes. She was disappointed but had no idea how to recapture the moment.

"Alright," she said pulling her cloak around herself as she stood.

He stood and gathered the blanket under one arm and invited her to take the other. She smiled as she placed her hand in the crook of his elbow and they began to pick their way through the rocks to the beach. Silence stretched awkwardly between them which only added to Jessie's confusion. She had no idea why their moment of intimacy had ended so abruptly and now his silence was unnerving.

They left the beach and walked back towards the parsonage. All the while Jessie tried to think of something suitable to say but came up empty-handed. As they neared her home she halted. "You'd best leave me here in case we're seen."

"Aye," he said dropping his arm.

He swallowed and in the fading light, Jessie thought he looked uncertain. She stood waiting for him to say something else. The seconds ticked by until she couldn't stand it any longer. "Well, good night then."

She'd only taken one step towards home when she felt his arm on her shoulder. "Wait."

She swallowed and paused before turning to face him. She wasn't mistaken, he looked nervous. "Can I see ye on Sunday afternoon?"

"Of course," she said with a sigh.

She could hear him breathing, quickly in and out as his eyes darted down the road and then back to her. "I…I wasn't sure if ye wanted to see me again."

What had given him that idea she didn't know and it only added to her confusion. She pressed her lips together while she deliberated her next words. "It would appear that we're at odds, Aaron. I would very much like to see you again."She felt like adding, but not if you're going to waste my time, but she bit her tongue and waited.

"Well then, I'll see ye on Sunday."

"I'll look forward to it." She smiled before turning and hurrying down the road for home. He was such a perplexing man and she wished she knew what had stopped him from kissing her tonight. One thing was certain, if he didn't kiss her on Sunday, then she would kiss him. She felt her cheeks warm and a flutter of nerves went through her at the thought. Could she be so bold?

***

Aaron watched her as she hurried toward the parsonage. He sighed and after giving her one last glance began the walk back to Orange Vale. He'd been a fool and clearly misread her. He'd had her right in the palm of his hand, or so he thought, but then she'd frozen like a statue. He groaned as an image of her pretty face swam before him. He saw the desire in her eyes, he'd been sure of it, but just when he was about to kiss her she'd stared at him like a frightened rabbit.

Damn it! He couldn't afford to frighten her. He had to be sure that she wanted him just as much as he needed her. And he had to make a move soon or he risked losing her altogether. He swallowed the rising fear that squirmed in his belly. She was his ticket to freedom and there may not be another.

***

Chapter Twenty Six

A Stormy Sunday in July

Sunday dawned wet and stormy. The wind had howled all night and Jessie barely got a wink of sleep. The rain was still now lashing against her window. She snuggled down under the covers and sighed. It would be cold and draughty at divine service this morning and she wished she could stay in bed. She groaned – everyone was expected to attend, no exceptions.

Half an hour later she was up and dressed and hastily swallowing a bowl of porridge. The Reverend had already left for the barracks, and she was to accompany Mrs Sharpe. She was sitting opposite sipping a cup of hot coffee. Mrs Sharpe grimaced.

"I do wish we didn't have to venture out in this weather," she said putting her cup down. "But Tom says we must set the example."

Jessie nodded. She didn't think Mrs Sharpe expected an answer, and so she went on eating her breakfast.

"My plans for the afternoon have also been thrown into disarray with this weather." She sipped her coffee and looked thoughtfully at Jessie.

Jessie did her best to keep her face unreadable. Her plans for the afternoon would no doubt also be disrupted. She had no idea what Aaron had planned, but she doubted they would be able to find a secluded spot indoors. She wondered what Mrs Sharpe would think of her association with Aaron Price, but she had no intention of revealing herself. The feeling that they wouldn't approve persisted.

"What about you my dear? What have you got planned for your afternoon off?"

"Nothing particular," she said shaking her head. "I had thought to go down to the black rock to watch the soldiers fishing, but not in this weather."

"No, it truly is ghastly."

Jessie finished her porridge and sat back in her chair. "Do you think divine service might be cancelled?"

"Not likely," she said rolling her eyes. "No - we must attend." She swallowed the last of her coffee and put her cup down with a clatter. "Come, let's get cleaned up and get down to the barracks. No point in putting off the inevitable."

Ten minutes later the two of them huddled under an umbrella as they made their way down to the barracks. The road was muddy and slippery and Mrs Sharpe gripped Jessie's arm to steady herself. Jessie hoped she didn't slip or they'd both fall. By the time they arrived, they were both mud-spattered and rather damp.

"Thank you," said Mrs Sharpe folding the umbrella. "I'll look for you after service?"

Jessie nodded. "Alright."

Mrs Sharpe started walking down the aisle to the front and Jessie went to find herself a seat near the rear of the room. She glanced around as she went – hoping to catch sight of Aaron. She thought she'd spot him easily amongst the redcoats of the soldiers, but there was no sign of him. She sighed as she sat down on one of the benches.

The Reverend began his sermon about the great work needed for salvation. His voice was muffled by the constant pitter-patter on the roof and Jessie let his voice drone over her. She was only half listening and was surprised when someone brushed against the back of her hand. She looked up into Aaron's smiling face as he sat down beside her.

She sucked in a breath but managed to smile in return and hoped he couldn't hear her heart hammering in her chest.

"Good morning," he said leaning in close so that no one else could hear. "I'm so very glad ye came out in this awful weather."

"I had little choice," she said with a rueful smile. "The Reverend expects me to attend no matter."

"Aye, well I'm glad ye did."

They sat in silence for the next few minutes. It was quite a comfortable silence as they listened to the Reverend drone on. However, Jessie was loathed to waste an opportunity and this may be the only time they would have together today.

"I expect we'll have to change our plans for this afternoon," she said turning her face towards him and leaning in closer. "The weather doesn't favour an outing."

"Aye." He slipped her hand into his and squeezed gently. "But we're here now."

A small gasp escaped her lips as a shiver went through her at his touch. He turned his face towards her and she leaned in closer and tilted her face upwards. Her breathing quickened as a nervous flutter that started in the pit of her stomach reached her throat and came out as a muffled moan. Their eyes locked and Jessie pressed forward – determined not to lose the moment.

He bent his head ever so slightly towards her and their lips met. At first, his lips barely brushed hers and then he pressed closer and she responded. It was a soft and gentle kiss that lasted no more than a few seconds, but it left Jessie with her heart racing.

His face was still almost touching hers and he grinned. "I've been wanting to do that since the day we met."

She felt her cheeks warm under his gaze and she swallowed and lowered her eyes. The people around them stood, and it was only then that she realised they were about to start singing the first hymn. Aaron let go of her hand and put his hand under her elbow and steadied her as they stood.

She was glad of the distraction which would give her a few moments to gather herself. Her first kiss had been wonderful but too brief and she hoped he'd kiss her again. She'd seen Charlotte and her husband kissing, and it had seemed to last a long time. Of course, she'd been in his arms and they'd been pressed up against one another in a passionate embrace. She glanced sidelong at Aaron. She imagined being in his arms with his lean body pressed hard against hers. A shiver went down her spine at the mere thought of it.

The hymn ended and the congregation retook their seats. The rest of the service passed in a blur for Jessie. Aaron's thigh was pressed up against hers and her hand was nestled in his. It was impossible to keep her thoughts from straying to their next meeting. Surely he would kiss her again.

When the service ended he leaned in close so only she could hear. "When can I see ye again?" He squeezed her hand in his before letting it go. “Make it soon,” he whispered.

She swallowed and licked her lips. She wanted it to be soon, but the weather was not inducive to a private tryst. The wind and rain would likely last a few days – it usually did.

“It will depend on the weather,” she whispered back.

The people around them began standing up and making their way to the exit. Jessie glanced around nervously. She didn’t want to be spotted by either of the Sharpes or any of their acquaintances. She stood and straightened her cloak.

Aaron stood as well and looked straight ahead. “Meet me on the first fine night, after supper by the black rock.”

“Alright,” she said as she brushed past him.

She made her way to the end of the aisle and walked sedately to the doorway, where she planned to wait for Mrs Sharpe.

“Who was that you were talking to?” said Mrs Sharpe coming to stand beside her with her eyes still gazing at Aaron.

Jessie jumped with fright. How much had she seen? “Oh…that’s Overseer Price.”

“What did he want?”

“Um…he was just saying hello,” she said in an unconcerned tone. “I delivered a message to the Reverend for him a while ago.”

“Hmm,” said Mrs Sharpe looping her arm in Jessie’s. “Stay away from him.”

She guided Jessie out of the barracks and into the drizzly rain. “This infernal weather,” she said as she opened the umbrella. “I’m in great need of a hot cup of tea.”

Jessie murmured her agreement as they began walking home, avoiding as many puddles as they could. So, she’d been right to keep her association with Aaron a secret. Mrs Sharpe didn’t approve and she was sure the Reverend wouldn’t either.

***

The inclement weather persisted for most of the week, and Jessie spent it shut indoors with Mrs Sharpe. She quite enjoyed her company, but she was anxious to see

Aaron again. She gazed out the window at the scudding clouds. There were patches of blue and even some weak wintery sun peeking through. Perhaps tonight she would see him.

After supper, Mrs Sharpe and Jessie retired to the parlour with mending in their hands. The Reverend had gone to visit a very ill man who Doctor Harnett did not think would last the night. Jessie wove her darning needle through the stocking she was mending. Her mind wasn't on her sewing, but rather, when could she retire for the night. The rain had eased completely and apart from a few clouds it was a fine evening, and she knew Aaron would be waiting by the black rock for her.

Mrs Sharpe would become suspicious if she feigned tiredness every time she wanted to meet Aaron. She glanced at her mistress. She was concentrating on her sewing and not paying her any heed. She sighed and put her mending aside.

"I think I might retire and read for a while before bed," she said getting to her feet. "You don't mind do you?"

"Not at all," she said looking up from her mending. "I expect Tom will be home soon at any rate. At least we should sleep better tonight now that the rain has stopped."

"Yes, it will be nice to not have the constant patter of it," said Jessie smiling as she left the room.

As soon as she was safely in her room she donned her cloak and slid open the window. A stiff breeze was blowing up from the sea which chilled her as soon as she climbed out the window. She shivered as she slid it closed and headed for the beach. She was glad of the quarter moon that was up – shedding enough light for her to make her way. The black rock loomed ahead of her and her heart rate quickened. A moment later Aaron stepped out from its shadow and grinned at her.

"I wasn't sure you'd be able to get away," he said taking her hands in his. He kissed the back of them and smiled. "It's good to see ye."

Jessie gasped as his hot breath brushed the back of her hand and then his lips. "It's good to see you too."

"Come let's get out of this wind."

He took her hand and led her to the same secluded nook between the rocks where they'd met last time. The wind immediately quietened and the rocks sheltered them. He let go of her hand and gazed down at her. Jessie licked her lips and looked into his eyes. She was sure she saw desire in their depths and her heart fluttered. He took a step closer and put his arm around her waist, pulling her closer to him. She instinctively put her hands on his shoulders but maintained the distance between their bodies. She imagined she could feel the heat emanating from him.

"I think ye know what I want," he whispered keeping his eyes on hers. "I see the way ye look at me."

She felt her cheeks warm under his gaze, but she didn't want to break the spell. She smiled and fluttered her eyelashes. "And how is that I look you?" Her voice sounded calm and steady, which surprised her because that's not how she felt. His nearness was driving all coherent thoughts from her mind.

He grinned as he pulled her closer until they were pressed together. She could feel his firm thighs pressed against hers and her lips tingled in anticipation. She was in his arms and she thought the next logical step would be a passionate kiss. She was more than ready for it.

He laughed softly and placed a warm kiss on her forehead before letting her go. “Sit, let’s talk and get to know one another.” He sat on the flat rock and patted the spot beside him.

Jessie hoped her disappointment wasn’t visible as she wrapped her cloak around herself and sat down. She really thought he was going to kiss her that time. He was infuriating and she wished she knew what was stopping him. He wanted to kiss her, didn’t he? If only she had more experience in these matters she might be able to read him.

“Well,” she said cocking her head to the side and looking at him. “Let’s start with you answering my last question. How did you end up here? You said you didn’t murder anyone, and I do hope that’s true.”

“Aye it is,” he said with a rueful smile. “I was a fool and ended up being sent out here for life.” He sighed and looked at her with a resigned look on his face. “I wasn't satisfied with that. When I got here I was sent up to the Hunter, and then I went bush with a few mad Irishmen."

"You were a bushranger?" Her eyes widened as she stared at him. She'd never met a bushranger before, in fact, stories of them had frightened her to death. Aaron didn't look frightening, on the contrary, he looked a bit remorseful.

"Aye. Then we were caught and three of us were sent here, and I think the others were sent to Morton Bay." He rubbed his face with his hands and peered at her. "I'm not proud of it."

"Are the other two still here, on the island?"

"No," he said with a shake of his head. "Paddy was murdered and Lawrie was sent to Cockatoo Island." He sighed. "Enough of me. Tell me how ye came to be here?"

"Ah, well that is not nearly such an interesting tale," she said clasping her hands together. "After my father died my stepmother arranged for me to go and work for the Reverend and his wife. They were living on the Hawkesbury River then."

The two of them spent the next few hours talking and getting to know one another. Jessie enjoyed his company immensely and they both lost track of time as they exchanged stories of their lives. Jessie deliberately withheld the small detail of her being indentured. It seemed trivial in the face of his life sentence.

***

Chapter Twenty Seven

Orange Vale – Love and Danger

The weather continued with squalls and storms for the next week and Jessie had no opportunity to see Aaron. She was confident their friendship or relationship, or whatever it was called was progressing, but she wished she had someone to talk to about it.

Since coming to the island she hadn't made one single friend. The civil establishment to which she belonged considered her beneath them. After all, she was a servant. The wives and daughters of the military had also been less than forthcoming. Not to mention that they didn't stay more than a few months and then were replaced with new soldiers. Even if there was someone amongst the prisoner population that she could befriend, Mrs Sharpe wouldn't let her anywhere near them.

Her eyes were glued to the road leading to Kingston. She'd arranged to meet Aaron on the road to Orange Vale after service today, but there was still no sign of him. She paced up and down until she finally spied him hurrying towards her. She stopped and smiled.

"I'm so sorry," he said coming to a halt and catching his breath.

"That's alright."

She looped her arm in his as they began walking down the road. "It's good to see you again."

"Aye," he said smiling down at her. "I haven't been able to think of anything but ye since we last met."

Jessie cast her eyes forward and smiled. So, he'd missed her. Surely that was a good sign. "So, what shall we do this afternoon?"

"I thought ye might enjoy a picnic down in the glen."

"I would."

They continued their walk down to Orange Vale in companionable conversation. Aaron pointed out his cottage amongst the others situated on a small hill above the Commandant's garden.

"Wait here," he said before ducking inside. He returned moments later carrying a small basket in one hand and a blanket in the other. "It isn't much, but I prepared us a small picnic," he said handing her the blanket. "Come."

He took her hand and they made their way down the path towards the grove of orange trees. There were no workers here today on account of it being the Sabbath, and the whole was quiet apart from the trees rustling in the breeze. Aaron came to a halt on the other side of the grove in a small clearing surrounded by guava trees and vines. It was rather romantic.

He put the basket down and took the blanket from Jessie. He tossed it on top of the basket before turning his attention to her. "What do ye think? It's rather pretty here."

She had to agree that it was rather pretty, but also very secluded. No one would likely come across them here and she licked her lips. A feeling of excitement tinged with nervousness pulsated in her veins. She sucked in a breath and smiled. "It's lovely."

"So are ye."

He took a step closer and reaching out his hand cupped her face and ran his thumb across her cheekbone. Their eyes locked and Jessie held her breath. His eyes burned into her with an intensity she hadn't seen before. It both scared her and thrilled her. He moved closer until she could feel his warm breath on her face.

Jessie didn't want this encounter to end like the last one. She pressed herself against him and wrapped her arms around his shoulders. He could not possible misinterpret her intentions as she tilted her face and pulled him closer. A soft moan escaped his lips as his arms came around her and he pulled her into a tight embrace. A split second later his lips were on hers. This kiss was not soft and gentle as it had been in the barracks during divine service. His lips demanded she respond and his tongue probed, urging her to open up to him.

A sensation between her thighs that she'd never expected or experienced before took her by surprise. She clung to him and surrendered herself as she allowed his tongue to explore her mouth and she tentatively reciprocated. When their lips parted her legs felt wobbly and she leant against him. He continued to rain little kisses on her lips and face, before squeezing her in a bear-like hug.

They stood there in a tight embrace for several seconds before Aaron pulled away and gazed down into her face. His eyes had deepened in colour with flecks of blue and green. The desire she saw in his eyes scared her just a little. She knew about men. She'd once convinced her grandmother's cook to tell her everything. Is that what he now wanted? Did she?

"I'm falling in love with ye, Jessie." His voice was barely above a whisper and sounded husky to her ears. "We'll take it slow. I don't want ye to be scared."

She sucked in a breath and slowly let it out. She was a little scared, but that was far less than the feeling of excitement that was thrumming through her. She was pretty sure she was already in love with him, but she didn't think she should tell him that. "I'm not scared," she said leaning closer to him. "But, I would like to be kissed again."

He chuckled as he drew her into his arms again. "I'm only too happy to oblige."

The next kiss was just as exciting as the first, and when they finally parted Jessie was breathless and giddy. She knew kissing him would be wonderful, but even she could not have imagined just how exciting it would be.

"Come, let's eat before we lose ourselves completely," he said reaching for the blanket. He spread it out on the mossy ground and waited for Jessie to sit before he joined her. He leaned over and kissed her again softly. "Ye are more than I ever dreamed of."

She wasn't quite sure what he meant but didn't care. This had turned out to be a perfect Sunday afternoon and she didn't want it to end.

***

Over the next month, Aaron and Jessie spent as much time together as they could. Jessie could barely think of anything except when their next meeting might be. As winter gave way to spring she had the distinct feeling that he was going to ask her to marry him.

She'd imagined it so many times. They were together in their private little glen. He'd take her hand in his and place a warm kiss on the back of it before turning it over and kissing the palm of her hand. A small thrill went down her spine as she imagined his warm tongue on the inside of her wrist.

Then he'd gaze into her eyes and say "Jessie, will ye do me the honour of becoming my wife?" And of course, she'd say yes and then she'd be in his arms and be so blissfully happy. She could almost feel his lips on hers as she imagined the joy of becoming Mrs Aaron Price.

"Jessie," called Mrs Sharpe from the parlour. "Come and help me put supper on the table."

She jumped as she was dragged back into the present. "Coming." She straightened her apron and hurried out to the kitchen. "I'm sorry I lost track of the time."

"It's alright," said Mrs Sharpe with a reassuring smile. "Take yours and Mr Sharpes, I'll bring mine."

She nodded as she picked up the two plates of steaming stew and potatoes. It smelled delicious and her stomach grumbled in anticipation. She made her way through to the dining table and put Mr Sharpe's supper down in front of him before seating herself. Mrs Sharpe joined them a moment later with a plate of bread. She bowed her head and waited for the Reverend to recite grace. A minute later she murmured Amen along with Mr and Mrs Sharpe.

"How was your day, dear," asked Mrs Sharpe as she passed the plate of bread to her husband.

"Thank you," he said taking a slice. "My day was fine, but three men were badly injured out at Orange Vale this afternoon. Two of them were buried under a mudslide and the Overseer took a bad fall."

Jessie's heart leapt into her throat and she stared at Mr Sharpe. "The Overseer? Do you mean Aaron Price?" There were many overseers, she knew that, but not out at Orange Vale. There were only the two of them.

"Aye, that's the one," he said before taking a mouthful of stew.

"Oh dear. Did they get them out?" said Mrs Sharpe with a furrowed brow.

"Oh, aye," he said nodding. "They're all in the hospital under Doctor Harnett's care."

Jessie felt like her stays had tightened and she couldn't breathe. How badly was he hurt? She stifled a groan as fear squirmed in her belly like a viper. He had to be alright.

"Are you alright?" said Mrs Sharpe placing her hand on her arm. "You've gone awfully pale, Jess. Is something wrong?"

"Ah…I…yes," she said pressing her lips together. "He's a friend of mine."

Mrs Sharpe exchanged a look with her husband and Jessie groaned inwardly. "A friend of yours?" she said looking intently at Jessie.

She only had a moment to decide what to tell them. Should she tell the truth? She put her cutlery down and folded her hands in her lap. "Well, yes. He and I have become rather close in recent months."

"Do you mean romantically?" she said still without taking her eyes off of her. "Is he the one I told you to stay away from?"

Jessie swallowed and lowered her eyes. "Yes." She couldn't lie, not straight to her face like that. She sighed as she raised her eyes and looked from one to the other. They didn't appear to be too surprised by the news.

"I'll accompany you to the hospital in the morning," said Mr Sharpe smiling kindly. "I'm sure he'll recover just fine."

"Thank you."

"And you and I will discuss this further when you return," said Mrs Sharpe in a tone that brooked no argument.

Jessie nodded. She would worry about dealing with Mrs Sharpe tomorrow, for now, she was relieved the Reverend had offered to take her to the hospital. However, she had a sick feeling in the pit of her stomach and her appetite had quite deserted her. She pushed her plate aside and got to her feet.

"If you'll permit me I think I'll retire." She had an overwhelming urge to be alone with her thoughts, not that she expected to get a wink of sleep. She would need to assure herself that Aaron was alright before she could sleep.

She thought Mrs Sharpe was going to protest, but the Reverend put his hand on her arm and squeezed. "Of course," he said.

***

Chapter Twenty Eight

The *Proposal*

Jessie was up early the following morning. She'd tossed and turned all night and although she was mentally exhausted, sleep had evaded her. She dressed in her simple day dress and pinned her braided hair on top of her head. She stuck her bonnet on and without even a glance in the mirror, she hurried from her room.

Reverend Sharpe was waiting for her by the front door. He smiled as she approached and opened the door before gesturing for her to exit. She stepped out into the spring sunshine and breathed in a large lungful of fresh air. It was only a short walk to the hospital which lay beyond barracks shaded by two large pine trees.

Once inside Jessie's anxiety only escalated. There was something about hospitals and doctors in general that always made her feel uneasy. She clung close to the Reverend as they made their way down the corridor. The smells of unwashed bodies, blood and other nasty things assaulted her nostrils. She grimaced as she retrieved her sweet-smelling handkerchief from her pocket and covered her nose.

Doctor Harnett appeared in front of them from behind a partition. “Ah, Reverend I wasn’t expecting ye this morning.”

“No. My servant, Miss Smith wishes to see Overseer Price. I believe he was brought in yesterday.”

“Aye, he was. He’s doing well. A dislocated shoulder and a mild concussion,” he said resting his astute eyes on Jessie momentarily. “Go through that door and he’s second on the right.”

“Thank you,” said Reverend Sharpe placing his hand on the small of Jessie’s back as he guided her towards the door.

He opened the door and stood aside for her to enter. Jessie smiled as she entered the smaller room. It had four beds and Aaron was sitting up leaning against several pillows in the one on the far right.

“Jessie,” he said as soon as he saw her. A wide smile spread across his face. “I didn’t expect ye to come.”

"Aaron. Oh, Aaron are you alright?" she said rushing to the side of his bed.

"I'll leave ye to your visit," said Reverend Sharpe with a nod.

"Thank you," said Jessie before turning her attention back to Aaron.

His left shoulder was bandaged with his arm in a sling. Jessie thought that would no doubt give his shoulder a chance to heal. He had a deep gash above his right eye which was half closed with a dark bruise visible down to his cheekbone. She could only imagine how he was feeling.

"What happened? I heard two men got buried," she said perching herself on the edge of the bed.

"Aye. There was a landslide below where I was. I saw it happen and I knew Rogers and Davidson were down there. They got buried under it and I raced to get to them, but I fell and hit my head on a rock I think." He grimaced and ran his finger over the gash in his head. "I don't remember much after that."

She shook her head. "Thank God you're alright. I was so scared when I heard you'd been hurt."

"Well, I've got a stinking headache and my shoulder aches something fierce." His good eye twinkled as he leant towards her. 'A kiss would surely make me feel better."

"Really?" she said with a smile before leaning forward and brushing her lips against his. "Like this?"

He moaned as he tried to press his lips firmly against hers, but she pulled back and grinned. "I see you're feeling better already."

She put her hand on the uninjured side of his face and obliged by pressing her lips to his. Her lips parted and she explored briefly with her tongue. He responded to her kiss which sent a shiver down her spine. Kissing him was always so thrilling and she thought she'd never tire of it. Moments later she ended the kiss –acutely aware of where they were.

"Ah – I do feel better, but one kiss might not be enough."

"It'll have to be," she said sitting back. "You're injured and I'll not be the one to set your recovery back." Her voice sounded so prim even to her own ears and she smiled. "I'm just so relieved that you're going to be alright."

"Aye," he said with a sigh as he relaxed against the pillows. "So tell me, does the Reverend now know about us?"

She sighed. "Yes."

"Ye don't sound happy about it. What's wrong?"

"Mrs Sharpe doesn't approve, and will be waiting for me when I get home to talk to me about you," she said folding her hands in her lap. "I didn't mean to tell them, but I couldn't lie directly to their faces."

He reached out and squeezed her hand. "There's naught they can do about us, Jessie."

She blew out her breath and looked at him. "Well, they might be able to."

"How?" he said with a puzzled look.

She knew now that she should have told him the truth from the start, but she honestly didn't think it would ever matter. Now she wasn't so sure. She sighed and glanced at him. "Do you remember me telling you that my stepmother arranged for me to work for the Sharpes after my father died?"

"Aye."

"Well, that arrangement's in writing. And it's a bit more than an arrangement – it's an indenture."

His eyes widened and he winced and put his hand to his head. "Ouch…an indenture? For how long?"

She licked her lips. One lie always seemed so innocent, but then it led to more lies, and now she was faced with having to tell yet another one. "Until I turn eighteen or…marry."

A wide grin spread across his face and he reached for her hand again. He brought it up to his lips and brushed a kiss across the back of it. "That's easily fixed then, isn't it? Marry me."

"What?"

"I mean it, Jessie. Marry me."

"No," she said shaking her head and pulling her hand free. "You're concussed and don't know what you're saying."

"I may be concussed but I know perfectly well what I'm saying," he said in a gentler tone. He sat up straight and sucked in a breath. "Jessie Smith, will ye do me the honour of becoming my wife?"

She pressed her lips together and looked at his poor battered face. He was serious and her heart started thumping madly at the intensity she saw in his eyes. She'd dreamed of this moment. It may not be the romantic proposal she'd imagined, but it was a serious proposal nonetheless.

"Yes."

He smiled and beckoned her with his good hand to come closer. "Come."

She shifted and leant forward and stared into his eyes.

"I promise to be a good husband to ye," he whispered before cupping her face with his good arm and pressing his lips to hers.

Jessie leaned closer and pressed herself against his chest. She didn't want to touch him in case she hurt him, and so the kiss was a little awkward. She'd just agreed to marry him and when their lips parted she was breathless and brimming with happiness.

"As soon as I'm able I'll ask the Commandant for permission," he said running his hand down her arm and taking her hand in his. "Do ye think the Reverend might agree to marry us?"

"I don't know," she said shaking her head. "But I'll ask him. He's a kind man and I don't think he'd refuse me just because he doesn't approve."

Aaron sighed as he released her hand and relaxed against the pillows. Jessie thought he looked tired and drawn.

"I think you should rest," she said standing and straightening her skirt. "I'll come and see you again tomorrow. Can I bring you anything"

"No, but I'd enjoy seeing ye again."

She smiled and took his hand and squeezed gently. "Until tomorrow then."

***

Jessie arrived home mid-morning with a feeling of trepidation in the pit of her stomach. Mrs Sharpe would waste no time in interrogating her, of that she was sure. She took off her bonnet and tied on her apron and glanced at herself in the mirror. Her anxious blue eyes stared back at her. She sighed as she left her room. It would be alright she reminded herself – there was nothing they could do to stop her from doing what she wanted.

She found Mrs Sharpe sitting at the kitchen table with a pot of tea in front of her. She smiled when Jessie entered and gestured for her to join her. "How's your friend?"

"He's going to be alright," said Jessie as she sat down.

Two spare cups were sitting beside the teapot and Jessie reached for one and poured herself a cup. It would help calm her nerves.

"Well I'm glad to hear it," said Mrs Sharpe taking a sip of her tea. "But I'm not going to beat around the bush, Jessie. We have to talk about this."

Jessie nodded and sighed. "I know."

"Good. Does he know you're only thirteen?"

Jessie put her cup down with a clatter. This was where the lies had first started and it sat uneasily on her conscious, but there was no going back. "No. He thinks I'm sixteen."

"I see. And how old did he tell you he was?"

"Thirty."

"Thirty!" She rolled her eyes and shook her head. "Well, it would appear that you've both been misled. He's much closer to forty than thirty."

Jessie didn't think so, and nor did she care. She shrugged her shoulders before taking a sip of her tea.

Mrs Sharpe sighed as she peered at Jessie over the rim of her teacup. "Do you imagine you love him?"

"I do."

The kitchen door opened and Reverend Sharpe came inside. He smiled at the two women. "Sails have been spotted off the bluff. It's the Government brig and I expect she'll be moored by nightfall." He seated himself and poured a cup of tea.

"Oh that's wonderful," said Mrs Sharpe in an excited voice. "It should relieve our isolation for a few days at least. Do you think there may be letters for us?"

"I expect so," he said with a warm smile. "I pray the desk I requested will be on board. It's most tiresome not having one for my own use."

Jessie was relieved that the news of a ship arriving had distracted Mrs Sharpe. She was sure she would continue her questions, but at least for now, she had more exciting news to discuss. The news of a ship in port would spread like wildfire and cause such excitement among the inhabitants. Jessie found herself wondering if there might be a letter for her from her grandmother.

***

Chapter Twenty Nine

The Brig Isabella

For the following week, the island was transformed. People stopped in the street to share news and gossip from the mainland. The inhabitants were so excited after months of no contact with the outside world. More prisoners arrived along with a new regiment of soldiers and their families to relieve those that had been on the island for many months.

Mr and Mrs Sharpe had both received letters and spent the time that the Isabella was in port writing their replies. The brig would be sailing tomorrow morning, but still, Jessie hadn't written a reply to her grandmother's letter. She sighed as she unfolded and read it for the hundredth time. Should she tell her about Aaron and her impending marriage? She'd been debating with herself for days, and still wasn't sure what to do.

My Dearest Jessie,

I was thrilled to receive your letter and to know that you have safely arrived on Norfolk Island. I expect you're very busy settling into your new life and getting to know your new neighbours. Do take care in that awful place, my dear.

I don't have any family news to share except that your dear sister Mary and her husband have moved down to Maitland. It would be nice to think that she may visit us, and I live in hope that she will.

George and William are both keeping very well. George has become Grandpa Joe's right-hand man and is an immense help to him. William is still a bit young to do any heavy work, but he's very good with the horses. By the time you see him again, he'll be a young man and you may not recognise him. He's getting so tall.

I pray for you every night and hope that you're happy there with the Reverend and his wife. And I trust they are taking good care of you both in body and soul.

It will be many months before you get my letter and I get yours. But know that you are in my prayers and in my heart.

All my love to you, Grandma

PS: While I believe I can still see well enough to read and write, Grandpa Joe insists on helping me. He's such a sweetheart and insisted on writing this for me.

She sighed as she dipped the quill into the ink pot. No -there was no need to tell her, at least, not yet.

***

The island returned to normal when the Isabella sailed, and Aaron was finally released from the hospital. They'd spent her entire afternoon off together and talked of how they would be married. Aaron had not yet applied for permission, but he'd promised to do it this week.

She had not yet broached the subject with the Reverend either. What with one thing and another and the ship being in port, everything had been shelved. She picked up her mending and made her way to the parlour for the evening. Mr and Mrs Sharpe were both there and they looked up briefly when she entered. She sat down and sucked in a breath. There was no time like the present.

"I wonder if I may ask a favour, Reverend?"

"Of course, my dear," he said looking up and putting the newspaper he was perusing aside.

Mrs Sharpe stopped sewing and looked expectantly in her direction.

She swallowed. "Aaron has asked me to marry him, and I was wondering if you'd be so kind as to conduct the ceremony for us?" she said as she twisted her fingers together. "Only after we've got permission, of course."

"I'm afraid I can't my dear."

It was not the answer she was expecting, and she stared at him with her brows raised to her hairline. "Why ever not?"

"Well, there are several reasons, the least of which is that I promised your grandmother I would take good and proper care of you," he said with a sigh. "But, the main reason is that I cannot. I've requested the Lord Bishop send me a marriage register, but it has not been forthcoming. So, you see, my dear I'm unable to conduct any marriage ceremonies."

Her shoulders slumped as she sat back in her chair. How was she supposed to get married if the Reverend couldn't do it?

"Well, I'm pleased he cannot," said Mrs Sharpe leaning forward in her chair. "You're too young to be even considering such a thing, and we will never approve of you marrying such a man."

She didn't think she needed their approval, but she certainly needed a minister. "Aaron and I are in love and determined to marry as soon as we have permission. Perhaps Mr Aitken can marry us?"

"You would be married as a Roman Catholic?" said Mrs Sharpe clearly scandalised at the thought.

"Mr Aitken isn't able to conduct weddings either, and I wouldn't stand by and allow such a thing," said Reverend Sharpe leaping from his chair. "I think the best thing may be for you to return to your grandmother on the next available vessel."

"You can't do that," said Jessie staring from one to the other.

"Actually, I can and I do believe it would be for the best. I'll write to your grandmother and arrange for you to return to her on the next ship."

"I won't go."

Mrs Sharpe looked from Jessie her husband with her mouth slightly agape. "You wouldn't really send her away, would you?"

"Aye, I think it's the only way to prevent from her throwing her life away on this scoundrel."

Jessie felt hot tears prick her eyes and she pressed her lips together. "You can't."

Mrs Sharpe put her sewing aside and got to her feet and went to Jessie's side. She put her arm around her shoulders. "It'll be for the best. You'll soon forget about him I promise you."

"I won't go, and you can't make me," said Jessie as two large tears rolled down her cheeks.

Mr Sharpe sighed as he gazed at her. "We have an agreement, Jessie. Your stepmother signed you over and into my care."

"But, you promised you'd never use that against me!"

"I'm not using it against you. I'm using it to save you from yourself," he said flatly. "You'll go on the next ship, and that's the end of the matter."

A sob escaped Jessie as she got to her feet and ran from the room. She heard Mr Sharpe telling his wife to let her go as she entered her room and closed the door behind her. She dived onto her bed and buried her face in the quilt and let her tears go. It was so unfair, and they'd promised not to use that damn piece of paper. She hoped Sophia would rot in hell.

She couldn't stop the tears that streamed down her face or the anguished sobs that escaped her. The situation seemed impossible. If she went to the mainland she'd never see Aaron again, and the thought of that was more distressing than she could bear. She sat up and did her best to wipe her tears away with the back of her hand, but they kept on coming.

She sat there for ages trying to think of some way that she could stay, but it was impossible. If she wasn't the Sharpes servant the Commandant would surely send her from the island. And how would she get back? She needed to see Aaron.

She got off the bed and pulled her cloak from the wardrobe and wrapped it around her shoulders. Slipping the window open she climbed out into the cool night air. It was dark and she paused, leaning against the house while her eyes adjusted. The minutes passed but still, she could only see the dark shapes of what she knew to be shrubs and trees. It was moonless and she was not likely going to see any better than she could right now.

She closed her window and started down the side of the house. She thought she'd be able to find her way to Orange Vale, even in the dark, but a nervous flutter in the pit of her stomach was making her feel uneasy. She licked her lips and glanced up and down the street. There was no sign of anyone. Grabbing her skirts in both hands she put her anxiety behind her and hurried down the road.

The road was slippery underfoot from the recent rains, and Jessie's boots squelched in the mud. She slowed her pace.

Her heart was hammering and she was breathing heavily as she entered the sheltered glen and made her way towards the Commandant's garden. She was sure Aaron's hut was just up from there on the hill. She made her way up the small rise and paused on the threshold. A soft light was glowing around the drawn blinds indicating that someone was home.

Her heart was in her throat as she knocked on the door. "Aaron, it's me."

A few moments later the door opened and Aaron stared down at her. "Jessie. What are ye doing here?"

Tears immediately sprang from her eyes and she threw herself into his arms. She clung to him and sobbed incoherently.

He held her in his arms, smoothing her hair with one hand. "Hush, hush. Whatever's happened?" he said kicking the door closed with his boot.

"They're…sending…me…away," she said between sobs.

Aaron pulled her closer and hugged her as he did his best to soothe her. He rubbed his hand up and down her back.

"Hush, come now. Dry your eyes and tell me what's going on."

She pulled herself free and wiped her tears with the back of her hand. She sucked in a deep breath and sighed. "I'm so sorry."

"It's alright. Here, sit down and tell me who's sending ye away."

She sat down on the only comfortable chair in the room and after several deep breaths managed to pull herself together. "The Reverend. I asked him if he'd marry us, and he can't, and then he went on to say that it would be best if I went to live with my grandmother." Once she started speaking the words tumbled out of her, one on top of the other. "He's putting me on the next ship. What are we going to do? We can't get married, and if I leave, I won't be able to come back." Tears threatened to overwhelm her again, but she swallowed and looked beseechingly at Aaron.

"Damn," he said running his hands through his hair. He pulled over a hard wooden chair and sat down. "Let me get this straight. He's sending ye on the next ship?"

"Yes."

"Well, we've got several months to find a solution before then," he said nodding.

"But…well, you can't leave and I can't stay and we can't marry here. There is no solution!" Her voice rose several octaves and ended on a shrill note bordering on hysteria.

"It may seem that way, but I promise ye I'll find a way to be on that ship with ye."

"You shouldn't make promises you have no hope of keeping," she said in a petulant tone. "What are we going to do?"

He got to his feet and knelt in front of her on the floor. "Do ye trust me?" he said taking her hands in his. He brushed his lips across the back of them before gazing up at her tear-stained face.

She swallowed and stared into his eyes full of love and worry - she nodded.

"Then trust me when I say I will find a way.

***

Chapter Thirty

Bound for Sydney, December 1837

Jessie pulled at the weeds in the garden with enthusiasm. She gripped a rather large one and after giving it a wiggle pulled with all her might. It popped out covered in the rich brown soil which she shook off before tossing it into her pail. Summer had arrived and the bees were busy buzzing around the flower beds and the sun was warm on her back. If only she could forget that she was leaving as soon as the next ship arrived.

She dreaded daily that sails would be sighted. There was a lot of speculation that the Government brig would arrive before Christmas. She hoped not. She glanced at Mrs Sharpe who was busy planting a row of spinach on the other side of the garden. Her pleas to her mistress to be allowed to stay had fallen on deaf ears, and Jessie felt resentment rise in her every time Mrs Sharpe looked at her. Her kind words and looks of compassion only made Jessie resent her more.

That evening, after supper Jessie retired to her room early. She didn't care anymore if she was discovered climbing out her window, and tonight was warm with a gentle breeze blowing. She left her window open as she headed for black rock, hoping that the fresh breeze would blow some of the hot stuffy air out while she was gone.

She smiled as she approached the rock – she could see Aaron's outline. He was leaning against it looking out to sea. She glanced towards the horizon when she reached him. "No sails I hope."

"No, not yet," he said grinning before taking her in his arms. He ran his hand down her spine before pressing his lips to hers. She responded by wrapping her arms around him and parting her lips so he could explore with his tongue. She pressed herself against him until she could feel the length of him hard up against her. A soft moan escaped her lips when he pulled free and ended the kiss. "Come, we much to discuss."

Her brows raised to her hairline. "We do?"

"Aye."

He took her hand and led her to the sheltered nook between the rocks. They settled themselves on a blanket and Aaron wrapped his arms around her. She rested her head on his shoulder where she could hear the steady beat of his heart.

"So, what news?" she said.

He placed a warm kiss on her forehead. "Well, it's not yet finalised, but I believe I'll have the Commandant's permission in a day or so. He's made every indication that he will indulge me."

She pulled free of him and looked into his eyes. "You really think so?"

"Aye, I do," he said pulling her back into his arms. "But, ye must not say a word about it. If the Reverend was to get wind of it he could put a stop to it."

"I promise I won't say a word. But I can hardly believe that the Commandant will truly let you go."

"Aye. I think he's only agreed to indulge me because of my part in putting down the mutiny last year." He tightened his arms around her and sighed. "But, if by chance he doesn't, ye must trust me, Jess. I'll find a way to get to the mainland. Tell me that you'll wait for me?"

Her heart broke at the anguish she heard in his voice. "I promise I will."

***

A week later sails were spotted on the horizon and fear gripped Jessie. She had no opportunity to see or speak to Aaron though. Mrs Sharpe was supervising her packing and was not letting her out of her sight. Jessie had no idea if the Commandant had given his permission for Aaron to sail to Sydney or not, and not knowing gnawed at her day and night.

By the time Christmas morning dawned Jessie was ill with fear and worry. She was up at dawn to prepare roast pork for the midday meal, but her mind was on the Isabella now moored off the coast.

Christmas morning was a blur for Jessie. She was glad to be busy in the kitchen but her mind was elsewhere. She accompanied Mrs Sharpe to divine service in the afternoon, but she paid no heed to the Reverend's words, which droned on and on.

She spent the entire time scanning the barracks for any sign of Aaron – of which there was none.

By the time she climbed into bed on Christmas night she was exhausted, but couldn't sleep. Her insides were tied up in knots and she had this dreadful feeling in the pit of her stomach like something terrible was about to happen. She spent several fruitless hours tossing and turning before she got out of bed and wrapping a shawl around her shoulders she crept out of the house.

It was a warm evening with a quarter moon and a sky full of stars. She wondered how the world could look so peaceful, and yet she could be in such turmoil. She wandered down the path in her bare feet and sat down on the garden bench sheltered by a large shrub. She wrapped her arms around her legs and stared into the darkness. If only she could speak to Aaron – to have some idea if all was well. She dared not venture down to Orange Vale in case she drew unwanted attention. She sighed. She could do nothing but wait and hope and pray.

***

Three days later she was escorted down to Cascades by Mr and Mrs Sharpe. They were intent on making sure she boarded the ship in plenty of time before she sailed.

"Do take care, Jess," said Mrs Sharpe with a look of concern etched on her brow. "I will miss you terribly, but I know this is for the best."

Jessie sighed and nodded.

"God speed, my dear," said Reverend Sharpe. "I've written to your grandmother explaining all. And I've made arrangements for Corporal Williams to accompany you and see you safely delivered."

She tried to hide the surprise on her face but failed dismally. "Corporal Williams?"

"Aye, he's going north with a contingent of soldiers and they'll ensure you're escorted to your grandmother's."

"Thank you." She was not foolish enough to think that she could get there alone, and was genuinely grateful that Mr Sharpe had arranged an escort for her.

"Oh, Jessie." Mrs Sharpe swooped on her and engulfed her in a tight hug. "I'm going to miss you so much. You've become like a daughter to me."

Jessie pressed her lips together as she did her best to bury her resentment. She wrapped her arms around her and hugged her in return. "I'll miss you too."

"If you're ready Miss Smith," said a soldier coming to a halt in front of them. "I'll take your bags."

"Thank you," she said handing her two bags to the soldier. She watched him walk to the launch and toss them in. "Well, this is it then," she said turning to Mr and Mrs Sharpe. "Thank you for everything."

"You're most welcome," said Mr Sharpe.

Mrs Sharpe nodded and tried to swallow the tears that had welled in her eyes. Jessie pretended not to notice and turned on her heel and walked down to the launch. One of the soldiers helped her climb in and she sat down and folded her hands in her lap. Well, this was it then, and still, there was no sign of Aaron. She wasn't sure if that was good or not. Perhaps he'd already boarded or was staying out of sight while the Sharpes were here. Either way, she would find out very soon if he'd been successful in his bid to travel to Sydney.

The launch pushed off and several crewmen took up the oars. Jessie watched as the cliffs and pines of Norfolk Island receded. She let out her breath and did her best to relax as the launch steadily made its way towards the waiting ship. She could feel panic rising from the depths of her stomach and through her chest. What if she never saw him again? Her throat felt constricted and she breathed in steadily through her nostrils as she tried to remain calm.

Twenty minutes later she found herself leaning against the railing of the Isabella. She brushed her tears aside as she gazed at the island she may never see again.

"Ma'am," said a young crewman sidling up beside her.

"Yes." She turned her tear-streaked face towards him and wiped them away with the back of her hand.

"Ma'am, if you'll come with me I'll show ye to yer cabin."

"Thank you."

She took one last glance at the island before turning and following the young man down below deck. It was dimly lit in the corridor with the only light shining in through a grate-like hatch. He opened a door and showed her to a small cramped cabin. Her bags had already been delivered and had been dumped on the narrow bunk.

"Thank you," said Jessie removing her bonnet and smoothing her hair.

"Ma'am," he said doffing his cap before leaving.

She sighed as she closed the door and leant against it. She slumped down on the bunk beside her bags and sucked in a deep breath. Thoughts of Aaron were going around and around endlessly until she thought she'd go mad. Not knowing if she would ever see him again was driving her to despair.

She spent all of the next day leaning against the railing of the ship as she scanned every launch for Aaron. Mostly, the launch was loaded with the soldiers and their families that had completed their tour of duty on the island. Late in the day, prisoners who had served their term or were being sent to Sydney for trial boarded. Aaron wasn't among them. Her anxiety reached new heights when she heard the crewman talking – the Isabella would sail the following day.

That night as she tossed and turned, she knew – knew in her heart that he wasn't coming. The Commandant had not given him permission and her heart ached for him. She rolled over and buried her head under the quilt as she tried desperately to go to sleep. She'd keep her promise – she'd wait for him – forever if she had to.

She must've fallen asleep in the early hours because she awoke with a fright. The ship was pitching and rolling and the timbers were creaking. They'd set sail and were underway. She buried herself back under the covers. She wasn't ready to face the day.

***

Chapter Thirty One

A Family Reunion

Jessie must've gone back to sleep because she awoke with a start. Someone was knocking rather loudly on her cabin door.

"One moment," she called before swinging her legs over the side of the bunk.

She rummaged through her bag and retrieved her shawl which she hastily wrapped around herself. She ran her hand over her hair, tucking several strands behind her ear and pulling her long plait over one shoulder. She opened the door and was immediately engulfed in a pair of very familiar arms.

"Aaron!" Her heart was thumping madly as she pulled herself free and stared into his smiling face. "I thought you hadn't made it. I was sure I'd never see you again." Tears of joy filled her eyes and she wrapped her arms around him and buried her face in his shoulder. "Oh my God, I can't believe you're here."

He pulled her hard against him and ran his hand down her spine. "I'm here. I'm sorry to worry ye so, but I didn't board until very late last night and I didn't want to disturb ye."

She tilted her face upwards and he oblige by lowering his lips to hers. She clung to him and drank him in like she couldn't get enough. She was breathless when their lips parted and giddy with relief.

"I'm just so happy that you're here, and we're going to be married."

He placed a kiss on her forehead as he relinquished his hold on her. "It's not quite that simple."

"What?"

"I don't yet have permission to marry ye," he said with a sigh. "Major Anderson couldn't give it because we're to marry in Sydney. He's written a letter of recommendation."

"You'll get it though won't you?" She couldn't help the little knot of fear that had formed in the pit of her stomach.

"Aye, I'm sure of it, but it'll take time. And there's another problem."

"Another problem?" She plopped herself down on the bunk and stared at him. "I just want to be married." She couldn't help the frustration in her voice.

"I know, I know. So do I. But, I'm still a prisoner, which means I have to report to the Sydney Gaol, and I'll have to stay there until things get sorted. But, the Commandants also recommended me for a ticket." A wide grin spread across his face. "I'll be free." He grabbed her and swung her around the tiny cabin before setting her back down.

She grabbed the side of the bunk to steady herself. He was going to be free - she couldn't have hoped for anything more and a wide smile spread across her face. "That's wonderful, but…well…I've got a bit of a problem as well."

"What?" he said raising his brows.

"The Reverend's arranged for Corporal William's to escort me to my grandmother's, and I can see no way out of it."

"No, no that's not a problem - that's perfect," he said with a shake of his head. "Ye go to your grandmother's while I get everything sorted. Once I've got permission I'll send for ye."

"Alright," she said with a nod. "Oh, I can hardly believe you're here." She wrapped her arms around him once more. "I love you so much."

"Aye." He held her and gazed down into her clear blue eyes "Me too."

***

A week later the Isabella docked in Sydney. Aaron and Jessie had said their goodbyes the previous evening, and now Jessie watched as he was led in chains down the gangplank. Her heart ached at the sight of him so restrained, but she consoled herself with the fact he would soon be free.

The morning was already warm and it was promising to be a hot day. Jessie waved her fan in front of her face trying to get some sort of relief. She wasn't looking forward to the day ahead on the road to her grandmother's – there would be little hope of escaping the hot sun.

"Miss Smith," said a soldier coming to stand beside her. He doffed his hat and smiled. "Corporal Williams' at yer service. I've been charged with seeing ye safely to the MacDonald River."

"Pleased to meet you."

"When you're ready we'll get going."

"I'm ready Corporal."

Corporal Williams seemed nice enough. Jessie thought he was probably in his thirties with a receding hairline and crooked yellow teeth. Still, he was polite and she expected he would see her safely to her grandmother's. He turned on his heel and headed for the gangplank, along with four other soldiers. Jessie sighed as she started after them.

A small cart sat at the foot of the gangplank which was loaded with their luggage, and Jessie's bags as well.

"We've left room for ye to sit in the back, Miss Smith," he said looking apologetic. "I'm sorry we don't have a more comfortable conveyance for ye."

She eyed the hard wooden cart and hid a grimace. "That will be perfectly fine." She noticed an upturned crate had been placed at the rear for her to use. She climbed onto it and settled herself on the back of the cart with her legs dangling.

She waited while one of the other soldiers climbed onto the driver's seat and with a click of his tongue, the horse started walking down the docks. The other soldiers, including Corporal Williams, marched alongside and behind the cart as they began to wend their way through the streets of Sydney. Jessie gripped the side of the cart and did her best to not think about what was happening to Aaron right now.

It was a long and dreary day on a hot and dusty road. By the time they reached Parramatta, her skirt was covered in a fine film of dust and the perspiration was dripping down the bodice of her shirt. Damp patches were visible under her arms and she was feeling sticky and clammy. They made camp a few miles north of Parramatta, and Jessie helped one of the young privates prepare a hearty supper of salt pork stew. It was a balmy starlit night, and the soldiers kept the fire smouldering all night. She didn't pull her cloak around herself until the cool morning air sent goosebumps down her arms.

They were up at dawn, and with nothing more than some hard-tack biscuits for breakfast, they continued on the road north. Jessie grimaced as she climbed into the back of the cart for another day. Her bottom complained at having nothing but hard wood to sit on which amplified every rut in the road.

The cool morning air quickly warmed as the sun rose over the horizon. It was going to be another hot day, and Jessie yearned for the cool of the MacDonald River. They hadn't gone far when Corporal Williams sidled up beside the cart next to her. He informed her that they'd be camping north of Wiseman's Ferry for the night, but that he'd personally take her to her grandmother's and meet up with his regiment later. She was grateful she wouldn't have to camp out with them again. She was desperate to get to the MacDonald River, and out of the unrelenting sun.

It was late in the day when Jessie and Corporal Williams parted company with their travelling companions. It was only a short drive through shady gum trees to her grandmother's house from here. It was a relief to be amongst the cool trees, and Jessie craned her neck to get a glimpse of the house. It was only now that she thought of seeing her family again and she couldn't wait. She could feel the excitement thrumming through her veins as they rounded the final corner and came to a halt in front of the house. It was exactly as she remembered it.

She jumped down from the cart and stretched and stamped her legs up and down to rid them of the numb feeling. Corporal Williams' leapt down and reached the veranda in two strides before he knocked loudly on the door. Jessie grabbed her bags and followed him.

A few moments later the door opened and Grandpa Joe peered out at them.

"Jessie, is that ye?" He brushed past the Corporal, ignoring him, and grabbed Jessie in a bone-crushing hug. "Ye grandmother will be beside herself when she sees ye." He released her and held her at arm's length. "What are ye doing here?"

"It's a long story," she said with a sigh. "I'd like to get settled and bathe in the river first though if you don't mind. And then I'll tell you everything."

"Corporal Williams at yer service," said Corporal Williams doffing his hat. "I'm charged with delivering Miss Smith safely into the hands of Mrs Margaret Smith. Is she here?"

"Aye," said Grandpa Joe eyeing the Corporal. "Ye can be sure you've delivered her. Thank ye."

"Ah…no. My instructions were very clear, and I have a letter that's to be handed only to Mrs Smith."

"Right," said Grandpa Joe with a sigh. "Wait here." He went back inside the house, calling Maggie's name as he went.

Jessie groaned inwardly. The Reverend had obviously followed through with his promise and had written to her grandmother. There would be no getting around the truth of the matter then. Not that she had any intention of lying, but the Reverend wasn't likely to paint Aaron in a favourable light.

Grandpa Joe returned a few minutes later leading Maggie by the arm. "This here is Mrs Smith. The Corporal's brought Jessie to us and a letter for ye."

"Ma'am," said Corporal Williams as he retrieved a battered envelope from his pocket. He handed it to Maggie with a bow. "I've executed my duty and now if you'll excuse me, I have to get back to my regiment." He stepped from the veranda before turning his attention to Jessie. "Miss Smith it has been a pleasure."

"Thank you, Corporal Williams."

He doffed his hat once more before climbing onto the cart and with a click of his tongue set off back down the road to Wiseman's Ferry.

"Grandma," said Jessie dropping her bags and hugging her grandmother. "It's so good to see you." She felt hot tears prick her eyes as she hugged her tight.

"Jessie what a surprise. What are ye doing here?" She pulled free of Jessie's embrace and cupped her face in her hands. "My how you've grown."

"I have. As I told Grandpa Joe, I'm so filthy from travelling and I want nothing more than to bathe in the river and to put on clean clothes. Then I'll tell you everything."

Maggie smiled. "I'll fetch a towel and accompany ye. There's nothing like the cool of the river after a hot day."

***

By the time she retired to the parlour after supper, Jessie was yawning and would've loved an early night. However, Grandpa Joe and Grandma both had expectant looks on their faces and were not likely going to wait until tomorrow for answers. George and William were lounging on the couch together and appeared disinterested. Maggie ran her fingers over the envelope sitting on the table beside her and sighed.

"So, Jessie. Are ye going to tell us what you're doing here, or should I read this letter? I presume it's from Mr Sharpe?"

"Yes I expect so," said Jessie nodding. "Before you read it, though, I'd like to tell you."

Maggie sat back in her chair and folded her hands in her lap. "Alright then."

Jessie sucked in a deep breath. Where to start? She thought it best to start with the fact that she was getting married. Once she started to tell them, it all came tumbling out. She told them about Aaron and how well he'd done for himself. He was a trusted Overseer and now had the Commandant's ear. She thought it best to tell them the Reverend didn't approve, but that he'd sent her away to prevent her marrying. And that Aaron was right now in Sydney applying for permission.

"And so, as soon as we have permission he'll send for me and we'll get married," she said finishing her long tale.

"Ye can't be serious?" said Maggie with a furrowed brow. "You're barely fourteen years old, an' ye think to shackle yourself to this man who's a prisoner? No matter that he's an Overseer an' such he'll likely never be able to leave the island."

"Listen to your Grandmother, lass," said Grandpa Joe leaning forward in his chair. "Surely ye can see ye can do much better than this man."

"No. I love him and he loves me, and I'm going to marry him," she said vehemently. "Anyway, he won't be a prisoner for much longer. He's been recommended for a ticket of leave."

"Bah," said Maggie reaching for the letter and tearing it open. Even with her failing eyesight, she didn't appear to have any trouble reading the letter. She held it close to her face as her eyes scanned it.

Jessie held her breath while she read it. What had the Reverend said? Her heart was thumping wildly as she tried to think of something to say to end this argument. George and William were looking expectantly at Maggie – their interest piqued at last. Before Jessie could think of anything further to say Maggie gave a scoff and handed the letter to Grandpa Joe.

"Read that," she said staring at Jessie. "Ye failed to mention that he's more than thirty years old. For goodness sake, Jess ye can't marry this man."

Grandpa Joe finished reading the letter and put it on the table. "The Reverend doesn't approve of this match, and neither do we. Ye can stay here with us, but you'll not be marrying this man, Aaron Price."

Jessie licked her lips and looked from one to the other. "I don't mean any disrespect, but you can't tell me what to do. And I don't need your approval to get married."

Maggie pushed herself out of her chair and glared at her granddaughter. "We're yer closest kin an' we have a duty to protect ye from yeself if needs be." She reached for Joe's arm as he got to his feet and stood beside her. "I don't wish to argue or disagree with ye. But we won't stand idly by an' watch ye throw yer life away."

Jessie swallowed. She had no desire to argue with her grandmother either. Perhaps in time, she could convince her that this was a good match. "I don't wish to argue with you either," said Jessie getting to her feet. She stepped forward and hugged her grandmother and placed an affectionate kiss on her cheek. "I'm really tired after two days on the road."

"Aye," she said patting her cheek. "Perhaps after a good night's sleep, ye'll see that we only have yer best interests at heart."

"I know that Grandma," she said smiling. "Goodnight."

***

Chapter Thirty Two

An Agonising Wait

Jessie was half dreading facing her grandmother following the conversation about her impending marriage. She'd expected her to continue to voice her disapproval, but she didn't. There was no further mention of it or Aaron, and over the following week, Jessie started to relax. She'd forgotten how peaceful it was on the river and how much she loved it here.

She settled herself in one of the wicker chairs on the veranda. A cool change with rain and thunderstorms had arrived late last night and drizzle rain had persisted all morning. It was now late afternoon and the sun had decided to make a brief appearance. She closed her eyes and basked in its warmth.

"I thought I might find ye here," said George slumping down in the chair beside her.

She opened her eyes, startled momentarily at his sudden appearance.

"Don't you just love it out here in the afternoon?" she said smiling.

"Aye. Though I don't usually have time to enjoy it," he said leaning his elbows on his knees - he pressed his fingers together. "I was hoping to have a private word with ye." His blue eyes stared at her with intensity for a brief moment before he lowered his lashes.

"Hmm," she said with a sigh. "Well, let's get it over with then."

"No. It's not like that," he said sitting up straight and putting his hands up in the air in mock surrender. "I…look are ye really serious about marrying this man?"

"I am." She sighed and gazed at her brother. "I know he's a lot older than me, and he's currently a prisoner, but none of that matters."

"Ye know Grandma will never agree. She'll try to stop ye."

Jessie nodded. She'd gotten that impression on her first night here, but there was nothing her grandmother could do to stop her. "Perhaps, but she can't. What about you?" She looked at her brother for any sign that he would also try to stop her.

He shook his head. "If it's truly what ye want I won't stand in your way. I just wanted to warn ye that Grandma will."

"Thank you, George. I appreciate that."

"There's just one thing," he said leaning forward. "Are ye sure ye want to spend the rest of your life on Norfolk Island? It's rather small and there can't be much to do there."

Jessie laughed. "I won't be spending the rest of my life on the island. In fact, we probably won't even be going back there."

"What do ye mean? He's a prisoner isn't he?"

"Well yes, but the Commandant's recommended him for a ticket of leave. It'll probably be granted at the same time as our permission to marry," she said folding her hands in her lap. "So, I expect we'll settle in Sydney. Aaron's a stonemason by trade and there'll be plenty of work for him there I'm sure."

"Oh, well perhaps ye should tell Grandma all of that. She might change her mind."

"Do you really think so?"

"No," he said with a laugh. "I don't think anything will change her mind."

Jessie smiled. She was relieved George didn't share her grandmother's opinion. She was also grateful for his warning. Even if Grandma tried to dissuade her further Jessie was confident everything would work out in the end. She would be married and soon her grandmother would realise there was nothing to worry about.

***

Jessie's confidence didn't last long. As the weeks passed, and she received no word from Aaron, her anxiety grew. She wondered if her grandmother had intercepted her mail. Surely even she wouldn't do that – but the thought nagged at her until she couldn't bear it.

She moved quietly through the house, keeping an ear out for any movement. There was none. She knew Grandpa Joe and her brothers were down in the stables – a new foal was born in the early hours and they were still with the mare. She was sure

Grandma was still in bed and Alice, the cook would be busy in the kitchen.

She sucked in a breath as she turned the key in her grandmother's writing desk and paused with her hand on it. With one last thought that she shouldn't be doing this, she lowered the front of it. She glanced nervously over her shoulder before turning her attention to the pile of letters tied in a bundle sitting in the middle of the desk. Untying the bundle she quickly flipped through them. They were all addressed to *Mrs Margaret Smith*, with the one from the Reverend sitting on top. She briefly thought about reading it, but then thought better of it. She needed to find any addressed to her, not her grandmother.

She retied the bundle and set them aside while she searched through the other papers. There was nothing out of the ordinary, and nothing addressed to her from Aaron.

"What do ye think you're doing?"

Jessie's heart leapt into her throat as she swung around and found herself face-to-face with her grandmother. "Ah…um…I just thought…well, I thought maybe a letter for me had got mixed up with yours."

"Did ye indeed," she said tapping her walking stick ahead of her as she came towards her. She brushed past Jessie and slammed the desk shut. "An' what did ye find?" She turned the key in the lock and removed it before tucking it into her pocket.

"Nothing."

"Aye, nothing," she said glaring at Jessie. "Do ye really think I'd keep yer mail from ye?"

"I don't know." Tears came unbidden and rolled down Jessie's cheeks. "I just thought I would've had word from Aaron by now. It's been three weeks and I can't stand not knowing." She wiped her tears aside with the back of her hand. "I'm sorry."

Maggie's face softened and she sighed. "Oh, child these things take time. I'm sure he'll write ye as soon as he can." She put her arm around her granddaughter's waist and urged her forward. "Come an' have breakfast with me."

"Alright," she said nodding.

Grandma was right, these things did take time and there was no way of knowing just how long it would take. She should’ve known her grandmother wouldn’t do such a thing as to take her mail. That was something her stepmother would’ve done and she winced at the pang of guilt that went through her for even thinking such a thing. She looped her arm through her grandmother’s as they made the out to the kitchen. She would make it up to her somehow.

***

Another agonising week went by before news finally arrived. Jessie had done her best to keep busy around the house, but nothing she did kept thoughts of Aaron and her impending marriage at bay. She could think of nothing else.

It was her grandmother who came to her bearing a creamy envelope with her name clearly written across the front of it. “Yer letter’s finally come, my dear.”

“Thank you, Grandma.” She took the envelope and held it to her breast. Relief flooded through her and she placed an affectionate kiss on her grandmother’s cheek. “This probably means I’ll be leaving soon.”

"We'll see," said Maggie easing herself into her favourite chair.

Jessie sat down in the nearest chair and sucked in a deep breath before carefully opening the envelope. She unfolded the crisp parchment and smiled at Aaron's familiar writing.

January, 1838 Sydney

My Dearest Jess,

I'm sorry this note has to be so brief, but I only have one sheet of parchment. And I'm afraid I don't have good news concerning our marriage. The authorities believe me to be married. I assure you this is quite untrue, I have never been married. I'm confident I can convince them of the error, but they will need to re-check their records, and that will take time. Do not lose hope. I promise we will be married in a matter of weeks - I'm sure of it.

I've been moved from the gaol to the Hyde Park Barracks. This affords me more freedom and I believe it's a good sign that my ticket will be granted any day now.

I pray that you are safe and well with your family. I will write again as soon as permission is granted. We will be reunited before you know it and we'll finally be free.

I'm missing you more than you can know, my love. Stay safe and keep well, and be ready to come to Sydney when you receive my next letter.

I am affectionately yours, Aaron

Her frustration from the past few weeks coupled with the news that she wouldn't be leaving for Sydney overwhelmed her. Tears welled in her eyes and an ache stretched across the back of her throat. She pressed her lips together as tears rolled quietly down her face. Nothing was working out as it should.

She'd quite forgotten about her grandmother until her hand touched her sleeve. She turned her tear-streaked face towards her. Maggie's furrowed brow and kind brown eyes only made Jessie cry even more.

"Hush, my dear child."

"Oh Grandma," said Jessie as she tried to stem the flow of tears.

"Obviously, tis not good news. Come, hush now. Tell me what's he got to say for himself."

Jessie sucked in a deep breath and wiped her face on her sleeve. "They say he's already married. He's not, but he's got to convince them of it."

Maggie's brows rose as she sat back in her chair. "Well, then."

Jessie folded the letter and slipped it back into the envelope and withdrawing a handkerchief from her pocket dabbed her eyes and blew her nose. "

"I think it's time ye forgot about this man, Jessie. He's lied to ye an' deceived ye, an' ye can't possibly trust him."

"But he hasn't. He's not married." She blew out her breath and tucked her handkerchief back into her pocket. "He wouldn't have asked me to marry him if he was already married."

Maggie shook her head and glanced sideways at her granddaughter. "Ye can't believe that. If they say he's married then I'm afraid he's married. He's deceived ye."

Jessie couldn't believe that. Aaron wouldn't do that to her – would he? She shook her head. "No, he loves me. I'm sure it's just a misunderstanding and Aaron will sort it out."

Maggie raised her brows and tilted her head to the side. "I know ye want to believe him, but this is a sign. A sign that this is not the man for ye. Forget about him – it'll be for the best."

Jessie didn't want to hear those words nor did she wish to continue this conversation. It was going around in circles and all Grandma was doing was making her doubt herself, and Aaron. She slipped her letter into her pocket and got to her feet.

"I think I'll go and have a lie down."

"Good idea, go an' have a nice rest an' I'm sure you'll see I'm right."

No, she wouldn't. But at least if she was alone she could think, and then she'd write to Aaron and assure him that she believed him.

***

Chapter Thirty Three

He's married – He isn't married – He's married

No matter how she tried, Jessie couldn't stop hearing her grandmother's words in her ears. He was married and he'd deceived her. By the end of February, she'd almost convinced herself that she must be right. A melancholy settled on her and there was only one thing that could end it – news from Aaron.

The hot weather continued and Jessie was grateful for the wide veranda that surrounded the house. It caught and funnelled even the slightest breeze into the house. She lay on her back on her bed staring at the ceiling – with thoughts of Aaron with another woman on his arm whirling around in her mind. She was driving herself mad.

Her bedroom door had been sitting ajar and was now pushed open as George popped his head in, and then entered the room properly. He grinned as he held up a creamy envelope for her to see. "It's for ye."

She gasped as she sat bolt upright and reached for it. Her name written in Aaron's now familiar script was scrawled across it. "Thank you. Oh, thank you, George."

"I hope it's good news this time," he said settling himself in one of the chintz chairs.

"So do I." She tore the envelope open and unfolded the parchment before devouring every word. A wide smile spread across her face as she read it, and then her eyes welled with tears. "He's sent for me. We've got permission to wed," she crushed the letter to her breast and grinned at her brother. "Oh my, I can hardly believe it."

George rose from the chair and crossed the room. He closed the door and leant against it. "I'm happy for ye sister, but don't let Grandma get wind of it. She'll try to stop ye for sure."

She knew he was right. "Does she know I got a letter today?"

"No. I got the mail."

"Thank you, George," she folded the letter and tucked it back into the envelope before slipping it into one of her bags. "I just have to work out how I'm going to get to

Sydney. I'll walk to Wiseman's Ferry and from there I should be able to get a conveyance of some sort."

"No need," he said with a shake of his head. "I wouldn't let ye go to Sydney alone at any rate – I'll take ye."

"You will? Really?"

"Aye, and the sooner ye leave the less likely Grandma will find out what you're planning. Did he say when you're to be wed?"

"Yes. The twelfth of March at Scot's Church. The banns are being read for us in preparation."

"Well, ye don't want to arrive too ahead of time, unless you've got plenty of money to pay for an inn."

"I've got money," she said sitting down on the edge of the bed. "But, you're right, I don't want to have to pay too much for accommodation."

"No. So how about we leave on around the tenth? That'll give ye a day of rest before your wedding."

"Perfect," she said nodding.

"So Saturday week," he said counting on his fingers. "We can't talk about this again just in case. So, meet me in the stables at dawn on the tenth. Got it?"

"Got it." She got off the bed and approached her brother before wrapping her arms around him. She placed a kiss on his cheek. "I can never thank you enough for this."

He grinned. "No need. What sort of brother would I be to let ye go off by yourself?"

***

The tenth of March couldn't come fast enough, but the closer the day came, the more nervous Jessie became. She'd retired early tonight and had her bags packed and ready for her dawn escape. Her heart nearly leapt out of her chest when Grandma came knocking on her door and she poked her head in.

"Are ye alright? I was worried when ye went to bed so early." She came in and sat on the edge of the bed and ran her gnarled hand across Jessie's brow. "Hm, ye don't feel hot."

"I'm not, I'm perfectly fine, Grandma. I'm just a bit tired – it was a hot day today."

"Hm, aye that's probably it." She placed a warm kiss on her brow before getting off the bed and feeling her way to the door. "Well, goodnight, my dear."

"Goodnight, Grandma."

Jessie breathed a sigh of relief when she left. She didn't appear to be aware that she was leaving at dawn, and Jessie was grateful for that. She would hate their last conversation to be another argument.

She did her best to settle down under the sheet, but she was so excited about her early morning departure that sleep evaded her. She tossed and turned for what seemed like hours until she fell asleep from sheer exhaustion. She awoke with a start and dived out of bed. She pushed the curtain aside and peered out the window. It was nearly dawn – the first rays of the sun were just peeking through the trees.

Her heart was racing as she divested herself of her nightgown and dressed in a light summer dress. She wrapped her shawl around her shoulders and shoved her night attire into her bag. Tying on her bonnet she took one last look around the room before grabbing her bags. She slowly opened the door. The hallway was dark and the house was quiet. She heaved a sigh as she tip-toed down the hallway to the sitting room and out onto the veranda. She paused – listening for any sound of footsteps or her grandmother's walking stick tapping on the floorboards – all was quiet.

She hurried to the end of the veranda and down to the stable. The stable was a ramshackle wooden barn of a building, situated down a shady path beyond the kitchen. The door creaked and complained when she pried it open. She breathed in the sweet scent of hay and horses, as she slipped inside. A single lamp was burning but there was no sign of George. She started to walk down to the other end passed the stalls when all of a sudden William appeared in front of her. She jumped in fright.

"Oh my God, you scared the life out of me. What are you doing here?"

"I've been sleeping out here since the new foal was born," he said with a lopsided grin. "Do ye want to see her?"

"I haven't got time," she said shaking her head. "I'm leaving for Sydney, please don't tell Grandma."

"Yeah, I know, George told me." He reached for her bags and she let him take them as the two of them continued walking. "Don't worry I won't tell. Come, George's out in the yard, he's already got the buggy hitched."

She couldn't help admiring her young brother as they left the barn. He'd really grown up in the last year and had become so tall and gangly – but he'd also matured with no sign of the little brother she used to tease. He put her bags into the back of the buggy and then engulfed her in a tight hug.

"Take care, Jess."

"I will, I promise," she said letting him go.

"Are ye ready?" said George appearing from around the other side of the cart.

"Yes. Goodbye, Willliam. I hope you're not going to grow any taller." She placed an affectionate kiss on his cheek before allowing George to help her onto the seat.

George climbed up beside her and gave her a reassuring smile. “All ready?”

“Yes.”

“Tell Grandma I’ll be back in a few days,” said George to his young brother who had sidled up beside the buggy.

“Aye. Don’t worry I’ll handle Grandma. Safe travels to ye.”

George grinned as he clicked his tongue and they started down the road to Wiseman’s Ferry. Jessie breathed a sigh of relief. They were finally underway and in two days she would be married. She could hardly believe that it was finally happening.

The day was already promising to be warm, but the overcast sky and recent rain had left the air humid and muggy. Jessie was glad George was setting a good pace, not only because the fresh breeze was most welcome, but because she was anxious to put some distance behind them.

***

The trip to Sydney was uneventful, and apart from feeling hot and tired, they were both in high spirits. They secured accommodation at the Newcastle Hotel in George Street, had an early supper and retired to their room. Jessie removed her best Sunday dress from her bag and hung it in the small wardrobe. It was badly crumpled, but she hoped the creases wouldn't be noticeable by Monday.

Having bid George goodnight, she climbed into bed and yawned widely. She'd barely slept the previous night, and although excitement was thrumming through her veins at the thought of seeing Aaron, she fell asleep almost as soon as she lay down.

They both slept late the following day and after a quick bite to eat they headed for the barracks. Jessie had no idea if she'd be able to see Aaron today or not, but she was anxious to let him know she'd arrived. She'd prepared a short note just in case they wouldn't let her see him in person which she had safely tucked in her pocket.

The Hyde Park Barracks was a three-story imposing brick building surrounded by a high wall. Several soldiers were standing guard by the main gates, and Jessie was glad to have George by her side.

"Good morning," he said approaching the soldiers.

"Mornin' to ye," said one of the soldiers eyeing them with suspicion.

"My sister here, would like to see her intended husband, Aaron Price," said George undeterred by the scowls coming from the two. "They're to be married tomorrow."

"No visitors."

Although she wasn't surprised Jessie's heart sank at those words. Aaron had been sure he'd have his ticket by now and he'd be free. What had happened? She hated not knowing and swallowed the small lump in her throat. She took the note from her pocket and nudged George as she slipped it into his hand.

"Well, perhaps ye'd oblige by delivering this note to him?" He held the note out to the soldier, who with a grimace and a nod took the note. "Thank ye," said George with a smile. "Good day to ye then."

Taking Jessie by the elbow he led her down the street away from the barracks. Jessie glanced back over her shoulder –

convinced the soldier would just throw her note away, but he didn't. She saw him tuck it into his pocket. She sighed as she turned her attention back to where she was going. At least Aaron would know she was here and that she'd be at the Church tomorrow morning. Would he be there? She knew in her bones something wasn't right. He should've been free by now.

***

Chapter Thirty Four

Scot's Church – 12th March, 1838

Monday dawned with the promise of being hot and sultry. After breakfast, Jessie enjoyed a sponge bath laced with lavender and dressed in her best Sunday dress. Most of the creases had fallen out of it overnight, and as she smoothed the tight bodice over her stomach she admired her womanly curves. Her breasts peeked out between creamy lace and the skirt ballooned over her hips in a most delightful way.

She twisted her long hair into a bun and secured it on top of her head. Several long tendrils hung loosely around her face which she thought gave her a most alluring look. She only had one bonnet, which would have to do. She'd brushed it down last night and cleaned it with a damp cloth as best she could. She put it on and tied the ribbon under her jaw before looking in the mirror. Her clear blue eyes stared back at her with a look of determination in them. She sighed.

“Are ye ready?” came George’s voice from the other side of the door followed by a soft knock.

“Yes, coming.” She gave herself one more look before opening the door and smiling at her brother.”How do I look?”

“Ye look just fine,” he said offering her his arm.

She took his arm and closed the door. Brothers had no idea about such things and she wished Mary or Charlotte could’ve been here with her today. It seemed a lifetime ago since she’d seen them and she wondered if she might be able to convince Aaron to take her to visit. She was sure he would.

George locked the door to their room and they made their way downstairs. The heat of the day hit her as soon as she stepped out onto the street. It was going to be hot and she was glad George had hitched up the buggy. He helped her onto the seat and she settled her skirts. It wasn’t far to the church, but in this heat, she would’ve been hot and sticky by the time she got there if they’d gone on foot.

Ten minutes later they pulled up outside Scot’s Church and Jessie felt her heart rate quicken. She wasn't at all nervous about getting married but she was worried Aaron wouldn't be there. So many doubts and what-ifs were swimming around in her mind. As she waited for George to come around and help her down a knot formed in the pit of her stomach. She breathed in and blew out her breath in an attempt to calm herself.

"Are ye alright?" he asked as he put his hands around her waist and helped her to the ground. "Everything will be alright, you'll see."

"Yes." She nodded and gave him a tremulous smile. It was perfectly normal for a bride to have nerves on her wedding day. At least she thought so.

They walked to the main doors of the church which were standing ajar. George pushed them open and stood aside while she entered. It was cool and quiet inside and quite void of people except for two soldiers who were standing just inside the door. One of them nodded to her as she passed him. She murmured a greeting before turning her attention to the end of the aisle - and there he was. Standing with the Reverend who would be conducting the ceremony was Aaron. She heaved a massive sigh of relief and the knot in her stomach evaporated.

"Miss Smith I presume," said the Reverend as he walked towards her. "Mr John Dunmore-Lang at your service."

"Good morning, Reverend," said Jessie in a low voice. "This is my brother."

"Pleased to make your acquaintance, Mr Smith," he said giving his attention to George briefly. "Mr Price has requested a private word with you Miss Smith before we commence."

"Oh."

"Please go ahead."

After giving George a final glance she quickened her step and hurried to the end of the aisle. Aaron smiled widely as he stepped forward and embraced her. He held her briefly and placed a chaste kiss on her cheek. Keeping his arm around her waist he led her to the end of the row.

"It's so good to see ye. I can hardly believe ye made it," he said grinning. "Thank ye for your note – it was a relief to know you'd made it to Sydney."

“They wouldn’t let me see you, and I couldn’t understand why. Is everything alright?”

“Aye, it’s just that…well, I got my ticket, but it’s not for New South Wales.” A look of disappointment flashed across his face. “It’s for Norfolk Island.”

“Norfolk Island?”

“Aye. It’s next to worthless but it’s the first step to freedom. I promise ye I’ll be free, but we have to return to the island for now.”

While Aaron was clearly disappointed Jessie was not. A sense of relief had surged through her at the news they’d be returning to the island. He would be freer than he was before and they could live their lives quite happily there, and he couldn’t leave. He couldn’t leave her or uproot her and she could finally settle somewhere long enough to call it home. No, she wasn’t disappointed in the least, and only hoped she could feign dismay for his sake.

“It’s alright. I know you’ll be free. I can wait.”

“I hoped you’d understand,” he said taking her hands in his. He raised them to his lips and brushed a warm kiss on both of them. "There's one more thing."

She looked into his earnest hazel eyes and saw the apprehension reflected in them.

"Whatever it is it'll be fine. We'll work it out," she said.

"Aye. Well, as I said, I'm not free, not until we board the ship back to the island."

She nodded, not quite understanding what he was trying to say.

He sucked in a breath. "I can't join ye, and ye can't come to the barracks. It means we can't be man and wife until we board the ship."

"Oh." She felt shy all of sudden at the thought of what that meant.

"It'll be a couple of days. The brig's not sailing til Thursday, and they won't board me until the night before. Ye can board tomorrow – it's the Governor Phillip."

"We can't delay any further, Mr Price," said the Reverend in a loud voice from the end of the row. "If you please." He gestured to them to join him.

"Of course," said Aaron placing his hand on Jessie's lower back he guided her towards the Reverend.

The ceremony was short and over before Jessie knew it she was saying *'I do'*.

"You may now kiss the bride," said Reverend Dunmore-Lang smiling benignly at them both.

Aaron's arms came around her and his lips brushed hers, tentatively at first, and then he pressed her hard against himself and his lips demanded she respond. She clung to him as her lips parted and she surrendered herself. His hand running down her spine sent shivers through her and when their lips parted she gasped.

"I love ye," he whispered before releasing her.

She felt her cheeks warm as she realised her brother and the Reverend had just witnessed that rather passionate embrace. She lowered her lashes momentarily before locking her eyes with his. "I love you too."

"Now, if you'll step this way and sign the register," said the Reverend. "I've filled in all the details and as long as they're correct, all you have to do is make your mark or sign." He indicated to a small table set up to the side with a large ledger open on it.

Jessie walked over to the table and sat down. Taking the quill in hand she scanned the register. She noticed Mr Dunmore-Lang had noted her age as seventeen. She paused as a pang of guilt went through her. She glanced up at Aaron before taking a breath and signing the register - now was not the time to confess.

A moment later Aaron joined her and taking the quill scrawled his signature above hers. "Well, how do ye feel Mrs Price?"

"Happy and relieved," she replied smiling.

"Sorry to break up this happy occasion, but it's time to go," said one of the soldiers as he approached them.

"Give them a moment, Corporal," said George intervening. "Surely ye can give them five minutes?"

"Our orders are to return Price as soon as the ceremony's done," he said ignoring George and glaring at Aaron. "Tis a shame ye pretty bride will be alone tonight."

"That will do, Corporal," said the Reverend before glancing at the register and snapping it shut.

"I'll see ye Wednesday evening," said Aaron brushing his lips against Jessie's again. He then turned to his new brother-in-law. "I trust you'll keep her safe and see her onto the ship, George?"

"Aye, I will."

"Get a move on," said the Corporal giving Aaron a shove towards the door.

Jessie watched as they marched him from the Church. It didn't feel real to her at all. She was married and yet she was already separated from her new husband. It all seemed like a dream, and even the memory of Aaron's lips on hers was not enough to shake the surreal feeling.

***

Supper was a subdued affair. George and Jessie had a small table in the corner of the dining room of the Newcastle Hotel. It was quiet and secluded and suited Jessie's mood perfectly. Her wedding day had not ended as she'd expected, and she couldn't help the feeling of despondency that had settled on her.

"I'll take ye to the docks tomorrow afternoon," said George before taking another mouthful of his supper.

"Hmm…oh yes. Thank you." Jessie pushed the potatoes to the other side of her plate with her fork.

"I know today didn't work out as ye expected." He reached out and squeezed her hand. "But, you'll be with Aaron before ye know it."

She looked up at her brother and smiled. "I know. It's just that…"

"What? Ye thought he'd be free and you'd be together? Well, of course, ye did, and ye will be."

She pressed her lips together and nodded. George was right, but it was more than that. There'd been no celebration, no family to wish her well, except for George of course. "I'm so glad you were there at my side but I really missed Papa today."

George sighed. "Aye, I'm no substitute."

"No, it's not that," she said shaking her head. "I needed you and I'm so thankful to have you. It just really hit me today that we're on our own, all of us.

"Aye we are, but we have each other." He smiled as he finished his supper and put the cutlery down with a clatter. "Don't forget that, Jessie. Ye have me and William, and ye should write to Charlotte and Mary. "

"I will. I wrote to them last year. Have you seen them in recent times?"

"Not Mary," he said shaking his head. "But I visited Charlotte and Tom not long ago. They're in Pitt Town – ye knew that?"

"Yes."

"She's got two little ones now. I believe Mary's expecting her first one in a few months, according to Grandma. She keeps in touch with them."

Grandma…she would write to her as soon as she was back on the island. Would she forgive her for running off and marrying Aaron?

"She'll get over it," said George appearing to read her mind.

"I hope so. I hate being at odds with her."

"Trust me, she loves us more than ye can know, and she's not so stubborn that she doesn't know when she's been out manoeuvred."

Is that what she'd done? Out manoeuvred her? She smiled as she imagined her reaction when she discovered she'd gone. Yes, she'd forgive her, she was sure of it.

***

Chapter Thirty Five

Homeward Bound

Jessie clung to George as hot tears splashed down her face. She had no idea when she'd see him again, and he'd been her rock in recent days. She pulled free of his embrace and wiped her face with the back of her hand.

"I'm going to miss you so much."

"You're going to have your husband by your side, and ye won't miss me." He laughed as he embraced her again, and then he kissed the top of her head and let her go. "I'll miss ye too. Be sure to write me."

"I will, I promise. Safe travels, George."

She picked up her bags and turned towards the gangplank and the waiting ship. This was it then. She had no idea when she'd be back in New South Wales, or when she'd see her family again. She glanced back over her shoulder – George was already up on the driver's seat with the reins in hand. He grinned and waved.

"Goodbye," she called and waved in return before returning her focus to the ship.

She walked up the gangplank where she was greeted by a spotty-faced soldier. He took her bags from her and led her below decks.

"This way, Mrs Price," he said gesturing to her as he opened the door to a cabin.

She followed him into a larger-than-normal cabin – at least for her. She remembered the first time she'd travelled to Norfolk Island had been in a cupboard, and this was certainly not a cupboard. A large bunk bed took up most of the available space, and a table and chairs stood against the other wall. He put her bags down on the bed and retreated to the door.

"If ye need anythin' just holler."

"I will thank you."

She closed the door behind him and leant against it. She was finally on board, and tomorrow Aaron would join her. Her heart thumped faster at the thought of finally being reunited. He was her husband now and while the thought of what that meant sent a shiver of excitement down her spine, a small part of her was also a little afraid. What would their first night together be like? Would it be like the time she'd seen the cook bent over the kitchen table while John, the farmhand, had rammed into her? She swallowed and pushed the image aside. Yes, she was just a little scared.

She spent what was left of the afternoon on the deck enjoying the sights and sounds of the docks. There was always a flurry of activity and men rushing to and fro. She retired early after supper and slept better than she had in days. When she awoke the next morning, she stretched and curled herself back under the covers. Aaron would be joining her this evening and she just knew the day would drag.

***

Jessie lit the lamp and set it on the table. She sat down and folded her hands in her lap for all of twenty seconds. Rising she paced to the door and opened it. She peered down the corridor - there was no sign of anyone. She sighed as she closed the door and walked back to the chair. It was way past supper time and still, there was no sign of Aaron. A small knot had formed in the pit of her stomach hours ago as she waited for him. She paced the small cabin again before grabbing her shawl and heading out the door.

She climbed the ladder and emerged on the main deck just in time to see Aaron being escorted up the gangplank. She stopped and pulled her shawl around her shoulders. She watched while the soldiers who were guarding him removed his shackles. Her breathing quickened as he looked up and their eyes locked.

"If you'll excuse me, I see my wife's come looking for me."

The soldiers laughed and one of them smacked him on the back. "I expect you'll be dancing the blanket hornpipe afore long."

"I'll thank ye to hold your tongue," said Aaron glaring at him.

The other soldiers laughed as Aaron turned and headed over to where Jessie was waiting for him.

"A little amorous congress heh?" another called after him.

Jessie blushed at their vulgar remarks and was relieved when Aaron reached her side. He took her hand as they went below decks. At the bottom of the ladder, he stopped and took her in his arms.

"Ah, Jess," he said gazing down at her. "I've dreamed of this day for so long."

He lowered his head and pressed his lips to hers. Jessie took his face in her hands as her lips parted and their kiss deepened. Aaron moaned and he ran his hand down her spine to her lower back and pulled her closer. She could feel his firm thighs pressed against hers and she thrilled at the feel of him against her. Their lips parted, but Aaron kept his arms around her.

Jessie felt a nervous flutter in her stomach at the look in his eyes. Was it desire? She thought so and briefly wondered if she was looking at him like that. She sucked in a breath and pulled from his embrace.

"Our cabin's just down here," said Jessie taking him by the hand.

She led him down the dimly lit corridor until she came to her cabin. She opened the door and went inside. He followed and seemed to take up all the available space. She stepped back until she felt the edge of the bunk against her legs. What had started as a flutter in her stomach had turned into a thrumming in her veins. She licked her lips as she removed her shawl and hung it over the back of the chair.

Aaron walked up behind her and wrapped his arms around her. He nuzzled her neck. "Are ye alright?"

"Yes," she said turning in his arms to face him.

His hazel eyes searched her face. "Would ye like me to leave while ye change into your nightgown?"

She lowered her lashes and nodded.

"Alright. I'll give ye ten minutes or so."

He kissed her forehead and in two steps he was at the door. He paused for a moment before opening it and disappearing down the corridor. Jessie heaved a sigh as she searched through her bag for her nightgown. It only took her a few minutes to divest herself of her clothes and slip her nightdress over her head. She carefully folded her clothes and tucked them into her bag.

The nightly ritual had distracted her mind from other thoughts, but now they returned to Aaron. He would be back in a few minutes, and she was determined not to be afraid. She pulled back the covers and climbed into the bunk – leaving room for Aaron to get in beside her. She could almost feel her heart thumping against her rib cage and her breath quickening.

She jumped when the door opened and Aaron poked his head in. When he saw her he smiled and came into the cabin, closing the door behind him.

"I see you're all ready." He unbuttoned his jacket and slung it over the back of one of the chairs. He sat down on the edge of the bunk and removed his boots.

Jessie watched him as he slowly and deliberately undressed. His shirt was next, and Jessie gasped when he pulled it over his head.

"What?" he said turning to face her.

"Your back…you've been flogged."

"Aye, once. I'll be glad if it doesn't happen again."

"Why? What happened?"

He laughed. “When I first got to the island I thought it’d be a good idea to go pig hunting. The Commandant did not agree.”

“I’ll be glad if it doesn’t happen again too,” she said tracing her finger along one of the thin scars on his shoulder blade. “Do they hurt?”

“No.” He took her hand and brushed his lips against her fingers. “I hope ye don’t think any less of me?”

“No.”

She sucked in a breath when he turned her hand over and placed a wet kiss in the middle of her palm. It sent an exciting feeling right to the core of her – one she’d felt before but still it was unexpected.

“Are ye nervous?” he asked.

Her heart was hammering and she thought it best not to deny how she was feeling. “A little.”

“Aye, so am I. Tis a long time since I was with a woman,” he said as he rolled over to face her and ran his hand down her bare arm.

He then placed little kisses where his hand had been moments before which sent shivers through her. He continued to run his hand down her body and over her rounded hip. A small moan escaped her lips when his fingers brushed her bare legs. She put her hands on either side of his face and pulled his face toward her until his lips met hers. He groaned as her lips parted and she explored with her tongue.

She felt warm fingers on her thigh as he lifted the hem of her nightgown. She ran her hands down his back and clung to him. They kissed again and she gasped when he squeezed her bottom. She ran her hand down his spine and copying him, she gently squeezed his firm buttocks. He groaned and buried his face in her neck before placing little kisses down her throat to her breast.

When his fingers found her warm womanly heart she arched her back and let out a low moan. Never in her life had she felt anything like it, and she spread her thighs to allow him to freely explore her. She closed her eyes as waves of pleasure thrummed through her veins.

Aaron fumbled with the buttons on his breeches until he was free. Jessie felt him shift and she opened her eyes to see him poised above her. He was positioned between her thighs and he pressed his lips to hers as he eased into her for the first time. Jessie gasped as pleasure was replaced by pain.

Their lips parted and he gazed down into her taut face. "I'm sorry."

Jessie shook her head. She'd known it was going to hurt the first time and it wasn't his fault. She thought he'd been as gentle with her as he could be. He thrust his hips several times and the pain began to ease as her body grew accustomed to the invasion. She was just thinking about moving her hips in time with his when he let out a long groan and collapsed on top of her.

He withdrew and lay down beside her and gathering her into his arms he kissed her forehead. "I'm sorry. I promise it'll be better for ye next time."

She looked into his eyes, full of concern and her heart melted. "It wasn't so bad."

He pulled her closer and she nuzzled into his neck and in no time she'd fallen asleep in his arms.

***

Jessie was disappointed when the Governor Phillip moored off the island a week later. It had been blissful having Aaron all to herself without any distractions, but life was about to invade. She leant against the railing and watched the launch moving swiftly through the water towards the ship. They would be disembarking next and she had a nervous knot in her stomach.

Aaron sidled up beside her and wrapped his arm around her waist. He kissed her cheek. "Are ye excited to begin our new life together?"

She gripped her skirt as a gust of wind swirled around her legs. "Yes…and no. I can't help but wonder what Mr and Mrs Sharpe will think." The closer they'd come to the island the more anxious she'd been feeling.

"Ye don't have to worry about them anymore," he said tightening his grip on her. "You're my wife and they no longer have any say over what ye do."

She nodded. He was right, she knew the agreement was no longer valid, but she couldn't shake the niggling feeling she had.

Would they cause trouble for Aaron? “I love you and I worry what they may do.”

He grinned. “I love ye too, and they can do naught.”

The launch bumped against the side of the Governor Phillip and Jessie sighed. What would be would be, and Aaron and her would face it together. Everything would be different now.

The End

Epilogue

MacDonald River, March 1838

George reined the horse to a halt at the front of the house. His grandmother was standing leaning on her walking stick in the middle of the driveway. He'd known she'd be waiting for him but hadn't expected her to ambush him as soon as he arrived. He sighed as he secured the reins and leapt down from the buggy.

She watched him as he walked slowly towards her. Her dark eyes narrowed and her knuckles whitened as her grip on her stick tightened. George pulled himself up to his full height and stared steadily back at her.

"Grandma."

"What do ye have to say for yerself?" said Maggie leaning on her walking stick.

He ran his fingers through his dark hair and sighed. "I'll not apologise."

"The devil ye won't," she said glaring at him. "Has she married him then?"

He nodded. "Aye."

"Ye haven't done yer sister any favours by helping her. She's now shackled herself to that scoundrel an' to that damned island."

"She loves him."

"Bah. She doesn't know what love is." She took a step towards George, who held his ground and stared steadfastly down at her. "I think twould be best if ye an' yer brother pack yer things an' go."

"What?" His brow arched upwards as he stared at her in disbelief.

She glared steadily back at him and then poked him in the chest with a gnarled finger. "Ye heard me."

"Ye can't be serious, Grandma." He reached out to hug her. She stiffened as his arms went around her shoulders and he pulled her close. "Please don't be angry with us."

"Let me go," she said pushing him from her. "What ye've done cannot be undone, nor easily forgiven." Her voice had risen several octaves and she shouted the final words at him.

George turned his gaze towards the veranda as Grandpa Joe came walking along. He paused and leant against the post as he surveyed the two of them. George kept his eyes firmly on Grandpa Joe as he silently implored him to intervene. Joe sighed as he stepped from the veranda and went to Maggie's side. He put his arm around her and ran his other hand over his face.

"This matter will not be settled out here." He squeezed Maggie and tried to urge her back towards the house, but she stubbornly refused to move.

"The matter's settled," she said flatly.

"I only did what I thought was right," said George shaking his head. "If ye really want William and me to go then we will."

"No one's going anywhere," said Grandpa Joe once again urging Maggie towards the house.

She seemed to reluctantly allow Joe to guide her towards the veranda. George heaved a sigh as he watched her walk slowly away from him. He was serious. They'd leave if that's what she wanted. He thought Uncle Joseph would take them in.

He'd done work for him on his farm before and he could do with their help. He didn't want to leave Grandpa Joe in the lurch though – he needed him. Over the past year or so he'd become Grandpa Joe's right-hand man, and he knew he couldn't run the farm without his help.

"Tis Jessie that's paid the price for yer foolishness," said Maggie over her shoulder. "When I think of that poor lass married to that brute I just want to scream."

"Come, Maggie calm yourself," said Joe opening the front door. "Ye go on ahead. George and I will be having a word."

"Hrmph." She said complying with his request. "Ye will not change my mind, Joseph Smith."

"Aye, I know. Ask William to come and take care of the horse and buggy will ye?"

"I'll send someone," she said glaring at George one last time.

Joe heaved a sigh and ran his hands over his face as Maggie disappeared down the hallway. He closed the door and turned to face George, who was looking after his Grandmother with a look of defiance.

"I only did what I thought was right," said George turning his gaze to Grandpa Joe. "Ye would've done the same, surely?"

"I cannot say what I would've done." He gestured to the wicker chairs sitting by the front door. "Sit."

George shoved his hands in his pockets and jutted his chin out. "I'd rather stand if ye going to tell me to go."

"For God's sake," said Grandpa Joe easing himself into a chair. "No one's leaving. Sit."

George kept his eyes on Joe while he seated himself in the other chair. "So, if I'm not leaving how are we going to get Grandma to agree? She's mighty mad."

"Aye, she is. But she'll calm down and see reason soon enough," said Joe. "So tell me. Has Jessie gone back to the island?"

"Aye," said George blowing out his breath. "She thought Aaron was going to get a ticket for New South Wales, but it was only for Norfolk Island. They had no choice but to return."

Joe sat back in his chair and ran his hand over his chin. “Did she seem happy?”

“What? Happy to be going back to the island? Aye. I think she feels safe there.”

A wry smile spread across Joe’s face. “That’s not exactly what I meant, but I can understand her being glad to be going back.”

“Ye can?” George sat forward in his chair and stared at Grandpa Joe.

“Aye. I spent many years on the island meself.” He smiled and the lines on his face appeared to soften as he thought about his time spent there. “The place has a way of getting under your skin and into your heart. Tis a special place – at least it was for me.”

“I never knew that. Were ye imprisoned there?”

“Heck no,” said Joe with a wave of his hand. “It wasn’t a prison back in those days. If ye must know, I stowed away on a ship hoping to get back to old Blighty and ended up there.”

George let out a snort followed by a chuckle. “I can’t imagine ye doing such a thing.”

“Well I was only a lad and life in Sydney was miserable. Anyway, I found my way to Norfolk Island and a man by the name of Darcy Wentworth took pity on me. I worked in his garden and I’ve never known a kinder man.”

George sat back in his chair and nodded. “Well, I hope Jessie finds her happiness there.”

“I expect she will. We just need to convince Maggie of it.”

***

Fact and Fiction

If you've read any of my other books, you'll know that my stories are inspired by my ancestors. Currency Girl is no exception.

Being based on my family history means I know the basic facts, but I have to work out the how and why of their lives. So, my interpretation of why Jessie went to work for the Sharpes at the age of twelve, is that she was indentured. Why wasn't her eldest brother, George also sent to work? That seemed odd to me.

So, the only way I could explain that was if her stepmother, Sophia had a special reason for doing so. Hence, the wicked stepmother scenario. It explains the factual events.

Currency Girl follows the actual events very closely where they're known. No record of her father, George's death has been found. We know he died because Sophia went on to remarry, we just don't know how or precisely when he died. I thought a quick sudden death was more likely than a protracted illness.

Some assumptions have to be made, and her brother's being sent to live with her grandmother is one of them. Of course, this enabled me to bring Maggie into Jessie's story, which I think gives you an idea of the whole interwoven family.

Maggie Smith's story is an interesting one and I may write a book about her in the future. She did eventually go completely blind and she would've been lost without Joe.

One of my biggest concerns with writing this book was the age gap between Jessie and Aaron. History doesn't allow for changing societal norms. What was considered perfectly alright in 1838 isn't anywhere near alright today. I hope you can see past that and still enjoy Jessie's story.

C J Bessell

Caroline Chisholm's Visit

In 1845 Caroline Chisholm visited Joseph and Maggie. She primarily came to interview Joe about the early days of the colony, but she also spoke with Maggie.

She described Maggie as being blind and that she acted as she spoke. The house was large and crowded with furniture.

Joe presented her with a loaded pistol as a souvenir of her visit. He pulled it out of his belt saying "Ye may depend on it."

Joe told her how he worked up and down the Hawkesbury until he saved enough money to buy his first farm. He now had a thousand pounds in cash, five hundred head of cattle and he owned several properties.

"We are never without a chest of tea," he told her. "Tea is a great comfort."

***

Author Notes

Thank you so much for reading Currency Girl. I'm an Australian indie author. As such, I maintain complete control of my work and self publish. That also means I have to market and promote my work, which I'm not very good at. I find it hard to self promote.

So, I'm taking this opportunity to not only thank you for taking the time to read my book, but if you liked it, would you mind leaving a rating or review on Amazon. It's the best way to show any author that you appreciate their hard work. It also helps other potential readers to decide if they should invest their time and money.

You already know that I write historical fiction, and you may have also realised that my stories are based on the lives of my ancestors. I've been passionate about family history for many years, and I've discovered so many amazing ancestors who led such interesting lives. So, I blend fact with fiction and bring their stories to life, and I'm so excited to be sharing them with you.

If you enjoyed this book, please consider reading one of my other titles.

Thank you

Jacob's Mob

How did one fateful decision land Aaron Price in New South Wales as an assigned convict?

He and his mate James were best described as petty criminals until they decided to try their hand at breaking and entering. What started as a grab for easy money, ended with them being sentenced to transportation to the colonies for life. Aaron may be lamenting his fate and the fact that he won't be seeing his sweetheart again, but is he content to serve his sentence?

Aaron knows only too well that bushranging is a hanging offence, and yet he once again allows himself to be persuaded. On the run and eager for revenge, he and his new mates wage terror on their previous master and the other settlers of the Hunter Valley.

However, Aaron isn't content to just wreak havoc - he's got an escape plan. If only he could find a way to get himself on board a ship bound for America. The British have no jurisdiction there, and he would be free.

Based on the true story of Aaron Price, who arrived in New South Wales in 1825 on board the convict transport Guildford.

Pioneers of Burra

From Cornwall to an untamed South Australia...

Based on the true story of the Bryar family, who left their homeland in search of a better life. Richard and his son Thomas secure free passage to South Australia, where they dream of a new beginning working in the copper mine of Burra.

After months at sea and a perilous journey from Adelaide to Burra, their families are finally reunited. Can they overcome the hardships of living in a dugout on Burra Creek to carve out a better future for their children? Will a disaster in the mine finally bring them together with hope for the future?

Margaret

From Bredgar House to Van Diemen's Land.....

Margaret Chambers never imagined she'd be forced to flee her family home and country to escape a hideous old man and an arranged marriage. Pretending to be a general servant she boards a ship bound for Hobart Town. It's 1837, and in order to get free passage out to Van Diemen's Land, she's agreed to work for Mrs Hector. There's just one problem, she's never done a day's menial work in her life and her lie is soon discovered.

Taken into the household of the Reverend Davies and his wife Maria, she not only finds kindness but friendship, and is employed as Maria's companion. She couldn't have hoped for a better situation, but when convict and scoundrel William Hartley crosses her path will it all come tumbling down? Seduced by the young and charming William she finds herself unable to remain with the Reverend and his wife. Maria doesn't want her to go but Margaret can see the conflict between Maria and her husband. Not wanting to be the cause of any rift between them she leaves.

William still has five years of his seven-year sentence to serve and he's not free to marry her. However, he stands by her side by stealing food for her and his unborn child until he gets caught. Sent away to work on the chain gang Margaret's left to fend for herself. Somehow she finds a way to survive until William's free to join her and when he gets a Ticket of Leave and permission to marry her, the future's looking hopeful.

My Very Occasional Newsletter

I love to connect with my readers and share updates with them. I don't send emails too often – but you'll be the first to know about promotions and upcoming releases.

Subscribe on my website.

www.cjbessell.godaddysites.com

Follow me on Facebook

I post regularly on my Facebook page, and it's a great place to connect and stay up to date with all things in my author world.

I'd love to connect with you.

https://www.facebook.com/CJBessell/

Printed in Great Britain
by Amazon